Dear Reader:

I am delighted to present to you *The Last Prejudice*, the latest novel by David Rivera, Jr. For those of you who have followed the author's first novels, *Harlem's Dragon*, *The Street Sweeper* and *Playing in the Dark*, you know that he is a talented writer who blends suspense with erotica. On the cover of *The Street Sweeper* is the incredibly sexy model from movies like Tyler Perry's *Madea's Family Reunion*. Yes, he was the stripper dressed as a police officer. He is hot and so is the author of this book: David Rivera, Jr.

In *The Last Prejudice*, Rivera detours from his detective series and addresses the adventures of three plus-sized women. We follow Noreen, Dahlia, and Kat through their wild, erotic odysseys from Jamaican resorts to S&M clubs. We also share in their sisterly bond as they deal with the ups and downs of romance and weight, discovering that true love and lust come in all sizes.

If you haven't read *Harlem's Dragon*, *The Street Sweeper* and *Playing in the Dark*, you will love them. The titles in the trilogy are all written without the need to read in a particular sequence, however, I would encourage you to read them all.

Thank you for supporting Mr. Rivera's efforts and thank you for supporting one of the dozens of authors published under my imprint, Strebor Books. I try my best to bring you cutting-edge works of literature that will keep your attention and make you think long after you turn the last page.

Now sit back in your favorite chair or, better yet, chill in the bed, and be prepared to be tantalized by yet another great read.

Peace and Many Blessings,

Zane

Publisher
Strebor Books
www.simonandschuster.com/streborbooks

ALSO BY DAVID RIVERA, JR.

Playing in the Dark
The Street Sweeper
Harlem's Dragon

ZANE PRESENTS

THE LAST PREJUDICE

DAVID RIVERA, JR.

SBI

STREBOR BOOKS

NEW YORK LONDON TORONTO SYDNEY

Strebor Books
P.O. Box 6505
Largo, MD 20792
http://www.streborbooks.com

ISBN-13 978-1-59309-235-1
ISBN-10   1-59309-235-0
LCCN 2009921902

First Strebor Books trade paperback edition April 2009

Cover design: www.mariondesigns.com
Cover photograph: © Keith Saunders/Marion Designs

10 9 8 7 6 5 4 3 2 1

Manufactured in the United States of America

For information regarding special discounts for bulk purchases, please contact Simon & Schuster Special Sales at 1-800-456-6798 or business@simonandschuster.com

DEDICATION

This book is dedicated to my father, Jose "Chemah" Melendez,
who told me that despite differences in culture, race,
and religion, everyone brings value to the world.
And through his unconditional love he taught me
that it was okay to love the person that
I see in the mirror every day.

ACKNOWLEDGMENTS

When I wrote my first book, *Harlem's Dragon,* I never suspected that a second—and now a third—book would come from it. So when I give thanks to Harlem Goju, wherein I first saw the principles that the main character in this series projected through my association with Grandmaster Sam McGee and Master Dwayne McGee, it is only fitting that I bow to them in humble appreciation.

To my writing mentor Zane, thank you for the opportunity to do what I was meant to do and helping me on the path to becomng a better writer. To Charmaine, who never seems to be disturbed when things aren't going exactly right. I am grateful for your patience. To Judith Lee-Sing Rivera who has to be credited with directing the photo shoots for every one of my book covers as well as putting up with the mood swings that writing causes in crazy folks like me, my sincere thanks and apologies. To Rehva Jones, who helped me flush out the story told in this last book through her first edits, it would have been extremely difficult without your help. Thanks to Keith Saunders for doing a marvelous job on the cover. He knows what we went through to get the right model. Shout-out to my sister Sheilla Rivera who is my biggest fan and greatest promoter.

Ultimately, I would like to thank everyone in my life who sings the blues with me in my dark times and those whom I hold close when the sun shines glaringly in my life path.

Peace and Love to you all

"There is only one happiness in life, to love and be loved."

—GEORGE SAND

Prayer:

May the evil man be good.
May the good man find peace.
May he who finds peace be free.
And may he who is free make others free.

CHAPTER 1
BEST OF FRIENDS

Dahlia looked down the bar at her ex-husband, Martin Gray. She was slightly drunk, and the sight of him was messing with her high. Her disdain for the man was palpable. He was sitting there with a beautiful, caramel-skinned woman, who looked to be about a size twenty-four, Dahlia guessed, categorizing the woman by her dress size the way she did all women.

Dahlia felt sorry for the woman. Her ex-husband was a piece of shit. It had taken her too long to figure out his true nature and hatred for women. It certainly wasn't obvious to her at first. Martin was a tall, dark-skinned, handsome man. He kept himself well-dressed and well-groomed; a manicure and pedicure was a part of his weekly regimen. He spent money like he had it to burn. He was a catch for any woman—at first pass.

Dahlia was married to him nearly two years before she finally let the gilded lenses she saw him through shatter, along with her self-esteem. Initially, he treated her like a queen, taking her out, buying her gifts and making love to her like no one else ever had. Soon after they were married, he started using her size, which he feigned reverence for, to belittle her which heightened her already keen feelings of insecurity. Still, his derogatory remarks hadn't kept him from climbing on top of her every night and humping away like some wild boar.

Months after Dahlia and Martin divorced, she inadvertently met a woman at the Laundromat who had dated him. Dahlia overheard a bit of female bonding between four women who were folding clothes and joined the conversation. While the woman spoke of her past love, how hot and intense the courtship began, how his love had turned cold and, finally, how he began to mutilate her with his words, it dawned on Dahlia that this woman was speaking of her ex-husband. She never let on that she and the woman shared something in common. By the time she finished folding her clothes, she reached the conclusion that her ex-husband had a fetish for abusing overweight women. First luring them in with his fine clothing, perfect manners, and good looks and then, when he had them hooked, go to work on their self-esteem. She became nauseated when she heard her own tale, told in excruciating detail, through the mouth of the woman at the laundry.

Dahlia caught Martin's attention and sneered at him through narrowed eyes.

Noreen had only agreed to meet with Martin after he begged her relentlessly to meet him one last time at the restaurant where they first met. She enjoyed the oysters there and had nothing better to do, so she went for the free meal. She knew she wanted nothing to do with Martin. He was too bogus, the way he gushed and swooned over her. She didn't know what he was after, but she knew the difference between a man who loved big women and a man that was just full of shit. Martin was definitely full of shit.

Martin kept staring over Noreen's shoulder at a woman sitting alone at the bar, tossing back chocolate Cosmos. Noreen had already finished her meal and was ready to give Martin the "brush-off." She'd suppressed her urge to see what he was looking at during the entire meal, and finally turned her head to see what was so interesting.

"Do you know her?"

"Yes," Martin sighed. "She's my ex-wife. She took to drinking right after we divorced two years ago, and I hear she hasn't been sober since."

Noreen looked back over her shoulder at the woman downing her most recent Cosmopolitan and then turned back to Martin. She picked up her napkin and wiped her lips, having decided that it was time to call this meal and this relationship to an official end.

"Goddamn!" Noreen said, throwing her napkin on her empty plate. "Who would think a woman could go on celebrating for that long?"

Martin stared at Noreen. Noreen stared right back at him, daring him to say anything else. Martin diverted his gaze first, and tried to play it off by raising his hand to call the waitress for the check.

Noreen decided she wasn't ready to go home quite yet. She got up from the table and patted Martin on the cheek.

"You can go on without me, sweetheart. I'm going to stay at the bar and get myself a drink." Noreen turned to go.

The waitress arrived at the table and looked from Noreen to Martin sensing that something more than she needed to know was going on.

"Leave her a big tip, honey, maybe it'll make up for what you're lacking in your pants."

"Fucking bitch," Martin said just loud enough for Noreen to hear.

Noreen turned back to Martin with a smile on her face and in her most sugary voice responded, "Oh, what a coincidence, I was just thinking the same thing about you." Noreen left the table and headed for the bar.

Two minutes later, Martin was leaving the restaurant. His ex-wife and ex-girlfriend were sitting seven feet from each other, and he could smell the hatred oozing from their pores. He was determined to walk past them without turning his head to look in their direction. He didn't like a lot of negative attention drawn to him. He had a reputation to uphold in the community and didn't need it tarnished. Harlem was his natural hunting ground. The selection of big beautiful women of color was plentiful and he didn't need anyone fucking that up.

Both of the women knew his style and neither of them was willing to give him a pass. He was walking with his head up too high and full of himself.

As it worked out, when he reached an equal point between the two women, they had the same idea. Both tossed the remnants of their drinks on him as if they had choreographed their movements and synchronized their watches.

Martin was embarrassed into paralysis as he stood between the two women with his jaw hanging open as he was completely stunned. He quickly composed himself and continued on his way without so much as a glare over his shoulder.

That was how Noreen and Dahlia met. They were two women, despising the same man, and out for a good night on the town. The kindred spirits became fast friends. They were both smart, professional, no-nonsense women. They shared other noteworthy physical characteristics that made them sistas, three times over. They were big, black, and beautiful.

CHAPTER TWO
HEDONISM

K at sat on a lounge chair skirting the perimeter of the pool at the Hedonism resort in Jamaica. It wasn't the first time she had been here. Years ago she'd visited with some girlfriends and they'd had a great time. Now, here she was thirty-five years old, trying to recapture some of her old glory. She'd tried to convince her one-time best friend Margarita to come down with her, but Margarita had begged off. Three years after getting out of jail, Margarita was still trying to get her life together, insisting that she couldn't afford to let her business go one day without her presence. *Once a control freak, always a control freak,* Kat thought.

Kat needed this trip. Her divorce was finally settled and she needed time to gather her thoughts and figure out what, if anything, she would do next.

When she and her husband, Kenneth, divorced, she took a job as a middle school social studies teacher in the New York City public schools system. She always thought she would teach if given an opportunity, but was really surprised when she went down to the board of education and, after a review of her college transcripts, was told that her sociology degree made her eligible to teach social studies.

Once she was sure that teaching was something that she could really do, Kat left Kenneth the limousine business they had built together. She was sure that he would continue to support their son, KJ, in the way they had discussed, prior to Kenneth leaving their home.

Kenneth was a lowdown, cheating son-of-a-bitch, but he did have one redeeming value—he took excellent care of his child. It was the only quality about the man that Kat hadn't been mistaken about.

After the many telephone calls that he explained away as wrong numbers, and late nights that he spent out of the house, Kat finally confronted him with his indiscretions. His response to her had been forthright and brutal.

"It's not my fault you let yourself go. Look at you! You've put forty pounds on since you had the baby. Your stomach is hanging over your skirt and you still haven't stopped eating."

Kat was so taken aback by his callousness that she didn't immediately have an answer. He was right. She had put on some weight after the baby was born. But he was wrong about the eating. She did realize that she put on too much weight and slowed down on her food intake. She had even tried three different diets that hadn't worked for her. But all of that, she had done for her own personal reasons. She missed the way men used to look at her before she had the baby. All her life men had eyed her, whistled at her and generally come on to her, even at the expense of raising the ire of whatever man she happened to be with at the time.

Kat never imagined she would ever get this big. She was a solid size 18. When she was younger, she and her girls would make fun of the full-sized women. Now she was "one of them"—a pretty face and fat ass.

She knew that her husband had been purposely cruel. He knew her pride would force her to throw him out and that was just what he wanted. Kat obliged and Kenny left their home for the last time that night. After he left, Kat spent a whole hour in front of the mirror. She didn't think she looked so bad. She was still pretty. Her breasts were now 38D. They sagged a little more than she thought looked sexy, but with her bra on, they still looked appealing. The one good thing about the pregnancy was that it made her hair grow thicker and longer. Her hair now went all the way to the middle of her back, tapering off just above her bra. She had never been able to grow her hair that long before and did not look a gift horse in the mouth. She took better care of her hair now than she ever had. She went to the Dominican hair salon every other week and let a lady named Miriam work her magic. She always got her nails, toes, and eyebrows done at the same time. The time and money Kat spent on herself was a small price to pay in exchange for having a taste of her former swagger, even if only sporadically.

Kat rubbed her naked belly as she frowned at herself in the mirror. She could feel the stretch marks that her son had left her with—badges of motherhood. *It's not fair,* she thought to herself as hunger pangs made her think of the chocolate cake in the fridge. Her hips were wider than she remembered them the last time she had looked in the mirror. Could it be that she was getting even bigger? Kat slid both hands up her waist feeling its thickness. It made her feel kind of sexy. Here she was feeling herself up in the mirror and there wasn't even a man there to enjoy the show. She couldn't remember the last time Kenneth had touched her, and now he was gone.

Kat had found out about this resort trip because she was on Strebor's listserv. Although she usually avoided giving out her email address on commercial web sites, she decided to join while searching for information regarding the latest book of her favorite fictional author, Zane. The web site gave details about Zane hosting a resort week at Hedonism. With the lack of sex in her life that she believed her extra girth had relegated her to, she thought that this trip would be the perfect opportunity to get her swerve back.

Now that she was sitting by the pool, hiding her huge, dimpled thighs with a sarong, she thought maybe this wasn't such a good idea.

Fifteen minutes after she had sat on her lounge chair, two other women sat directly across from her. They were big women, cute, but still big. They waved to her nonchalantly as they settled in their own lounge chairs. Kat nodded and smiled back at them. She didn't want to be unfriendly, but she also didn't want the area where she lay to become the "Big Girlz" section. If memory served her correctly, they always seemed to travel in herds. Kat felt it was going to be hard enough to attract a handsome man looking the way that she did. She didn't want to add any pressure on any would-be suitors by having competition around her.

Hedonism was definitely the place to be if you were looking for love without conditions. She and Margarita had slayed many would-be playas the last time she was here. Kat believed they coined the phrase, "What happens in Hedonism, stays in Hedonism."

Kat didn't have to wait long before her first suitor rolled up on her. The empty lounge chair was an obvious invitation. The minute she looked over to see what had plopped down on the chair next to her, she knew it wasn't going to happen.

This man is definitely long in the tooth. Kat didn't think he was too old. She was really referring to his two long, yellow front teeth. They draped over his bottom lip like an old blanket on a sofa.

He had a drink in his hand and it was obvious that the brown liquid in his glass was acting as a courage potion. There was no way that a man who looked like this, had the confidence to approach women of Kat's caliber sober. Kat knew she wasn't the hot chick she used to be, but there was no way she could have fallen this fast…and that far. She knew she had to get rid of him quickly, if she was going to have a chance with anyone else on the island. If he were seen next to her for too long, other ugly men would think they had a chance and the good-looking brothers would think she was beneath them.

"Hey beautiful, you mind if I sit here a while?" Toothy asked.

Kat gave him an annoyed look and shrugged her shoulders to show she didn't care if he sat or not. Toothy took this as a positive sign and smiled his most sunshine yellow smile.

"So what's your name, Miss?" Toothy asked.

Kat acted as if she didn't hear him, but this did not deter him.

"My name's Carl Hancock," he said, extending a hand for Kat to shake.

Kat continued to act as if she did not see or hear him and he withdrew his hand still smiling.

"I'm a White House staffer in Washington, D.C." Toothy seemed to like to hear himself talk. Kat ignored him but he continued to talk about his job a mile a minute.

"I meet with the president and his top aides on occasion. They're pretty smart people, for the most part. But, our first president, he was a very smart man. John Hanson knew how to get things done when no one else did. I bet if he were running the country now, we wouldn't have all these terrorists making crazy threats. That damn 'W' just sat for ten minutes while the country was being bombed." Toothy sat back, very secure that he'd just sprung some new news on the lovely sista, thereby effectively enhancing his chances as a serious contender.

Kat knew his kind well. She had worked with politicians before and this guy was no politician. He was probably some grunt. It was obvious that he thought working in the White House made him an authority on American history. She had heard the Hanson myth many times over, and it was always "shared" by grunt guys like Toothy trying to impress with information and intellect.

Kat waited for him to pause and then turned to him and spoke. "John Hanson was not the first president of the United States."

Toothy looked at her still smiling and let out a chuckle. "Well, you can speak after all."

"Yes I can speak, when I have something to say. And like I said, John Hanson was not the first president of the United States."

Toothy sat on the lounge chair ready to make a point. He spied the two women that sat across from Kat. They were perking up and listening carefully to the exchange.

"Do you have a two-dollar bill in your purse?" Toothy asked.

"No I don't," Kat said, barely concealing her disgust at Toothy's insistence for passing off fiction as fact.

"Well, if you did, you'd see that the back of the two-dollar bill has an engraving of the signing of the Declaration of Independence. In the image is a man who has dark skin and wearing a powdered wig while sitting at the table just to the left of the men standing in the center of the engraving. This dark-skinned man was a Moor, or a black man, if you will. His name was John Hanson, and in his position was president of the continental congress.

"The new country was actually formed on March 1, 1781 with the adoption of the Articles of Confederation. Once the signing took place in 1781, a president was needed to run the country. John Hanson was chosen unanimously by Congress, which actually included George Washington. No one would run against him because he was a man to be contended with during the revolution, and was an extremely influential member of Congress. He took office at the time the Revolutionary War was ending. The army was demanding to get paid, but there was no money to pay them. As a result, the army threatened to overthrow the new government and put Washington in place. Congress decided to leave him holding all the weight, as the only guy left running the government.

"If anyone were to come back from the past that was fit to run the country now, it would definitely be John Hanson. As president he ordered all foreign troops off American soil, as well as the removal of all foreign flags. And, as you must know, this couldn't have been an easy thing to do considering how many European countries were occupying the United States since Columbus landed."

Toothy was caught up in his lesson and didn't notice the look of caution on the faces of the ladies that were listening intensely.

"Hanson established the seal that is now used on all official presidential documents. He established the first Treasury Department, the first Secretary of War, and the first Foreign Affairs department. He even declared that the fourth Thursday of every November was to be Thanksgiving Day—"

"I don't know about all you just said," Kat interrupted, "but I can see…"—Kat took the time to let her eyes wander down to Toothy's extended gut—"…that you clearly know when Thanksgiving is."

Loud snickers could be heard from the women across from them.

"Are you finished?" Kat asked impatiently.

"Yep. What more is there to really say?" Toothy offered.

"Well maybe you should think about this. The claim that John Hanson was the first president of the United States is a flat-out lie, anyway you try to slice it. The foundation of the lie started in 1876 by a guy named George A. Hanson whose only motivation was enhancing the careers and backgrounds of his ancestors and anyone else with the last name Hanson. George Hanson's hallucinations were treated as fact in 1932 by Seymour Wemyss Smith who wrote a book called *John Hanson: Our First President.*

"In real-life history, Hanson was the third president of the Continental Congress. He was the first to serve a full one-year term, and the first to formally use the title President of the United States in Congress Assembled. However, the office of the President of the United States in Congress Assembled was, despite the name, not an executive post. It was more like what's now the Speaker of the House or the Vice President. The office was in existence from 1781 to 1788, under the Articles of Confederation, and was replaced by the modern office of President of the United States when the Constitution took effect in 1789.

"As for all that hype about paying troops for the war, history annals will show that the only issue was about paying the secretary who reported to the Board of War—not the president. Congress passed the final resolution on that issue on October 1, 1781 before Hanson became president.

"George Washington, John Adams, and Abraham Lincoln all declared a national day of thanksgiving, after all, the holiday had been celebrated since the 1600s. However, it was FDR—that's Franklin Delano Roosevelt in case you can't keep up—that actually made the date of Thanksgiving a matter of federal law on December 26, 1941."

Toothy wasn't going down without a fight.

"You know, you're so pretty, I would believe just about anything that fell from those sexy lips of yours. But the fact still remains that Hanson was black." Toothy thought he had her.

Kat took a deep breath and closed in for the kill. "You know, you really shouldn't believe everything that's written in black ink. There was a Senator John Hanson, a politician who was involved with the resettlement of freed slaves to his homeland of Liberia, West Africa. He was indeed black, but was no relation to John Hanson of Maryland and lived about a hundred years too late."

Kat sat back in her chair and closed her eyes thinking that Toothy would leave her alone now.

"I like a smart woman," Toothy started again. "What else can we talk about?"

Kat sat up again.

"What do you want to talk about?" she said, feigning interest in showing him up again. Toothy thought hard for a moment, trying to think of a subject that a woman would not likely have a lot of information on.

"Why don't we discuss nuclear power," he said, believing that Kat would not have anything to say on the subject.

"Sure we could discuss nuclear power," Kat agreed. "That could be a real interesting subject, but let me ask you a question first."

"Sure, ask me anything you want." Toothy flashed another smile.

"A donkey, a cow, and a deer all eat grass, right? Yet deer excrete little pellets, while cows turn out flat patties, and donkeys produce clumps of dried grass. Why do you suppose that is?"

"Damn, baby, I have no idea."

"Well then," Kat said. "How the hell you feel you're qualified to discuss nuclear power, when you don't know SHIT!"

The two women sitting across from Kat burst out in fits of laughter. Toothy's smile was no longer visible. He mumbled something incoherent under his breath and then got up and left.

After the two women stopped laughing, they formally introduced themselves to Kat. Coincidentally, they were both from Harlem, too.

"Girl, we thought you were some stuck-up heifer from California or somewhere," Noreen admitted to Kat later that day, after they'd all had a few drinks. Kat hadn't come to find friends in Jamaica, but after no other man approached her that first day at Hedonism, she was glad to be around some decent sistas. These women were no different to the women she used to hang with before the kid and the marriage. If anything, they were more mature, less preoccupied with self and even more fun.

CHAPTER THREE
SLIM PICKINS

The three women spent the first three days together at Hedonism. They danced every night, if not with each other, then with whichever gentleman asked them. After the first day at the resort, the men and women who were there to hook up did just that. Everyone else who was only there to have a good time weren't disappointed either. During the morning, Noreen and Dahlia would meet Kat in her room and then they'd spend the day by the pool or at the spa. On the third day, Noreen made an announcement to Dahlia and Kat.

"I signed up for The Dating Game this afternoon."

Every afternoon since they had arrived at Hedonism, Zane hosted a Dating Game contest by the biggest pool at the resort. All three women would look on and laugh at the contestants, enjoying the questions and responses from the three women or men who were brave enough to participate in the fun.

Neither Dahlia nor Kat seemed surprised by Noreen's announcement.

"I knew you were going to do it," Dahlia said.

"After you got up on the open mike last night and did your poem, 'Big Juicy,' I knew you were going to do something else to prove that you're as good as the skinny girls." Kat chuckled.

"And why shouldn't I?" Noreen asked.

"The charcoal-black chick did her poem, 'Midnight Love.' All she was doing was advertising how much better extra dark punany is, than regular brown punany. Why can't I put the word out, how good *Big Juicy* punany is? I know I got some good stuff and I'm not ashamed of it," Noreen said, turning over onto her back on the reclined pool chair.

"Anyway, what does my poem and signing up for the Dating Game, have to do with anything?" she said, turning to her side and leaning on her elbow while she spoke.

"Nothing, except anytime you see some small woman getting something that you want, you go all out of your way to do something about it," Dahlia said, remaining relaxed on her back.

"And what's wrong with that? I'm proud to be a big beautiful woman and I'm not letting life shortchange me out of anything. You can keep trying to diet if you want, Dee, it's not going to change who you are."

Dahlia remained quiet. She was not ready to admit that Noreen was right, again. She stayed on her back and continued to look at the blue sky through her Versace sunglasses.

Noreen turned to Kat waiting to see if she had something to add.

"Why are you looking at me? You know how I feel. I'm going to diet and exercise until I get this weight off of my fat ass, and if that doesn't work, I'm gonna get me another job until I can pay for some liposuction. Then maybe I'll find a man that deserves this good pussy. It won't be fat, it won't be funky black, but it will be good."

All three women laughed. They had already had this discussion the first day when they met. Kat and Dahlia had sided with each other on the issue of why big women settle for whatever man they can get. Noreen made the point that she was fat, happy and never settled for second best. She had even bragged that she could get any man whom she really wanted.

After three days of seeing Noreen manipulate and seduce all sorts of men, Kat was ready to believe her. Dahlia had seen Noreen in action and had never doubted her. All Dahlia knew was that she didn't have that same power over men.

An hour later, Noreen was sitting behind a makeshift partition with two other women. They were definitely not as pretty as Noreen, but they were not big women. All three women wore bathing suits with a sarong wrapped around their waists. Noreen's suit was the tightest. She had an incredibly flat stomach for such a large woman. Her hips flared out widely over the stool she sat on, and when she crossed her legs you could see more of her evenly brown thighs than the other two contestants. Noreen was bachelorette number three.

The bachelor was named Dennis. He was a thin, handsome, brown-skinned man. His face was clean-shaven if not for the pencil-thin mustache that outlined his upper lip. During the introduction of the contestants, Dahlia and Kat whispered and joked with each other how he would never be able to carry Noreen to bed.

"She will break that little man in two," Kat said, giggling behind her hand.

There were approximately a hundred people by the poolside. This daily event had quickly become the entertainment of the day for the resort. Everyone stopped swimming and people stepped out of their rooms to enjoy the show. Noreen waved to her girls and they waved back, not wanting her to become suspicious of their little joke.

Noreen was not attracted to skinny men at all. She liked her men to be big and strapping. She liked feeling petite in a big man's embrace or when lying underneath him in bed. She also liked the feeling of being "handled" in bed. You couldn't be too big for her taste. If she knew it was a skinny man that she was competing for, she would have walked right off the makeshift stage. Her girls had promised her that if it was a skinny or ugly man, they would give her the high sign. She would then give bad answers so that there was no chance she would get stuck with a lemon—so much for friendship.

"Bachelorette Number One, if I were at a fruit stand and you were the fruit I was looking for, what fruit would you be?"

Dennis had a voice that was so deep and rich it made all the contestants' eyebrows raise. Bachelorette Number One sat up a little higher in her seat and then smoothed her sarong before answering.

"Honey, I would be two big melons," Bachelorette Number One said, holding her two large breasts together for everyone else but the bachelor to see. The men who were watching clapped a little, but it was a very obvious answer.

"Bachelorette Number Two, same question."

"Baby, for you, I would be a grapefruit, because although I could be called high yellow, I'm definitely pink and all juicy on the inside."

More men clapped for that answer than the first, but the women were still not giving it up.

"Bachelorette Number Three, would you like to try your hand at that same question?"

Noreen smiled easily before opening her mouth.

"Dennis," she said, letting his name linger in the air. None of the other contestants had said his name. You could tell he liked the way she said it, by the smile that came to his face.

"I couldn't be anything other than a quince if you were looking for me."

"A quince?"

"Yes, the quince was the fruit that Eve allegedly tempted Adam with in the Garden of Eden. The only difference is that biting me is not a sin. And if you bite me right, I'll bite you right back."

The crowd liked her response and both men and women gave her a loud clap. The game continued for about another thirty minutes. Noreen gave the cleverest and sexiest answers. If Dennis were to pick anyone else, he would be a fool. At the end of the question-and-answer session, Zane, the resort's hostess, asked, "So Dennis, who will it be? Bachelorette Number One, Bachelorette Number Two, or Bachelorette Number Three?"

After Dennis picked Noreen, the other two women came out to meet him. He didn't seem wholly disappointed that he didn't pick the other contestants. He gave them both a perfunctory kiss on the cheek before they went on their way.

When Noreen came from behind the partition to meet Dennis, the crowd was momentarily hushed. It was as if now that they were standing next to each other, the crowd could finally see how they each opposed the other's physical appearance.

For his part, Dennis smiled and held his arms out to welcome Noreen in a warm embrace.

Noreen's response was not as warm. As she allowed herself to be hugged by Dennis, she looked over his shoulder at her two friends. They did not look back in her direction. Instead they acted as if they were in some very interesting conversation with one another. Noreen gave a dirty look in their direction and then pulled away from Dennis's grasp.

Zane announced that their prize for participating in the game was a private lunch at the most exclusive restaurant at the resort. Everyone clapped their approval as the pool crowd started to dissipate. Now that Dennis and Noreen were left to be with each other without the benefit of a hundred onlookers, Dennis voiced his mind.

"Hmm, not too pleased with what's behind door number one, huh?"

Noreen seemed shaken out of her thoughts by Dennis's voice.

"Pardon me?"

"I must not be exactly what you expected."

"I have to be honest with you, Dennis, and mind you, I never judge a book by its cover, but I'm not sure that we're at all compatible."

"Compatible? I see. Am I too short? Too skinny? Too lightskinned? Which one is it?" Dennis smiled good-naturedly.

"Yeah, that's it." Noreen made an awkward face.

"Whoa! All of the above, huh?"

Noreen shook her head yes, and folded her arms against her chest, uncomfortably shifting her weight from one foot to the other.

"No problem, I feel you," Dennis said, raising his hands to chest level, as if to ward off a blow. "But there is still the issue of a special lobster lunch.

The all-inclusive buffet is all right, but I don't eat lobster enough to just throw away this opportunity."

Noreen wrinkled her nose as if she had just smelled something fishy, but then decided to put her own prejudice against thin men down for a second.

"You certainly make a good point…Dennis, right?"

Dennis smiled at her and nodded slowly, not wanting to scare Noreen away with too much enthusiasm.

"All right, Dennis, let's do lunch."

Dennis's smile widened showing his perfectly white teeth and a pair of abnormally long canines for the first time. Noreen made a note of that slight oddity and tried not to stare.

"Great, if we go right now, we can be seated and enjoying lunch, and more of each other's company in about fifteen minutes."

Noreen wanted to go over to her friends and give them a piece of her mind, but let the thought go. She could feel them looking at her and Dennis from across the pool. They were probably laughing themselves silly with their little prank. She thought it would be better to let them think it didn't faze her. Or if they knew better than that, then at least she could keep them in suspense over when she was going to give it to them good.

Dennis put his arm out for her to take a hold of and she grasped it, hesitating only slightly before looping her arm through his. Noreen held her head high and found her most regal and dignified gait. She heard her two friends laugh uproariously as she took a few more steps and she couldn't help herself anymore. She turned around and shook her fist at them as Dennis continued to lead her out of the pool area. The women laughed harder. They knew they were in for it, but they were enjoying their moment of triumph.

CHAPTER FOUR
DAMN, BABY!

This was going to be Noreen's fourth date with Dennis. Kat and Dahlia were in the room with her as she prepared to go out for her last night at Hedonism.

"What the hell is it about this guy that's so special again?" Kat asked.

"I told you before, I don't know. He's just different." Noreen was irritated that she didn't have a better explanation.

"I know what it is," Dahlia offered. Both Noreen and Kat turned to her at the same time.

"It's the fact that he hasn't tried to do anything with you yet. You're obsessed with the fact that he hasn't tried to get into your panties by now—and here at Hedonism, no less. My girl couldn't get laid in the only resort where anybody that wants to get laid, will get laid."

"Please, that is so not true. We have kissed."

"Listen to her. 'We have kissed,'" Dahlia mocked Noreen.

"This from a woman that drags me all over New York checking out all of the hot spots for guaranteed love connections. If I thought you were getting any, I'd say you were dick whipped."

"For your information, if I really wanted to, I would have already had him in my bed."

"Uh-uh, not in this bed, you wouldn't," Dahlia said, bouncing heavily on Noreen's disheveled bed.

"I am not sleeping out by the pool like you had me do when we were in Cancun. Hell no! Not this time!"

"I did not have you sleeping by the pool in Cancun."

"Like hell you didn't. You left the dance floor with that big doofy guy you met. Darren or Derrick or…"

"Darrell."

"Darrell. That was his name. I get back to the room, by myself, and I hear all kinds of animal noises going on."

Dahlia made her voice deep and gruff and added a Southern drawl for her imitation of Darrell. "Slow down, baby, slow down. Oh damn! I didn't know it was going to be like that."

All three women cracked up at Dahlia's imitation.

"He wasn't that bad. He was kind of cute," Noreen tried to explain,

"Well, cute or not, I am not spending my last night out by the pool."

"I'll tell you what," Kat said. "I've got the single room, so if any of us feels like we want to be alone with a guy, we'll just use my room, okay."

"Okay with me," Noreen said.

"Of course it's okay with you. I know I'm not sleeping with anybody I meet tonight."

"Me neither," Kat agreed.

"Well, I guess you can give me the keys now then," Noreen suggested.

"'Cause tonight is definitely the night."

"You don't mind me bunking with you, do you, Dahlia?" Kat asked, as she handed the keys over to Noreen.

"As long as you don't snore, I don't mind."

Kat gave her a sideways glance.

"You do snore, don't you?" Dahlia accused her. Kat nodded matter-of-factly.

"Dammit, I can't get a break."

"Well, you grind your teeth," Noreen said.

"I do not." Dahlia was indignant.

"Please, you grind your teeth so much, I'm surprised you have any left."

"I do?" Dahlia looked heartbroken.

"It's no big deal, just another little Piccadilly for your great personality. We all have those little idiosyncrasies that make us special," Noreen said with a honey-dipped voice.

Dahlia didn't think it was so special. She didn't need another flaw to make her feel even more inferior to everybody else.

✢✢✢

When the girls reached the club, the party was in full swing. Everybody was letting it all hang out for the last day at the resort. Dennis met them at the door and he immediately swept Noreen out onto the dance floor.

It took Kat and Dahlia a drink and a trip to ladies room before they were asked to dance. The men who asked them were not the finest men in the place, but luckily or maybe because of the way they carried themselves, the men were no losers. Both men were handsome with average builds. They came over to Kat and Dahlia together as if it were planned. Like women they figured that there was safety in numbers and less likelihood of rejection. The girls were just glad that the men were not fat. They both hated when fat men thought that they were what big women were supposed to end up with.

After a few dances and just as many drinks, Noreen coaxed Dennis out to a secluded grove outside of the club. They kissed passionately, touching each other's faces tenderly for several minutes before Noreen took him by the hand and tried to lead him toward Kat's room.

"Where are we going?" he said, stopping abruptly before they went more than a few yards.

"To my room." Noreen smiled devilishly.

Dennis looked up into the night sky as if trying to figure out the mystery of the heavens before he looked back into Noreen's eyes.

"I don't think that's such a good idea," he finally said.

Noreen blew out an exasperated breath.

"Are you gay?" she said in annoyance.

"What? Gay? No! I'm not gay. Whatever gave you an idea like that?"

"Whatever gave me an idea like that? You gave me an idea like that. I've done everything but smack you with it and you won't even try to touch me below the waist."

"That doesn't mean I'm gay."

"Well, what does it mean, Dennis, 'cause I'm all out of answers to that question."

Dennis looked at Noreen closely, gauging what she might accept.

"I just don't have sex that often, that's all," he finally said, looking at the ground.

Noreen had been holding her breath for a moment and when she heard his explanation, she let it out easily. She smiled, feeling better that he hadn't said that he had some disease or that he had someone else back home.

"Is that all?" she responded, reaching out for him and squeezing him about the waist.

"You're just a little shy because you don't have sex often."

"No, that's not it." He wriggled out of her grasp uncomfortably.

"Then what?" Noreen was once again annoyed.

"I'm not shy, Noreen."

"You could have fooled me."

"I just don't want to hurt you, is all."

"Hurt me? I thought you said you don't have anyone else in your life."

"I don't."

"Well, what is it? Are you embarrassed to be seen with me?"

"Don't get crazy, we've been with each other all week, we look good together."

Noreen had a different opinion on that subject, but did not bother to elaborate on her own feelings.

"Well?" Noreen said, waiting with her hands on her hips.

Dennis mumbled something under his breath that sounded like, *I'm going to be sick.*

"What? You're going to be sick?" Noreen was suddenly more concerned.

Dennis shook his head.

"No, no."

"Then what, Dennis, what is it?"

"I've got a big dick," he said, raising his eyes to meet hers.

Oh no the hell he didn't. This motherfucker did not just say, 'I've got a big dick.'

"You've got a what?"

"I've got a big dick."

"I heard what you said. I just wanted to make sure my ears weren't deceiving me. You've got a big dick. That's what all the secrecy is about? That's the reason you won't touch me below the waist? That's the reason you won't go to my room with me? I have heard some lame-ass excuses before, but that has got to be the funniest shit I've heard yet."

"Noreen, you don't understand."

"Oh I understand." *Another man with delusions of grandeur,* she thought.

"No, I don't think you understand. I put the last two women I was with in the hospital."

"Uh-huh, I see."

"No, you don't see. I'm not kidding, I'm really big."

Noreen stopped for a second and slowly allowed her gaze to go downward toward Dennis's crotch for the first time. She tried to remember the pants that he had worn since she'd met him. He had been wearing long shorts, down to his knees, on the day they had met. During the evenings his pants had always been baggy. She assumed that he wore baggy pants because he was thin and wanted to give the illusion that he was bigger than he actually was.

"Let me see it."

"What?"

"I said, let me see it."

"Right here, right now?"

"Yeah, right here and right now."

Dennis looked around the surrounding area and then shook his head no. "Not here," he said. "Maybe if we go to your room ..."

"Okay, let's go to my room." Noreen thought this was turning out to be more trouble than it was worth. She had played this game with men before. That is, the game where men try to make you believe that they're not really into you in a sexual way, so that you'll be more intrigued and go after them more aggressively.

Noreen opened the door to Kat's room. It was no different to the room that she and Dahlia shared, except that it had a king-sized bed in the middle of the room instead of the two double beds on opposite sides. The maid had cleaned the room so that everything was in its proper place. Generically speaking, this room could have belonged to anyone.

Noreen held the door open for Dennis, who appeared as if he were more than just a little reluctant. When he finally entered, Noreen quickly closed the door behind him.

"Okay, let's see what you've got," she said, choosing to bypass the formalities of foreplay. Having dated nothing but big men as an adult she had seen many big penises. It wasn't true that all big men with big feet had big penises, but it was common enough that she'd seen her share of them. It could also be said that if a man had a big penis, it would be common for him to brag about it or at the least be very proud of it. Dennis was taking another path to show off how well he was endowed, but like any man, he was only trying to set a better stage for his display, Noreen thought.

"Before I show you, you have to promise me something."

"What?" Noreen asked, now sure that he had set up this entire scenario for this promise that he was going to try to extricate from her.

"You have to promise that you'll still see me, even after I show you."

Noreen didn't know what she expected, but she certainly hadn't expected this.

"Okay." She was trying to get on with it.

"No, you have to promise."

He was really taking this thing too far, but Noreen went along.

"All right, all right, I promise."

Dennis unbuckled his pants and unzipped his zipper. He proceeded to pull down his pants and Noreen almost started to laugh. He had on boxers that were at least four sizes too big for him. The elastic on the waist was so wide that he needed the help of a large safety pin. Dennis pushed his pants down to mid thigh and then wriggled his waist a little to make them fall around his ankle. Now Noreen couldn't help but smile a little. Dennis looked ridiculous in his underwear. The diamond pattern reminded Noreen of her five-year-old nephew's pajamas. They went so far past his knees they could almost be capris. Dennis looked embarrassed as he started to fiddle with the safety pin. He was having problems undoing it.

"Here, let me help you," Noreen offered, taking a step toward him.

"I can do it." Dennis turned around to keep Noreen from getting to his waist. Noreen waited impatiently for a moment and Dennis finally said, "There, I got it."

Dennis turned back toward Noreen with the elastic of his underwear held up daintily between his right thumb and forefinger. Dennis looked Noreen in the eyes.

"Please, just don't run."

This guy's got jokes, Noreen thought.

"Well…" She threw up her hands impatiently.

Without further ado, Dennis let go of the elastic. Noreen was looking at his groin area at the exact time that he let the underwear drop. She was definitely not prepared for what she saw.

"What the fu…?"

She couldn't complete any of the words or the sentence that came to her mind as she took a step back out of a sudden fright. Dennis took a step forward.

"Don't," was all he was able to say as he tripped over the pants and underwear around his ankle. He caught himself against the dresser and righted himself quickly before he fell. Before Noreen could say anything else, Dennis picked his underwear up to his waist along with his pants. He didn't bother trying to put the safety pin back on. Noreen watched him scramble to get himself together and fought with herself not to run out the door. She had seen some big penises in her life, but what she had just witnessed scared the shit out of her. She was as surprised as Dennis when she heard herself saying, "Wait. Don't put it away."

Noreen stepped in front of Dennis and put her hands over his as he tried to cinch his belt. Dennis didn't struggle with her. He let his hands come away, accepting hers in their place. Noreen prided herself on facing and overcoming all of her fears. That's why she always went hard, when anyone tried to keep her from the things that she desired. Noreen took a deep breath in an attempt to get over her initial anxiety at seeing Dennis's monstrous member and then undid his pants again. When she let the pants waist go, the underwear slid down with them, exposing his huge organ to the brisk climate of the air conditioned room. Noreen thought she saw it twitch and slowly reached out to touch the cable-sized vein that traveled the length of it. Dennis flinched when she touched it and now she definitely knew it had twitched.

"My God, Dennis, how big is it?"

Noreen reached down with both hands and held it one hand over the other, trying to hold it like a baseball bat. Noreen knew she had big hands for a woman, she had held Dennis's hands a few times and hers were larger. She wondered how he held it, as her own hands found it awkward to handle.

"It's about sixteen inches long."

"Sixteen inches long, flaccid?"

"Yes, but it doesn't get much longer when it's hard. Only about another two inches. The problem is, it gets thicker, a lot thicker."

"It's already as thick as my wrist."

"Yeah," was all Dennis could muster, as he felt himself starting to swell in Noreen's hands. She stared into her hands mesmerized by how hard the penis was becoming. The head had swelled to the size of a Granny Smith apple, and started to leak clear fluid. Noreen couldn't help herself. She wanted to know just how big this monster could get.

"Please don't, I don't know if I can stop."

"Sshhh, just close your eyes, baby. You don't have to stop. I'm going to take good care of you."

Noreen's voice was hypnotic and Dennis slowly closed his eyes. Noreen stroked, pulled and tugged on the enormous appendage as best she could and was starting to become afraid that it would never stop growing. Her fascination overwhelmed her fear and she continued with her mission. Her awkward strokes were causing larger amounts of pre-seminal fluids to leak from Dennis, and she used that to lubricate the head. She allowed her palm to cover the two-inch-long slit in the crown, again and again, coming away with moisture to soak the shaft. It wasn't going to be nearly enough to cover its entirety, but from the look of ecstasy on his face, Dennis wasn't going to last much longer anyway.

The look on Dennis's face made Noreen feel good. She prided herself on being able to satisfy any man, and this would be her masterpiece, her pièce de résistance, as it were. Noreen had the urge to let her head go down and lick some of the pre-cum from the crown, but remembered that she had never spoken to Dennis regarding his health status. *Damn, I want to lick it so bad.* Noreen threw caution to the wind and started to bend her head toward the dick head anyway. *Ah shit,* but she was too late. Dennis was already cumming. Rope after rope of sperm arced out of the thick spongy head. Noreen put both hands around the crown and continued to massage. She was trying to get the last vestiges of cum out of him. Dennis was shaking from head to toe, and it was making Noreen hot to watch. It wasn't going to be enough for her to just lick. Now she wanted to feel that monster inside her. Dennis opened his eyes. They were wild with fulfilled lust. Noreen pushed him and he allowed himself to land easily onto the king-sized bed.

"I'll be right back," she said. Dennis couldn't get to his feet fast enough to stop her. Instead, he called out to her as she reached the door.

"Where are you going?"

"I have to get a condom."

"No, condoms don't fit me," he called out.

Dennis knew she had heard him, but she never slowed down. Two minutes later, she opened the door and slammed it shut behind her. Dennis was still in the same position sprawled on the bed. He hadn't bothered to try to put his penis away.

Before tonight he hadn't had sex in more than six months. His penis was still hard and there was no way it was going to fit back into his pants.

"What's that?"

Noreen put a small plastic package to her teeth and ripped it open.

"It's a female condom," Noreen answered. She was already on her knees in front of him trying to fit it over the head.

"It's supposed to go inside of the woman," she said, grunting to stretch the rubber over the head, "but in your case, I think it might just work this way." It took her a minute, but she was finally able to get the rubber sheath over the head and halfway down the shaft of his penis. *That would have to suffice.*

Dennis looked up at Noreen as she shimmied quickly out of her panties. He watched as her big beautiful ass rippled with its own weight. She pulled her dress over her head and he was surprised by the size of her breasts. He hadn't thought they would be as large as he now saw.

"My God, you're beautiful," he said.

"Not too big?"

Noreen was fishing for compliments; she loved hearing the voice of a man that truly adored her. She knew Dennis was attracted to big women from the start.

Before he could answer she was up on the bed with both feet flat on either side of his hips. She already had the blunt head of his dick at the entrance to her wet vagina. He didn't want to spoil it and just shook his head no.

Noreen gritted her teeth and let her knees give way. Lights exploded in her head.

When the girls picked her up from the resort clinic the next morning, she had an ice pack between her legs.

Their plane was leaving at one o'clock in the afternoon. They had to leave the resort by eleven thirty. It was only eight, so they decided to have breakfast before starting to pack.

During breakfast Noreen explained to them what had happened. She and Dennis had tried to have sex all night long, in vain. The head would just not fit into her small vagina. At one point they had gotten a fraction of it into her, and she had just rubbed herself back and forth until she came. Dennis had been a gentleman the whole night. He let her try over and over again, all the while content to just nibble on her breasts and kiss her clit. She had cum a second time while banging the head continuously into the opening of her already raw pussy. Her orgasm was so strong that she lost consciousness. When she awoke in the morning, Dennis was gone and she was so swollen that she went straight to the resort clinic. The resort doctor had a suite that was connected to his office and saw her right away. Apparently this sort of morning visit was common. It was after she was treated that Noreen called the girls.

Dahlia and Kat didn't laugh at Noreen openly. They waited until she was in the shower, then they cracked up. Noreen heard them as she soaped and took her time rinsing to give them time to get it out of their systems.

At the airport, Dennis found Noreen and apologized for leaving the room without saying good-bye. He explained that he had gone to his room to shower and change clothes and when he returned to the room she was no longer there.

"I was worried about you, No. Where did you go?"

Noreen's family and very close friends were the only ones that shortened her name like that. She sort of liked the easy way that Dennis did it, too. Noreen forgave him and they made plans to see each other in the States. Dennis lived in New Jersey and worked in Manhattan. Noreen liked him enough to continue to see him. She had already thought he was a special man; after last night she knew just how special.

On the plane Dahlia graciously switched seats with Dennis so that he could sit with Noreen. It was a relief. Those seats weren't made for two voluptuous women to sit together.

Dahlia was enjoying her second plane meal. The cute man sitting next to her didn't want his. He watched as she finished off the meal, then the dessert. She tried to start a conversation with him after she finished, but he seemed to want to doze. She stopped trying and closed her eyes and went to sleep.

Kat was in first class alone. She thought about her son and how she missed him. Her mother and he would be picking her up at the airport. She hadn't gotten laid at the resort, but it didn't bother her. She had made two good friends.

CHAPTER FIVE
PLEASE, MA'AM, THANK YOU

Kat told the girls that she would meet them downtown later, but they had insisted that they would meet her at her place.

Kat and Kenny had bought their brownstone six years ago while they were still trying to get their limousine company off the ground. When they found the property, it was a shell between two other crack-infested buildings. Kenny fought with Kat for over six months about wanting to build a new building between two that were inhabited by junkies, but Kat saw the bigger picture. She saw it as an investment property as well as a home. Her plan was to build a duplex on the bottom two floors where she and Kenny could live and to make individual apartments of each of the two floors above her. Harlem was gentrifying very quickly and she wanted to get in on it before it was too late. The Mount Morris Park section of Harlem was central to all the subways and buses and would be a prime area once the crack heads were forced out. At the time Kat had big plans with very little capital. She was out of a high-paying job with the city. Her best friend in the world had been responsible for getting her hired and also responsible for her being fired. Margarita Smith was the only person she knew that had the kind of money she needed, so Kat went to her for a loan. She didn't like to say that Margarita owed her, but she did.

Margarita had only one stipulation—all the property be under Kat's name. She was leery of Kenny and wanted to protect her friend. Kat had grudgingly agreed to the stipulation and this year, thanked God that Margarita had insisted. Her divorce went smoothly because of it. Kenny had no claim to the assets that they once shared. If it weren't for the fact that she didn't want to run the limousine company, he would have been left with nothing. She still owned the company, but she allowed him to run it, and give her fifty percent of the profits. This way they didn't have to argue over child support. Her share didn't make her rich by any stretch of the imagination, but she was supporting her son and living comfortably in the big city.

Kat's tenant on the third floor was a young, gay, white boy named Billy, and on the fourth floor was a young black couple that was always arguing. The rent from both the apartments more than paid her mortgage. Last year the rent for one full floor in a brownstone had gone up to $2,400 a month. This meant Kat was living in her space for free, with a little change left over for incidentals.

Noreen pushed the bottom bell and when the door buzzed, she turned the doorknob hard and entered the building. Dahlia was right behind her and stepped on the back of Noreen's heel as she took a step forward. Noreen turned quickly and gave Dahlia a dirty look.

"These are my favorite Bruno Maglis; if they have a scuff on the back, eeeeww."

"I'm sorry. Damn, you're in a bad mood. You're acting like you haven't gotten any in weeks."

Kat slid one of the double doors to her apartment open just as Noreen was about to light into Dahlia.

"Who hasn't gotten any? Noreen? Ha ha! Come on in and tell me about it, baby girl." Noreen looked annoyed, but she let Kat put her arm around her and lead her into the parlor that lay behind the double doors.

Noreen and Dahlia were both appreciating the size of the room.

"Oh, this is nice," Dahlia said, looking up at the twelve-foot ceilings.

"I don't mean to get in your business, girl, but your ex-husband is handling his business. This place is posh."

"My ex had nothing to do with it. This is my place."

"You mean he doesn't help you with the rent anymore."

"No, I mean I own the building. He never owned any part of it. Shit, he
tried to talk me out of buying the property when I first wanted to do it."

"I'm sure he's kicking himself in the ass now," Noreen said, holding her
hand up to Dahlia for a high-five. They all laughed at Kenny's expense and
then Kat showed them around the rest of the apartment.

Kat's mother was downstairs putting KJ to bed.

"Ma, this is Noreen and this is Dahlia." Kat's mother was a thin frail woman.
She looked to be the meek and quiet type. It was a deceptive posture she
enjoyed. It was from her that Kat had gotten her disposition and her man-
nerisms. There had been no man in the house when Kat was growing up,
only Ma.

"So you girls are going out for a night on the town, huh?" Kat's mother asked.

Noreen and Dahlia only smiled and nodded their heads.

"Well, you girls be careful, okay. There are men out there who just love
to get their paws on some big-ass women."

"Maaa!"

"I'm just saying the truth," she said, looking at Noreen to confirm what
she'd just said.

"And it's usually a man with a big thing that's looking for a big girl, so you
better watch out."

Noreen blushed and looked at Kat accusingly.

"Maaa! I swear I didn't tell her anything," Kat implored Noreen.

"What did you have to tell me? You think you girls are the first to go out
on the town trying to find a man. When I was your age…" she said, looking
at Dahlia this time, "I had all kinds of men trying to date me. Fat, tall, skinny,
short, but I never had the problem my girlfriend Nidia had—she was big

like you girls. There was always some man with a big thing trying to get with her. Men are so dense. They thought that all big girls were going to have a big opening between their legs. We know it ain't so. Nidia was very small down there. We were best friends back then and sometimes we would tell each other who had a big one and who had a small one. Of course she liked the small ones and I—"

"I think it's time for us to go now, Ma," Kat interrupted, giving the girls an apologetic look. "I'll probably be home late so don't stay up waiting for me."

Kat kissed her mother on the cheek and gave her a hug. The girls said their good-byes and nice-to-meet-yous before Kat was able to rush them upstairs and out the door.

Once they were in Dahlia's car, Kat tried to apologize for her mother's brutally candid personality.

"Please, don't even trip, girl," Noreen interjected. "Wait till you meet my mother. She has a Bible in one hand and a bottle of beer in the other."

"Oh yeah, your mom is a trip," Dahlia agreed.

"What, you talking about my momma? Your momma ain't no better," Noreen accused.

"What was wrong with my mother?" Dahlia asked.

"You know what's wrong with your mother. I don't need to tell you."

"No, I want to hear it, what's wrong with my mother?"

"She comes from a farm in Puerto Rico, right?"

"Yes."

"And your father is a doctor and African American, right?"

"Right."

"Then why can't she just try to speak normal English. She's always trying to keep up with your father's conversations. Why is she always trying to use big words that she doesn't even know what they mean?"

Dahlia was pulling away from the curb, but stopped to turn toward Noreen.

"My mother does not do that."

"Oh yes the hell she does. Last time I was at your house, your father asked me if I ever thought of switching from being a nurse and going back to school to be a doctor. Your mother breaks into the conversation and says, *Ju know. Dahlia, eh wonted to be a vegetarian when she was eh leetle girl.*" Kat had to stifle a giggle at Noreen's imitation of Dahlia's mother.

"If your father hadn't corrected her and said, *veterinarian*, I might have thought you wanted to go on a diet from the time you were five."

"That is not funny, Noreen."

"I'm not trying to be funny"—she winked at Kat when Dahlia turned away—"I'm just telling it like I see it."

The conversation went on like that the whole drive downtown. The only time they stopped bickering was when Noreen had to tell Dahlia which way to turn to get to the club.

They were somewhere around Eleventh Street in the meat packing district when Noreen said, "Pull over there into that parking spot."

"Where's the club?" Kat asked from the backseat.

"Right there." Noreen pointed to the entrance of what used to be a meat packing plant. In front of the door were two men. One black and one white. If size were the only factor, they could have both played in the NFL. They were dressed in black from head to toe including their leather jackets. The dark shades they were wearing at this time of night were overkill, but who would have the nerve to tell them.

"There's no sign, no awning. What kind of club is this, Noreen?" Kat asked, leaning over into the front seat.

"You'll see, don't worry we're going to have a good time."

"This better not be one of those cheesy places you've taken me to before," Dahlia said, turning off the ignition.

"The last place you took me had every old Superfly, used-to-be old player in Harlem in it."

"This is not that type of club. First of all, it costs two hundred dollars a head to get in and second of all, you have to have a special invite."

"And how the hell are we getting in? I am not paying two hundred dollars to get into any club," Kat said, sitting back in her seat.

"Kat, get your ass out of this car," Noreen said, opening her car door. "I know someone at the door. We're not paying to get in."

Kat reluctantly got out of the car. Dahlia was already out and was using the car's side mirror to touch up her hair. Noreen got out of the car, saw what Dahlia was doing and decided to check her reflection in the car door window. She looked pretty as ever. *Fine as wine, good as gold, the best and first for all to behold,* Noreen thought.

"Will you two come on? We all look just fine."

The three women were a breathtaking sight as they walked side by side taking up the entire sidewalk. They were each very beautiful in their own way, but together they looked like awesome forces from Mother Nature.

When they reached the darkened doorway, the black bouncer stepped forward to greet Noreen. He was about six feet eight inches tall and it was an effort for him to bend down to kiss Noreen on the cheek. Noreen made no effort to reach up to kiss him, fully acting the part of the Queen Bee.

"What's up, No?"

"Hi baby, these are my friends, Dahlia and Kat," she said, gesturing toward one, then the other.

"Girls, this is my baby brother, Eric."

Both women said, "Hi," and he turned his attention back to Noreen.

"Did Momma go back down to Atlantic City this weekend?"

"You know she did. She and her whole church gang go down there every weekend."

Eric shook his head in disbelief.

"I'm going to stop giving her my money if all she's going to do is spend it on—"

"Eric, baby, we're not here to discuss family business. Can we go in now?"

Eric smiled apologetically at Dahlia and Kat.

"Sorry, ladies, go right in. Have a good time." Then he leaned over and whispered to Noreen, "When Momma comes home tomorrow, you tell her to call me?"

Noreen pretended not to hear him and flipped her hair in his face as he held the door open for the girls to enter.

Inside the club Kat said, "Shit, girl! That was your baby brother? Your mother doesn't make anything small, does she?"

"I knew you had a brother, but damn he's fine. Why didn't you ever introduce him to me before?" Dahlia asked.

"Oh, he's always in some sort of trouble. When we were younger, he always wanted me to hook him up with my friends. I didn't do it then, and I'm not doing it now."

Dahlia looked longingly back at the closed door they had entered. "Mmm, maybe it's time for you to reconsider that one."

"Girl, please, come on, let's have a good time."

The girls walked past a second security person and a woman behind a desk. Noreen nodded to them and they smiled and nodded back. Kat supposed that they were the ones assigned to taking money or tickets or whatever got everyone else inside. Noreen walked through the doorway that was covered by a red velvet curtain. Kat and Dahlia followed closely behind.

The curtained doorway led them into a huge loft space half the size of a football field. Kat guessed rightly that the small doorway outside was to give the illusion that the space inside was small and exclusive, when in actuality it took up the whole block.

Kat was intrigued and amused at the scenes she saw around them, but Dahlia appeared to be shocked and dismayed. She wasn't saying anything, but her mouth hung open as she followed closely to the left of Noreen who walked in like she owned the place. The three women walked to the closest bar, which was only ten yards from the entrance. There were three empty barstools and they each climbed up on one.

"Well?" Noreen said to the girls.

"Noreen, this is an S and M club," Dahlia hissed.

"I know what it is. I used to come here all the time."

"Yes, you do seem to know your way around here," Kat added.

"Well, I haven't been here in about a year, but I used to come all the time when Eric first got the door."

"Noreen, these people in here are freaks," Dahlia said, looking around the room.

"Since when did you become such a prude, Miss Why Didn't You Introduce Me to Your Brother Before?"

"That is different. Look at these people around here. Some of them have all of their clothes off," Dahlia said in a hushed whisper.

"Nobody is telling you to take your clothes off, Dahlia. You can just watch if you want. Or you can just talk to someone. Or you can just dance. Nobody is going to judge you here."

All of a sudden there was a voice behind them.

"Mistresses, may I offer you a drink?"

The bartender was a young man of about twenty-five and had on a full tuxedo. He was one of the handsomest men that Dahlia had ever seen.

Kat was ready to swing.

"First drink is on me," she said, reaching into her red Dooney & Bourke for her wallet. Noreen put her hand over Kat's stopping her from reaching into her bag. She directed her attention to the beautiful bartender.

"Three Cosmos, sweetheart."

"Right away, Mistress." He turned away from them.

Noreen spoke to Kat, "The entrance fee includes all drinks. If you want, you can tip the bartender, or one of the submissives, but you better not come out of your pocket with anything less than a hundred dollars." Kat took her hand out of her purse immediately.

"A hundred dollars?"

"Mmm-hmm."

"Damn, this may not be so much fun after all."

"Believe me, we're going to have a lot of fun here and we're not going to spend one thin dime."

The bartender came back with their drinks. Dahlia, who had not said another word to either Kat or Noreen in the last few minutes, took her drink from the bartender and took a big swallow of the red liquid. Noreen and Kat both looked at her for a clue, as to what she was thinking. Dahlia took another long swallow of the liquid and then looked at her girls again.

"All right, I'm good. What do we do next?"

"Now that's my girl," Noreen said, putting an arm around Dahlia.

Before any of the women could move, Kat spied a half-dressed, middle-aged white man coming toward them with a leather paddle.

"Noreen, what the fuu…!"

"Be cool, be cool," Noreen said, barely moving her lips. Dahlia moved closer to Noreen, trying with all of her will not to run screaming out of the narrow door that they'd come through.

"Mistress, I'm here as your servant," the man said going down on one knee in front of Noreen. Dahlia and Kat, who were on either side of Noreen, both leaned away as if she had some unseen force field around her. Noreen had an annoyed look on her face. She turned and set her drink on the bar before speaking.

"Get up, slave," she addressed the kneeling man.

The half-dressed man got up immediately, but kept his head bowed, refusing to meet Noreen's eyes.

"Can't you see I'm here have a drinking with my friends," she said, taking on the air of an Egyptian queen. "How dare you disturb me!"

With that, Noreen reared back and backhanded the man across his face. Kat and Dahlia both jumped back with their hands up in a fighting stance. Where they came from a slap like that was surely going to cause a fight, and although Noreen had started it, they had their girl's back. Noreen shot them both a fierce look of disapproval and they simultaneously and cautiously put their fists down. She turned her attention back to the humiliated man in front of her. "Go and wait for me in the salon. I'll come for you myself."

"Yes, Mistress," the man said as he left, ever careful not to show Noreen his back. Noreen turned back to the bar, picked up her drink and took a sip. Both her friends were giving her funny looks.

"What?"

"What the hell was that about?" Dahlia asked.

"That was no big deal. He's a regular in here. He will pay you to beat him."

"He's going to pay you to beat him?" Dahlia asked, stunned by the information.

"No! The only people that can take money in here are the ones that work as submissives. Those people are interviewed and chosen by the club and work here for tips. Then there are submissives that come here on their own accord and want to find a Dom to submit to. The Doms usually outnumber the submissives. Most of the time, you see more than one Dom working on a submissive at one time. That's why they hire out submissives, there just aren't enough to go around. The gentleman that you just saw was a regular here when I used to come about a year ago. They tell me he's rich. He once offered to have me come to his house and beat him, but I turned him down. I just came here for fun. I wasn't trying to make a living out of it."

"I can tell you something for sure," Kat said, taking a sip of her drink. "I know for damn sure I'm not a masochist, 'cause if somebody slaps me the way you slapped that man, it's on fo'sho."

Dahlia was still looking uneasy. She followed the shape of the man that Noreen had slapped, as he went in and out of the crowd. He finally disappeared behind a wall of people wearing leather, and Dahlia turned her attention back to her drink. She downed the last of it and Kat looked thoughtfully at her.

"Girl, you're shaking. Are you okay?"

"Mmm-hmm." Dahlia nodded her head yes. Noreen didn't chance a look at Dahlia until she saw the concern on Kat's face.

"Are you feeling okay? You really don't look good. We can leave if you want."

"No, I'm okay. I don't want to mess up your and Kat's good time. I just need another drink to loosen me up."

Noreen signaled to the bartender and moments later they all had fresh drinks. The girls drank in the sex scenes that were unfolding before them as their drinks relaxed them further. Every now and then one of the girls would direct the other two's attention toward some especially funny scenario or another particularly unsavory one. When they finally finished their second drinks, Noreen draped her arms over each of her girls' shoulders and pulled them into a huddle.

"Okay, girls, this is what we're going to do. First of all, in this place, we're not the flavor of the month. We're more like a Rocky Road banana split, when everyone else has a vanilla cone. For these bankers and lawyers that are bossing, controlling, and generally fucking people over all day, there is nothing more relieving and cleansing than handing over the steering wheel for someone else to do the driving. Now if you think about the psychology of it, it's really twisted. A man that wants to be punished for all the naughty things he's done. Well, in their minds, who better to punish you than the very people that you're subjugating. In the workplace it's usually the woman. So you get this dominant little woman to beat you down and control you for an hour or two and it makes you feel better. But what if you're a real sack of shit at home and in the workplace you're fucking over the troops and the common folk. That's when you need the real deal. A representation of all of the people that you have beat down. And that's where we come in.

"We are big, black, and beautiful. We represent the women and the people of color that are being taken advantage of. We're big enough to intimidate and finally, we are beautiful to look at while it's all happening. We are the complete package to a submissive man. We are in our own kingdom here and everyone knows it. Haven't you seen the way everyone has been looking at us since we got here? They're just waiting to see what we're going to do. I'm sure a few of these people remember me from when I used to be a regular."

Kat was all into it.

"All right, so what do we do?" She sounded overly excited.

"Just follow my lead. Walk with your head up, like you own the place, and everyone will think that you do."

"I don't know if I can do this," Dahlia squeaked, looking into her empty Cosmopolitan glass.

"Come on, Dee, you've never punked out on me before. Remember when we first met? Remember that bully of an ex-husband of yours? You wanted to whip his ass, didn't you? All you have to do is make believe one of these guys is him. Shit, they want to be him. They want you to let loose on them."

"Can I have just one more drink?"

"You can have one at the bar, in the salon. I'm sure Silas is getting impatient waiting for us. I think that's his name."

Noreen wasn't waiting anymore. She turned from her girls and gazed across the room. When Kat and Dahlia got up from their seats, it seemed as if everyone within fifty feet of them followed their every move. Noreen had been right. They were three queens amongst "want to be" throne usurpers and a village of loyal servants. Noreen led the way to the salon. She walked slowly and regally; Kat and Dahlia mimicked her every move. Other smaller female Doms nodded to them, deferring to their superiority. Bigger female Doms smiled at them regarding them as equals. Noreen didn't smile back, so her partners didn't either.

The salon was located at the back of the club. They made their way through the crowd to a secluded area with assorted chairs, leather-covered carpenter horses and a stockade. When they reached him, Silas was standing alone next to a carpenter horse. Kat remembered seeing one similar to it, but less decorated when the carpenters put major lumber into her house. Other Doms, males and females alike, were working their submissive over one piece of equipment or another. When Noreen, Kat, and Dahlia stopped in front of Silas, some of the female Doms whipped their submissive harder, in an attempt to get the jealous looks out of their eyes. Noreen stood in front of Silas with Kat and Dahlia standing to the left and right of him. She cupped his chin in one of her big hands.

"I'm disappointed, Silas. You picked the horse and not the stockade." She gestured toward the medieval piece of equipment that was ten feet away. She felt Silas quivering in her hand and she smiled a deliciously wicked smile.

‡‡‡

Two hours later, the ladies were back in their vehicle. Dahlia asked Noreen to drive.

"I drank too much," she lied. The truth was, her legs were still shaky and she hoped that now that she and her two friends were out of the club, they would not be able to detect the strong musky smell coming from between her legs. She was almost high from the activity that she and her friends had just participated in.

"You didn't drink too much. Your arm is just tired from using the paddle on Silas," Kat kidded her.

"I didn't get tired," Dahlia tried to defend herself.

"Damn right, you weren't tired. You were whipping his ass for two hours straight. If Kat and I hadn't been ready to go, you would probably still be in there spankin' that ass." Kat and Noreen gave each other high-fives and were laughing at Dahlia's expense.

"I was only copying what you two were doing," Dahlia said, slamming herself back into her seat.

"We gave the man a couple of good smacks on his butt, Dee, but you were trying to hit home runs on his ass. *KAPOW, BAM, SLAP,*" Kat mimed a baseball player swinging a bat.

Noreen looked into the backseat and noticed her good friend had her arms folded, and her bottom lip was protruding.

"We're just joking, Dee. You didn't do anything wrong. We just never saw that side of you. You're usually the voice of reason between me and Kat. Personally, I loved seeing that side of you come out. I haven't seen you that riled up since the first time we met. Remember? We were both feeling like kicking your ex-husband Martin's ass. We have to watch you, girl. A few drinks and you get violent."

The warm smile on her face told Dahlia that Noreen was aware of her sensitivity to their joking and was trying to change the direction of the conversation.

"You were both going to kick Dahlia's ex-husband's ass? You never told me about that."

"We never told you that story? That's how Dahlia and I met. Let me tell you…"

Dahlia was glad Noreen was telling the story. She liked to hear Noreen's rendition of that night, a crazy beginning to their friendship. Dahlia was surprised that Noreen hadn't brought it up sooner, since they had all been spending so much time together.

Dahlia closed her thighs together tightly as her thoughts moved away from the story Noreen was telling and back to what had transpired in the club.

Dahlia remembered how Noreen cajoled her into taking the leather paddle from her while she took another sip of a new drink. Dahlia was enthralled by how Silas was bent over the leather-covered carpenter horse. Noreen had made him unbuckle his pants and turn away from them, at which time she grabbed his pants by the waist and ripped them down to his ankles. Silas was obedient and remained still, enduring his shame. He had already been topless and was now naked except for the pants around his ankles and his shoes. Noreen didn't speak to him. She bent him over at the waist, posi-

tioning him with his chest supported by the leather horse. This made Silas'
ass protrude more, like an offering to the girls. Dahlia couldn't help but
admire Silas' body. His well-muscled back expanded and contracted with each
breath that he took. His skin was stark white, but it was flawless. Dahlia
could tell that he had removed all his body hair with a professional waxing.
If it had been done with a razor, there would have been telltale stubble.
Dahlia wanted to reach out and touch this man's creamy skin, but did not
dare. She had never seen a white penis before and was surprised at how large
it was. She had never even dated a black man with a penis as large as the one
she was now looking at. It was getting longer and harder as she stared at it.
She took a sip of her drink to give herself an excuse to tear her eyes away.
Dahlia's eyes focused on Noreen as Noreen moved slowly toward Silas' side.

Noreen raised her big hand over her head and let it come down on Silas'
left butt cheek with a resounding *SMACK*. Noreen didn't lift her hand after
the smack. Instead she let it stay there and she massaged the ass cheek that
was now turning cherry-red in contrast to the rest of his body.

"You like that, don't you, Silas?" Noreen asked, grabbing a handful of Silas'
hair and yanking his head back, so that his back arched and his buttocks
rose higher, showing the brown ring of his anus in contrast to his ivory skin.

"Yes, Mistress."

"That's right, you love it," she said, letting her hand raise off of his ass
again, then letting it drop just as fast. *SMACK, SMACK*. The second hand
belonged to Kat. Dahlia couldn't believe that Kat was participating so quickly
and without any prompting. She was as crazy as Noreen, but it usually took
something extra to get her started. Kat laughed wickedly and let her hand
land again and again. Silas never let out a peep.

Dahlia could feel the heat emanating from between her legs as she watched
Kat and Noreen beat and humiliate the man with the perfect white skin. As
much as she wanted to join her friends, she continued to lay in the cut,
aware of her growing desire to join them.

When Noreen finally thrust the leather paddle into her hands, Dahlia reluctantly shook her head no, trying to give the paddle back. Noreen made a face at her and pushed the paddle back into her hands.

"Come on, Dee, everybody is watching. You're going to make us look bad," she said, whispering through clenched teeth.

"Just give him a few smacks on his ass and act like you're bored with him." Noreen thrust the paddle back into her hands. This time she took it, albeit with some hesitation. Dahlia took a last sip of her drink and then put it down on the table to her left. She walked over to Silas who was as still as a statue; leaning over the side of the carpenter horse. Kat was standing next to Silas, and when she saw Dahlia coming with the paddle in her hand, she whispered dangerously into Silas' ear.

"Oh baby, you're in for a real treat now. We've saved the best for last and your ass will never be the same."

Silas heard Dahlia's stilettos creak against the floor close to him and goose bumps crept up his naked back. He lost his nerve for a moment and tried to turn his head to see what was coming, but Kat caught his chin with her freshly manicured left hand and held it straight.

"Uh-uh, no sugah, you don't get to see it coming."

Silas tried to relax and put his head down only to have it snapped back up by Kat's razorlike fingernails again. This time Kat didn't whisper in his ear; she forced him to look into her eyes to see the trouble that he was in. Kat giggled and nodded to her friend to commence with the punishment when Silas' eyes pooled like a kitten's and begged to be released from her malevolent stare.

Dahlia raised the paddle over her head and hesitated again for a moment, which gave Noreen an opportunity to saunter past her to the left of Silas' side and grip his thickly muscled-ass cheek. As if on cue Kat grabbed the other ass cheek and gripped it tightly; the flesh of it turned a rosy hue between her fingers. The sight of her two friends gripping a stranger's ass excited her in a bizarre way she had never experienced before. Dahlia felt herself get moist between her legs. The weight of the paddle felt good in her hand and when Kat winked at her and let go of Silas' ass, Dahlia let her arm arc downward with all the might she could muster. The explosion Silas felt on his ass coincided with the explosion Dahlia suffered in her vagina. The initial shock of it straightened her like a volt of current, and she let the paddle fall from her hand as she watched the blood in Silas' body rush to the area of his buttocks that she struck making it a bright red.

It took Dahlia a few moments to recuperate from that first orgasm. She realized that her experience was not the same as her friends and she averted her eyes from theirs, hoping that the panty liner she always wore was up to the task of absorbing her secretions. It was Kat that picked up the paddle and handed it back to Dahlia. Dahlia held the paddle loosely this time and as her friends encouraged her through a chorus of catcalls.

"Wax that ass, Dee. Let him feel it."

"He likes that shit, Dee. I think he's laughing at you."

Her friends' words were not needed as she raised the paddle again and again, a tiny orgasm exploding in her pussy with each strike that Silas took from the weapon in her hand.

Noreen was flying up the Westside Highway at top speed telling Kat the story of how she and Dahlia first met. Kat laughed raucously as Noreen intermittently sprinkled her exaggerated version of the tale with her sense of humor. Dahlia sat in the backseat of her own car half listening to what was being said, but she was already trying to figure out how she was going to get her friends back to that club again next weekend.

CHAPTER SIX
HANDYMAN SPECIAL

I t was eight o'clock in the morning and the cold was whipping through the floors of Kat's brownstone duplex apartment. Just a half-hour earlier she'd informed the two tenants on the upper floors that there would be no heat for the day. The boiler was broken this Sunday morning. Kat broke out the Yellow Pages and began her campaign to find a repairman who would be willing to come out on a Sunday. But the only thing she could accomplish was conveying the urgency of her dilemma to the answering machines of repairmen that were within her budget.

Kat was bundling up KJ for the frigid weather. Fortunately, her mother had been too tired to go home at three in the morning when Kat got home from her night out with the girls. Now instead of preparing to sit down to a full-fledged Southern breakfast, complete with cheese grits and homemade biscuits with molasses, Kat was preparing to take her mom and KJ back to her mom's apartment until she could get the boiler fixed.

Kat returned home around nine a.m. frozen and still slightly hung over, she lay back down and immediately went to sleep. She was awakened by the annoying ring of the phone which was broken and making a weird whining noise. *Shit is really starting to break down around the house.*

Kat patted around the bed searching for the handset she'd dropped after leaving a message for the last boiler repairman. Somewhere around the eighth ring, she found it under the pillow by her head and pressed the *ON* button before grumbling into the phone.

"Hello?"

"Hey, Katty."

Kat recognized Dahlia's voice and tried to clear her head enough to talk. She pulled the comforters tighter around her and sat up a little.

"I just called Noreen. Can you believe she actually got up this morning and went to church with her mother? After all that drinking we did last night, I don't know how she did it. I just woke up five minutes ago and my head is still spinning."

"I've been up for a minute already. My boiler broke down early this morning, I had to pack the baby up and send him to stay with my mother until I can get this damn boiler fixed. I hope I can get somebody here tomorrow. Most likely, I'm going to have to call in to the school and take a day off to get shit straight again."

"It's thirty degrees outside. You're sitting in that big house with no heat?"

"I've got my long johns on, a pair of pajamas, two pairs of socks, and I'm under three blankets and a comforter. I'm not feeling a thing."

"What about your tenants?"

"My tenants are handling it okay. They know these things happen. I lent them each one of my electric heaters. That just leaves me under the blankets for the rest of the day. All day in bed and no man to share it with—that is the story of my life."

"Oh, oh, oh, I have an idea," Dahlia interrupted.

"What, what is it?"

"I don't want to get your hopes up. I'll call you back in a minute."

Dahlia hung up before Kat could argue with her. Kat lay back down, but before she could get comfortable again the phone rang. This time she picked it up on the first ring, intuitively knowing that it was Dahlia again.

"What's up?"

"I got someone to fix your boiler."

"Who?"

"My cousin. He's a super of a building in the Bronx. He knows how to fix boilers and just about anything else."

"Dee, I can wait 'til tomorrow," Kat said not wanting to insult Dahlia by disclosing that she didn't want anyone but a licensed professional to mess with her boiler.

"It's not a problem. My cousin owes me more than a few favors. I already gave him your address. He should be there in thirty minutes or so. And anyway this is going to be free. I'm sure a house call to fix a boiler costs a grip."

"Dahlia, I can't ask your cousin to come to my house on a Sunday and fix my boiler for free. Call him back and tell him not to worry about it."

"Why? Do you want to be in a cold house for the rest of the weekend and have to take a day off tomorrow? You know it's freezing out there. I don't know a lot about buildings and stuff, but won't your pipes freeze and maybe even burst if there isn't heat going through them when it gets this cold?"

Kat had momentarily forgotten about the pipes, but now dreaded thinking about how much more she would have to pay a plumber if the pipes burst, on top of possibly needing a new boiler. It was only sensible that she have somebody come take a look at the boiler today if it could possibly be fixed at all.

"I'll just pay him for the time that he spends here then, Dee."

"If he's able to fix it, you can try to give him something, but I doubt if he'll take it. I told him you were family. He's really big on family. He's my favorite cousin on my mother's side. When we were little, he used to beat up anybody on my block that tried to make fun of me. Just one thing, Kat, he doesn't speak English all that well."

"He doesn't speak English! I thought you said you grew up together."

"We did. His parents used to send him to New York to stay with us every summer. He lived in Puerto Rico the rest of the year, but don't worry, he knows his stuff. He's licensed with a professional-level HVAC certification. He fixes commercial heating systems in those large corporate buildings in midtown."

Kat had her misgivings, but unless a repairman returned her phone call within the next twenty minutes, she was going to have to go with Dahlia's impromptu plan.

More than an hour had passed and Kat was back under the covers having a very sexy dream about her ex-husband when the ring of the doorbell dragged her back to the harshness of her cold reality.

"Uugghhhh!" she cried in frustration, feeling the heat and moisture as she pried her hands from between her legs. *Damn, just when it was getting good.*

RRIIINNGG! The doorbell rang impatiently again and Kat poked her head from under the paisley Halston comforter. The cold air in her bedroom stung her nose and Kat pulled the comforter tightly around her as she got up to answer the door. She took two steps on the cold wooden floor and tiptoed back to the side of the bed to slip on her wool-lined, Australian-made UGG boots. They were funny-looking shoes but they kept her feet warm and this was no time to look cute.

RRIIINNGG!

The doorbell rang yet a third time and Kat yelled down the stairs to whoever was at the door.

"I'm coming, I'm coming."

Kat made her way down the stairs pulling the comforter even tighter around her as the cold attempted to creep through its seams.

The only person Kat was expecting at this time was Dahlia's cousin and she didn't know what he looked like. She wouldn't have been able to see him anyway because her door didn't have a peephole. She had forgotten to ask Dahlia what her cousin's name was, but stood on her side of the door with her ear inches from the dark oak.

"Who is it?"

"Librado, for de boila."

Kat unlocked the door glad that the person on the other side of the door understood at least that much English. His accent was very thick and Kat smiled as she remembered how Noreen had made fun of Dahlia's mother's accent. When she swung the door open, Kat was not prepared for what was on the other side. It was a good thing she said "hello," before her eyes met his because when their eyes did meet she was struck speechless.

Librado stood on the other side of her threshold, six-foot-two, dark-caramel skin with the deepest set of brown eyes that she had ever seen. He had shocks of wavy jet-black hair and a cleft on his chin. His clean-shaven face had the smoothest-looking skin she had ever seen on a man. His only flaw was his nose, which was a little too big for his face, but the slight imperfection is what made his face a real masterpiece.

She noticed Librado's teeth were perfect as he smiled at her for a full five seconds before she realized that her response to his looks was a source of amusement for him. She forced her slack mouth shut and invited him in.

"Come in. Lee…bra…doe, right?"

"*Jes*, Librado. *Jou* are Kat, *jes*?"

Kat only nodded her head in affirmation, suddenly very conscious of her appearance.

Although he gave no indication of it, Librado was more than pleased with Kat's appearance. She was a true natural beauty with her simple ponytail and unpainted face. Kat stepped to the side to allow him entry into the foyer. Librado entered quickly, but never allowed his eyes to lose sight of Kat's derriere. Kat felt Librado's unabashed eyes roving over her body through the comforter that was wrapped around her. All of a sudden it wasn't so cold anymore and Kat shrugged the comforter off of her shoulders allowing his eyes to further access the best of what her mother had passed on to her. Kat knew she was being an overt flirt, but it had been a long time since any man had gawked at her the way Librado was now doing, and her natural coquettishness took over. Kat closed the door and turned the latch of the bottom lock. When she turned around, Librado wasn't looking at her anymore. He was standing just inside of her parlor and looking up at the ceiling. Kat sidled up next to him and looked up to see what he was staring at. Without looking away from the ceiling, Librado answered the question Kat wanted to ask.

"De molding around the ceiling, it is original. More than one hundred years old."

"Yes, that's right. The previous owner made a point of that when we were haggling over the price after I went into contract."

"*Jou* were very lucky to get a place like this. It has many original features. The fireplace, the mirrors, even the floor is original, no?"

"You seem to know a lot about brownstones, Librado."

"*Jes*, I own three small ones on the East Side."

"You own three brownstones?"

"Mmm-hmm."

Librado turned to face Kat again.

"But none of them as beautiful as this one. When I bought my buildings they were only shells. Now they are all new inside. No character, no feeling. This, this is timeless."

Librado spread his arms in a gesture of wonder and reverence. Kat could feel the passion in his voice and it made the hair on the back of her neck stand up. She felt herself become enveloped by the tone of his voice and was almost ready to swoon when he snapped her out of it abruptly.

"So where is de boila? The basement stairs are over there, no?" Librado pointed to the basement door as if he had been in the building before. Kat was taken aback by his familiarity with her home and then realized that he had probably been in many brownstone buildings and they all were basically set up the same.

"Yes, it's down there. Let me show you."

Kat led the way down the stairs to the basement, but she had all but forgotten about the broken boiler. As she took each step down the steep basement stairs, she attempted to give her hips just a little more swagger in hopes of getting Librado to take a second look at her. She had enjoyed the feeling of his eyes on her. She had not received a look like that from such an attractive man since before the baby was born.

Kat wished it had not been so cold in the house. It would look peculiar for her to take her sweater off. As cold as it was upstairs, it was coldest downstairs in the basement. Kat could feel her cold hardened nipples pressing through all those layers of clothes she had on. She wished that the sweater she wore was a bit more revealing. Now she couldn't tell if they were hard because of the cold or because of the excitement of having a fine man undress her with his eyes.

They reached the bottom of the stairs together and Kat's fingers searched along the wall to the right for the light switch. Her fingers found the switch and in an instant the inset lighting lit a finished basement complete with a large leather couch and ottoman. The floors were textured red tiles from Brazil and there was a fifty-inch Sony flat-screen television hanging on the wall.

Librado let out a low whistle.

"Wow, baby, this is nice. You did this yourself?"

"You're kidding, right? I'm good with my hands, but this is way out of my league. It was the only part of the house that didn't have all of the original pieces in it when I bought it. Sometime in the seventies someone had decided to put wood paneling on the walls and shag carpet on the floor."

Librado's upper lip curled in disgust making his face look like a cartoon character.

"That is a shame that they do that to such a beautiful place. But it is beautiful again. *Jou* have very good taste, *Mamita.*"

"Pardon me?"

"I say *jou* have a very good taste."

"No, the other thing you called me."

When he was nervous Librado's accent became thicker.

"Oh, I'm sory, Meeses Kat. I don mean no desrepek. We say *Mamita* or *Mami* as a term of, how you say, dearment."

Kat struggled not to blush.

"I've heard *Mami* before, but that other way…"

"*Mamacita.*"

Librado let the word dance off of his tongue.

"Yes, that way it sounds so different."

"I will not use it again if it offends *jou*, Meeses Kat."

Librado let a smile play around his lips as he realized that she was indeed blushing.

"No, I like it…I like it…Uh, it's this way to the boiler."

Kat motioned to her right, not knowing what else to say without sounding like a little girl.

They walked along a narrow corridor toward the boiler approximately twelve feet from the bottom of the stairs.

"Here it is."

Kat pressed herself against the wall to allow Librado to pass, but she couldn't press against it enough to avoid his body touching hers entirely. His chest barely grazed her breasts, but to Kat it felt like he raked his hot breath across her nipples. Her heart skipped a beat and she was suddenly conscious of the moisture that thoughts of her ex-husband had caused in her previous to Librado entering the house. She hadn't bathed since she came in last night. She just hoped that Librado couldn't smell it. Kat tried to suck her stomach in, but it was a futile gesture. There was just too much of it. Librado's abdomen pressed against hers and she winced as the muscles in his stomach brushed against her jelly belly.

"Escuse me." Librado reached past Kat and bent down to examine the boiler.

Kat let her breath out and could feel the roll of fat assume its place over the elastic of her pajama pants again. She was only self-conscious about it for a moment before deciding that it was too late to try to hide it now.

"Ah, I see the problem right here."

"Can you fix it?"

Librado looked over his shoulder and smiled as devilishly as he could at Kat.

"For you, *Mamacita*, I can fix anything."

Kat managed to stifle a giggle and instead offered Librado some coffee.

"I'm going to make a pot of coffee. Would you like some?"

"*Jes,* coffee would be good. It is a leetle cold down here."

Librado rubbed his calloused hands together and blew on them before picking a wrench from his tool bag.

"Coffee coming right up."

Kat left Librado fixing the boiler and went up to the kitchen and put a pot of coffee to percolate in the Cuisinart coffeemaker that her mother had given her for Christmas.

After putting the coffee on, she climbed the stairs to her bedroom and took off all of her clothes. She knew there was no hot water, but she couldn't make herself go back down to stand next to Librado when her lower regions were fast and furiously firing off pheromones.

Kat stepped into the shower and the cold spray of water felt like needles piercing her skin. It hurt like hell, but she was trooping it. She quickly soaped, careful to give special attention to her vagina and the deep crevice that her ass had become. It didn't take her more than two minutes to get clean, but she had lost the feeling in her feet by the time she got out of the shower stall. Kat dried quickly giving her feet an extra vigorous rub in an attempt to get the feeling back into them. She couldn't very well put an evening dress on to go back into the basement, so she picked one of her nicer Baby Phat sweatsuits from her closet. Kat put a cold-wear Under Armour shirt on underneath to keep her warm and keep her fat from bulging, then put on her running Nikes. She looked like she was on her way to the gym or out for a run. Kat looked in the mirror one last time before leaving her bedroom and decided that her hair was still holding together from her visit to the Dominican hairstylist yesterday. She patted an errant lock of hair back into her ponytail and made her way down the stairs to the kitchen again. Kat took two identical mugs from the dishwasher and filled them with coffee. She added a drop of milk and two spoons of sugar to one of them and left the other black. She'd neglected to ask Librado how he took his coffee. She decided she would ask him when she reached downstairs and she would drink whichever one he didn't.

Kat looked at the clock on the kitchen wall. Only ten minutes had passed since she'd left that fine-ass man downstairs fixing the boiler.

Kat used her foot to open the door that led to the basement stairs and carefully made her way down, a scalding hot mug in each hand. She was careful not to spill any of the coffee.

When she reached the bottom of the stairs, Kat pulled her stomach in again and walked to the back of the basement where Librado was bent over the boiler twisting some screw on or off, she couldn't tell which.

Kat took a moment to admire the broadness of his back and the way it tapered perfectly to his waist and down to his round buttocks before clearing her throat to disrupt him from his work.

"Aheemm…I have your coffee here…I didn't know how you take it, so I just put a little milk and sugar in one of them."

She offered him the cup with the lighter liquid.

"Regular, that is perfecto."

Librado took a sip from the steaming mug and sighed.

"That is very good coffee, you must tell me your secret."

"No secret. Just add water and coffee to the machine and turn it on."

"This coffee comes from a machine? My mother, she would laugh to think that I drank coffee from a machine. She doesn't drink coffee unless she makes it herself."

"You still live with your mother?" Kat responded a bit incredulous.

"Why? Is that such a bad thing that a man should stay with his mother?"

"No, I didn't mean it to sound offensive or anything…"

Librado laughed at her discomfort and then soothed her.

"I was just teasing you, *Mamita*. No, I do not live with my mother. My mother is still living in Puerto Rico. She refuses to leave her little house with the chickens and mango tree in the back. I have tried many times, but she will not come."

Librado took another sip of the coffee and handed the mug back to Kat. "Thank *jou*."

Librado bent back down to work on the boiler again and Kat was left holding two cups of coffee. She felt dismissed and almost turned to go back upstairs when Librado started talking again.

"It will take me another thirty minutes or so here. I had to take most of the heating core apart to get to the coil spring. After I clean it, it should work, but I'm going to have to come back tomorrow and replace it with a new one or by next week *jou* will be without heat again."

The only thing that Kat could say was…"okay."

Librado turned away from his work again and looked up at Kat.

"*Jou* are on *jou*r way to the gymnasium? I could finish this and wait for *jou* to come back, if you would like."

"Oh, you mean these clothes? No, no, this is just what I wear around the house. I mean sometimes I go to the gym, but not today. I have a lot to do today."

Librado turned back to his work for a moment, but then stopped as if pondering a riddle before turning to Kat again.

"If you do not mind me asking, why does a beautiful woman like you go to the gymnasium?"

Kat was taken aback by his blunt question, but tried not to look too ashamed.

"As if you hadn't noticed, I could stand to lose a few pounds."

She rubbed her midsection aware that she was still holding it in.

"Ah, I understand. *Jou* want to be like those women in the magazines? But those are not real women. They have no shape, they have not lived. *Jou* are a woman that has lived life. *Jou* have a baby, a job, *jou* eat, *jou* drink, *jou* make love. These women in the magazine, they cannot do all of this. *Jou* are a real woman."

"Thank you. You're being kind."

"No, *Mamita*, I'm not being kind. I am telling you the truth. If *jou* were my woman, I would never let *jou* go to the gymnasium where other men could look at you. I would keep *jou* home and exercise you myself." Librado gave her a knowing look and Kat got his meaning.

This time she did blush and Librado turned back to work on the boiler again. Within the thirty minutes that it took Librado to fix the boiler, Kat and Librado exchanged information about family, work, children, some likes and some dislikes.

"There, it is finished." Librado flipped the switch on the boiler and it hummed back to life.

"Oh God…thank you! Thank you so much, Librado! I don't know what I would have done if you didn't come by."

"Well, remember, I have only fixed it temporarily. I have to come back tomorrow with a new part so that it doesn't break down again. As a matter of fact, I think I should stay around a few more minutes just to make sure it stays on."

"You don't have to do that, Librado. I've already taken up too much of your time. It even sounds better than it sounded all of last winter."

"Still, *jou* cannot be too sure with these things. I would feel better if I stayed for a while."

"I can make another pot of coffee, if you want."

Librado shook his head no and followed Kat to the front of the basement where the leather couch was.

"Is there a place that I can wash my hands?"

"There is a bathroom right behind that door." Kat pointed to the far left of the room.

Librado entered the bathroom and Kat decided to follow her instincts. They had both told each other that they had recently broken up with their spouses. He didn't have any children, so there was no mama drama. And the only time he took his eyes off of her was when he was working on the boiler. Not to mention he was his own man. He worked as a superintendent in a high-rise apartment building, but he also owned rental property. And the man was fine as hell.

Damn, he is fine, fine, fine. Kat, do not mess this up. Girl, DO NOT mess this up.

The house was already heating up. She knew that the basement would get warm first and then the rest of the house. She thought she would invite him upstairs, but it would still be uncomfortably cold and down here, where it was already getting warm, she would have an excuse to take off her jacket. Maybe her big breasts would inspire him to ask her out. She thought to go upstairs to get them some wine, but before she could Librado was already coming out of the bathroom.

Kat had just hit *PLAY* on the iPod that was connected to the Bose iPod speaker system and a Marc Anthony song came through the speakers that surrounded the room.

"All right, that's my thing, baby. You dance salsa, *Mamita?*"

"Just a little. My ex-husband and I took lessons together a long time ago. You know…to try and get the magic back and…"

Kat didn't finish her sentence. Librado took her in his arms and was twirling her around the room. He was a much better dancer than she was, but the way that he guided her around the room made her feel graceful, elegant, and light.

The Marc Anthony song finished and Biggie came through the speakers.

Kat normally liked to listen to some Biggie, but damn, this was not the right time. Librado stopped dancing and held her at arm's length.

"Put on another song we can dance to."

"That was it. That's all the salsa music that I have."

"Then put it on again. You dance like an angel."

Kat went to the iPod stand and tapped the reverse button twice. Marc Anthony's voice came through the speakers again and Kat glided into Librado's arms. Kat loved the way that Librado was handling her again. He kept constant eye contact and with just the slightest of touches let her know which way he wanted her to move. She was already sweating and she wished that she had taken the jacket off when she had the opportunity. They twirled and spun, laughed and smiled for the full four minutes that the song played and then it was over. Biggie's voice was booming out of the speaker again, and Kat let go of Librado's arms to stop the music before it totally ruined the romantic mood.

She tapped the STOP button, but before she could turn around again, she felt Librado's arms wrap around her and his hardened penis press against her backside.

Kat tried to turn around to face him, but he held her still and kissed against the soft part of her neck, just under her ear. It had been too long since she felt a man kiss her there, and it left her susceptible to the longing of a woman who needed to be loved. Already she felt the moisture in the cleft of her pubic area gathering and threatening to soil her pink silk panties. Before she knew what was happening, Librado dipped his hand beneath the elastic of her sweat pants and past the delicate elastic of her panties to cup her vagina.

Before Kat could object, he slipped his middle finger deftly between her pussy lips, gently gliding over her engorged clit and then quickly pulling his entire hand out of her pants in one motion.

"....Don't." For a millisecond Kat didn't know whether she was going to tell him...*don't do that or don't stop*. When she did turn to face him, she was stunned to see the finger that had recently stroked between her pussy lips was now between his lips. Librado was sucking on his finger the way you suck a finger you had just dipped in your mother's homemade cake batter. He seemed to be savoring the taste, reluctant to let the finger out of his mouth.

Kat's mouth hung open at the sight of him sucking his finger. She hadn't been this turned on in longer than she cared to remember. Librado finally released the finger from his mouth and spoke.

"*Mamita*, you taste like a ripe mango. I wanted to make love to you from the time I seen you at the door."

"Librado, we can't..."

"Here, taste."

Librado pressed his mouth to hers, slipping his tongue into her as swiftly as he had done with his finger.

Kat had no time to argue, and for the first time, she tasted her own vagina from a man's mouth. The taste was syrupy as he had said it was, and she was not revolted as she thought she might be. The few times that any man had gone down on her, she had not allowed them to kiss her again until they washed their mouths out. It was the practice that she had learned from dating black men, as they had not allowed her to kiss them after she had gone down on them.

Kat embraced her taste. She enjoyed it as Librado fed it to her over and over again fucking her mouth with his tongue.

As they kissed, Librado was guiding Kat over to the leather couch. She was aware of where he was leading her and allowed him to take her there.

The back of Kat's leg touched the leather couch and she allowed Librado to gently lay her back against it without ever losing the connection of their lips.

Librado was careful not to lie on top of her. He lay next to her, continuing to kiss her softly as his hands roamed over her body.

His right hand reached each of her full breasts and squeezed her nipples gently until they hardened. His fingers traced a line down her abdomen. Librado felt her trying to pull her stomach in again and purposely let his hand stay there massaging and kneading the fleshy area around her waist. Kat finally got tired of sucking it in and let it go. More fatty tissue flowed between Librado's fingers and he seemed to revel in it. He groped and kneaded her belly a while longer before plunging his hand into Kat's pants again. Kat felt not one, but two fingers, slide between the lips of her vagina and attempted to open her legs to allow him easier access. Before she could really open her legs, he had already pulled his fingers out and had brought them to his lips again. This time he put both fingers in his mouth and sucked at them ravenously.

After a moment, Librado pulled the fingers out of his mouth and looked down at Kat. Believing that he was going to kiss her again, she closed her eyes and parted her lips ready to receive his offering from her vagina again. When she felt Librado tugging at the top of her sweat pants, she almost pushed him away. He felt her hesitance and had the presence of mind to soothe her with his disarmingly calm voice.

"Let me taste it, *Mamita*, I just want to taste *jou*."

The sound of his voice was like a long-lost melody that Kat was trying to remember. She wanted to remember it. She needed to remember it. Kat lifted her hips allowing the sweat pants and underwear to be dragged past her hips and down past her knees to her ankles. She still had her sneakers on and the pants and underwear just bunched around her Nikes as Librado pushed her knees apart and ducked his head into the damp mound of her vagina.

Kat had not bothered to trim her pubic hair in months. Realizing that her pussy must look like something out of seventies porn, she opened her mouth to apologize for the extra fur, but before she could utter a sound, Librado's tongue touched her clitoris, sending a bolt of lightning up her back. Kat's heels dug into the leather sofa and pushed off, simultaneously splaying her legs further and pushing her pussy harder into Librado's face.

"AAAAAhhhhhhhhhhhh…..oh God, oh God, oh Ggggooddd."

Librado pulled his face away from her pussy and pushed her hips gently back down to the leather couch.

"Easy, *Mamita*, easy."

"Okay, okay, okay, okay," Kat chanted.

She tried to calm herself down, but as soon as Librado's tongue touched her pussy again she couldn't stop shaking. Librado was using long sweeping strokes of his tongue on her pussy. He was starting at the bottom, using his tongue as a ladle to scoop up all of the juices that were flowing out of her and sweeping upward. He finished each stroke off with a flick of his tongue on her clit to make her shudder from head to toe.

After only moments, Kat started to chant again. "I'm gonna cum, I'm gonna cum, I'm gonna cum, I'm gonna cum."

When Librado heard this, he stopped tonguing her immediately. The cessation of his tongue only caused her to chant something different.

"Please don't stop. Please don't stop, please don't stop, please don't stop."

"SSShhhh, *Mamita*, Shhhhhh. Wait for me, we'll do it together."

Librado's voice was leading her to be calm again, but she was barely containing herself.

"Turn over for me, *Mamita*, turn over."

"What?"

"Onto your stomach."

"Onto my stomach? I can't. My shoes…"

Before she finished the sentence, Librado had ripped off both of her sneakers and was now peeling her sweat pants and panties past her toes.

Kat didn't know what to expect next. Librado wasn't trying to take his pants off, or even pull his zipper down for that matter, so he wasn't trying to fuck her. He guided her with a slight touch of his hand like he did when they were dancing, and she new which way he wanted her to turn. Kat turned where he said and found herself lying on her stomach. She felt Librado behind her. He was kissing slowly down her back. His tongue danced lazily around each of her muscles making them twitch every time he stopped to pay special attention to a small knotted group of muscles.

As he made his way down her back, Kat became more and more agitated. She loved the feeling of his gentle kisses, but she knew if he started to tongue her pussy again from this position, he would not be able to reach her clitoris. Librado reached the crack of her ass with his kisses and Kat was shaking with anticipation. She tried to turn back over so that he could kiss her pussy again, but he held her firmly on her stomach. She was about to protest when she felt his tongue start to lick down into the crack of her ass. She thought maybe she was imagining it, but she wasn't. He was going deeper and deeper into her ass. When his tongue couldn't go any deeper on its own, Kat felt Librado's strong hands, one on each cheek, prying them apart. Kat had only tried anal sex one time with her husband, Kenny, but it hadn't worked out. She had been willing, but it hurt too much and she made him stop. No one, including her husband, had ever even attempted to eat her ass out.

Kat started to shake uncontrollably again as Librado's hands pried her ass cheeks apart. She could feel the cool air hitting her sphincter and it made her clench. Librado held her cheeks open against their will, and Kat could feel his hot breath against the rubbery aperture.

Oh my God, he's going to do it. He's really going to do it. I can't believe he's going to eat my ass.

Librado's tongue found its target and Kat felt the lightning shooting through her again. Kat's back arched and pushed her ass against Librado's mouth hard. She felt his tongue slide into her ass for the first time and wondered if she would ever be satisfied with ordinary sex ever again. She shook violently from head to toe, reaching again and again for a climax but never quite getting there.

She knew what she needed. She needed more of that tongue in her ass. She needed to feel it deeper inside of her. She concentrated on relaxing the muscles in her ass so that Librado's tongue could reach the spot that she wanted it to reach. She felt more and more of his tongue sliding into her, until she thought his tongue must be at least six inches long.

"Right there, right there, don't stop. Right there." Kat felt her anus balloon open on its own, somehow knowing that it needed to open further to get what it really wanted. Kat's asshole was sucking on Librado's tongue, as Librado tried desperately to go deeper.

"Oh God, it's going in, it's going in."

For the second time in just minutes, Kat felt close to an orgasm. Her body started to vibrate again and it was Librado's clue that her orgasm was imminent.

"Baby, I'm going to come, I'm going to come."

Librado pulled his tongue out of Kat's ass.

"Not yet, *Mamita*. Not yet."

Kat felt Librado behind her, crawling between her now splayed legs. It wasn't until she felt the heat and thickness of his penis nestle between the crack of her ass that she realized that he had taken his pants off while eating her ass out. Her body was still shaking from the tongue lashing her ass had taken and when Librado's hand snaked past her belly and cupped her pubic mound, her body shook at an even more intense rate.

Kat was finding it impossible to remember even to breathe.

"I don't want…No, not the..!"

She felt the head of Librado's condom-covered penis pressing against the normally tight ring of her asshole and was both disturbed and elated to find that it entered her with no discomfort. The pressure of the penis in her ass compounded by the hand that found her clitoris so easily was making Kat thrash about, almost dislodging Librado from her ass. Librado felt her bucking beneath him. The head of his dick was slipping out of her ass, forcing him to bear down with his hips. The result was that he slammed his cock into Kat to the hilt making her scream in pleasure pain and commencing the long drawn-out orgasm that he had engineered.

"Aaaaaaaaaaahhhhhh!"

Librado pulled back to alleviate her pain, but also to alleviate his own pain. The dull pain he felt at the head of his penis was an indication that he might have injured himself with that last thrust. Undaunted by the pain, Librado pulled back slowly enjoying the whispering sigh that escaped Kat.

"Oooooooohhhh…"

And then slower this time Librado entered Kat's dank, warm hole again.

"Aaaaaaarrrrgghh!"

It was Librado's lone scream that echoed throughout the basement this time.

Kat mistook the scream of pain for a premature orgasm and attempted to finish her own. Librado tried to pull back, but Kat clenched her ass cheeks and bucked backward trying to cum and keep him inside of her.

"Fuuuuuck…I'm cuuuuuuummiiinng!"

"Aaaaaaaarrrrgghh!"

The pain in Librado's loins was excruciating, but he knew that Kat was coming and being the stereotypical Latin lover that he was, the pleasure and orgasm of his partner was of paramount importance to prove the superiority of his skills as a cocksman. Kat shook with the last vestiges of her orgasm and slumped onto her stomach. She felt Librado pulling out of her backside and the shame of how she'd allowed her abstinence-induced horniness to consume her made her turn quickly over onto her back as if hiding her ass would erase the act she had just participated in.

"Hisssssssssssssssssssss…."

Kat turned in time to see Librado hissing painfully through clenched teeth as he gripped his penis with both hands. As Kat's lust-glazed eyes started to focus, she saw the cause of Librado's pain.

"Awwwwppp."

She gasped, if not in surprise, then certainly in embarrassment. Librado grimaced and steeled himself against certain pain. The look on his face reminded Kat of a movie where a character that Wesley Snipes played sewed up his own bullet wound. Librado's left hand loosened its grip around the shaft of his penis, and he used the thumb and forefinger of that hand to gingerly touch the still swollen head of his penis. Librado winced once and then reached into the wide hole of his penis head and gripped the embedded item with the two fingers. Wasting no more time, he yanked something out. Librado didn't make a sound, but Kat could see by the look on his face that he was in some distress. His lips were pressed tightly suppressing a scream. In his hand he held the biggest kernel of corn that Kat had ever seen.

Kat was even more mortified that he held the kernel of corn above his head like some golden trophy.

God, I haven't even eaten corn in a week.

"Whewwwwwwww..." Librado exhaled loudly letting Kat know that he was okay.

But Kat was not okay. She was a mother and recently divorced woman and now after the pressure of not having sex for over six months was released, she was thoroughly ashamed of herself. She reached for her sweat pants and pulled them on quickly without bothering with her underpants. Librado did not know what was going on, so Kat helped him out. While still holding onto the cords that held up her sweat pants, she bent to pick up the pants that he'd left at the foot of the couch and literally threw them in his face.

"Out!"

Librado was caught by surprise and snatched at the pants that were in his face. The look on his face was almost comical as he tried to form words, then suddenly looked hurt. Kat knew the look was merited, but she was not taking it back.

"Let's go, my mother is going to be here any minute," she lied.

Librado knew it was a lie, but started to put his pants on in a rush anyway. A minute later he was gathering his tools in silence and soon after Kat was thanking him and pushing him out the door. Librado was being very understanding and allowed her to move through these motions that would allow her to maintain dignity. He left without any further discussion knowing that he would bide his time until he returned tomorrow to fix her boiler again. He had not made love to a woman since breaking up with his girlfriend three months ago and allowed his penis to think for him again. When he saw her tomorrow, he would apologize and properly invite her out to dinner. She was the type of woman he enjoyed. Smart, passionate and big boned. She reminded him of his mother.

"What time should I come tomorrow?" he tried to ask her before the door closed.

"I'll call Dahlia tomorrow and let her know," Kat answered him from the other side of the door. She genuinely liked him, but after that embarrassment, she had no intention of seeing him again. She would call the boiler repair person in the morning and have them fix the boiler properly. Then she would call Dahlia and tell her that her cousin didn't have to come over again after all. It made her sad to think that she would not see Librado again. She chastised herself all that night lamenting how nice a relationship they might have had if she had not let her libido get the better of her—again.

CHAPTER SEVEN
HOW LOW DID YOU GO?

"Even if he wasn't your cousin, I still wouldn't date him."

"You're prejudiced, admit it. You won't go out with him because he's Puerto Rican and has a little bit of an accent."

"A little bit of an accent!"

"Aha, aha. I knew it, I knew it."

The two women were standing in front of Noreen's building waiting for her to let them in. She had called both of them and told them to meet her at her place. She had something special that she had to talk about.

Dahlia and Kat had both reached the apartment building thirty minutes earlier than they had agreed and found that Noreen was not at home.

"Will you lower your voice? Everybody in the neighborhood doesn't have to hear our business."

The doorman was looking at them through the large plate glass window. When they arrived almost simultaneously and found that Noreen had not arrived from work yet, he invited them to wait in the lobby for Ms. Klein. Both women were weary from having been stuck indoors behind their desks all day; Kat marking test papers and Dahlia auditing accounts at the Harlequin National Bank branch that she managed. They declined, instead opting to enjoy the brisk winter air that blew up from the Henry Hudson River onto Riverside Drive.

They were still having a heated conversation when Noreen came walking down the street and met them in front of the building. Noreen saw them before they saw her and she managed to put a warm smile on her face where moments before there was only fear and questioning. As she got closer Noreen was astonished to hear the two women were arguing. Since they had all started to share company, it was usually her and Dahlia who shared more history that argued over petty differences. Kat's role had become one of a referee. She usually didn't take sides, but was almost always consoling Dahlia who got the worst of Noreen's biting sarcasm.

"What are you two arguing about?" Noreen greeted them both with a kiss on each cheek and then chastised them.

Dahlia opened her mouth to answer and was quickly shut down.

"Ah…save it," Noreen cautioned, "Mr. Furley over there is trying to read your lips."

She was referring to the doorman who shared a remarkable likeness to Don Knotts from the old sitcom *Three's Company*. He was straining to look at them through the lobby window and attempted to look nonchalant when Dahlia and Kat turned to look, after Noreen gestured toward him. The doorman reached the door well before the three women and smiled politely as they passed him each of them nodding their thanks. They all held their tongues until they reached the elevator. When the elevator door opened, all three ladies entered. It was the first time Kat had ever been in an elevator with her two friends and she noticed how much room they actually took up in this small space. Dahlia had already started arguing with her again, but Kat did not hear her. She was focused on the sign hanging over the elevator buttons: *Maximum capacity 1200 lbs.* It was an old elevator and she was distracted trying to figure out approximately how much of that capacity she and her friends took up. The embarrassing episode the night before last was making her think more about food and her obesity.

When they reached the fourth floor, the door opened. Noreen stepped off followed by Dahlia who was still ranting and then Kat who noticed how the elevator raised slightly when her two friends were not on it. Noreen's apartment was painted in pink with gray trimming. The furniture in the living room was sparse, but what there was of it was tasteful. It was a small apartment but Noreen moved around in it gracefully. She gave Kat the ten-cent tour of the place and invited her to sit in the living room while she went into the kitchen to get them something to drink. Dahlia, who had been in the apartment many times, sat in the floral-patterned wingback chair mumbling something about rice and beans and watermelon to no one in particular. Kat knew they would have to have some closure on the subject, but wanted to wait for Noreen to return. She needed an ally and Noreen always made fun of Dahlia's family, anyway. Maybe she would take Kat's side.

Noreen came back from the kitchen with three champagne flutes and an open bottle of Cristal. She handed each of her friends a flute and let the champagne flow. After a bubbly sip, Dahlia was jolted out of her own thoughts. She stared at the glass in her hand for a moment and then turned to look at the bottle of Cristal that Noreen held as she lounged on the sofa next to Kat. Dahlia remembered that this bottle sat in Noreen's refrigerator for over a year waiting for a special occasion.

"Mmmm, what's the occasion?"

Noreen looked back at her and held the bottle high over her head.

"Life, Sweetheart. Today we are celebrating life."

Kat took another sip and held her glass up.

"To life!"

All of the friends raised their glasses and each took a long pull. Dahlia knew Noreen better than Kat did. Something was wrong and she was waiting for the other shoe to fall.

"So what were you two arguing about?"

Noreen refilled her glass and put the Cristal bottle on the glass-top coffee table in front of her.

"Ladies, I asked what are you two arguing about?"

"We weren't arguing," Kat offered.

"Like hell we weren't," Dahlia responded as she set her glass on the coffee table. She talked with her hands and liked to have them free when making a point.

"No…Kat is prejudiced against Puerto Ricans."

Noreen knew that Dahlia was prone to exaggeration, but turned to Kat for a response.

Kat sucked her teeth.

"Tsk…Dee, will you stop saying that. I am not prejudiced against Puerto Ricans. You're Puerto Rican and I love you."

"I'm only part Puerto Rican. And I've never asked you out for a date."

"You're not my type. Sorry, sweetie, I'm strictly dickly."

"Then why won't you go out with my cousin?"

"Is that what this is all about?"

Noreen was perturbed by how truly trivial their disagreement was.

"Hell yes, that's what this is about." The drink was already making Dahlia more emotional than normal.

"Are we talking about that tall, caramel cutie cousin of yours? The one with the nice nose? What's his name, Lee?"

"Librado."

"He said I could call him Lee," Noreen said, dropping her voice an octave lower for effect.

Kat snapped her fingers at Dahlia to remind her who she was talking to.

"That man is fine. I regret having to turn him down myself."

"Huh?"

"That was news to Dahlia."

"Well, I would have turned him down if he asked, but I was seeing Johnny back then, you remember?"

"Yeah right."

Noreen gave Dahlia a dirty look, but did not dignify her sarcasm with a response. She turned back to Kat.

"So he asked you out. What's the problem?"

"She's prejudiced, that's the problem. She doesn't like Puerto Ri—"

"Shhh! You've said enough," Noreen snapped.

Kat pointed an accusing finger at Dahlia.

Dahlia didn't finish her sentence and although she knew Noreen was just being motherly, she didn't like the thought that her best friend might be taking her new good friend's side. She reached toward the table a picked up her drink again.

"Is it his accent? That man does fuck up the English language."

"Noreen…!"

"Well, he does."

She turned back to Dahlia for a moment.

"And that can be a turn-off for some women."

"Hmmff!" Dahlia huffed and crossed her arms, spilling some of her drink.

The good champagne was quickly working its magic on Kat too. She actually felt a need to discuss her mixed emotions about Librado. She took another long swig of the golden fluid in her flute, downing the last drop in the long glass while her friends waited. When she put the glass down on the table and looked up, she saw that the two women waited with unabated curiosity on their faces.

"I like him." She paused for either of her friends to respond to her confession. When neither of them went for the bait she continued.

"Something happened between us on Sunday when he came over to fix the boiler."

Dahlia almost started to say something, but Noreen held up her hand to stop her without looking in her direction before she could interrupt.

"Go on," Noreen urged.

"After he finished fixing the boiler, we were listening to some music. We started to dance and one thing led to another…" Kat stared at the coffee table no longer able to look her friends in the face.

"You kissed him!" Dahlia said in disbelief.

Kat's eyes didn't leave the table.

"You fucked him, didn't you?"

"Noreen!" Dahlia was appalled.

"She's not like you, tramp!"

Kat's eyes looked up from the table and met Noreen's.

"Like hell she's not! You did, didn't you? You did."

Kat nodded her head yes, confirming Noreen's suspicion.

"Yes, yes, yes. I knew it. I knew it." Noreen stopped abruptly. "Was he good?"

"Noreen…! Kat, don't answer. Don't stoop to her level."

Kat looked from one friend to another and the liquor got the best of her modesty.

"It…was…reeeaaal good."

"Aawwp." Dahlia always made that funny noise when she gasped.

"Details. Give me details," Noreen encouraged.

"I'm not sure I want to hear this." Dahlia already felt a little incestuous knowing her cousin's sexual business.

Kat reached for the bottle of Cristal and poured herself another glass. There was a time when she would have called her old friend Margarita and given her the juicy details, but her she was busy with other things these days. After all she and her new friends had already shared some rather intimate moments. Kat described the sexual acts that she participated in with Librado and they *ooohed* and *aahed* at all the appropriate moments. She was rolling along smoothly giving them the "blow by blow" until she got to the deed that she had only performed with a few choice men.

"You let him get the booty his first time out of the box? No pun intended," Noreen asked incredulously.

"Girl, I could not help myself. He knew all the right strings to pluck and I haven't had anyone touching me in months. Let alone the way he was doing me."

"Damn, girl, then what's wrong. He wants to see you again. So he either really likes what you were doing, too, or, at the very least, he wants more than just the booty relationship."

"Kat, he really likes you. He never even hinted that you two did anything," Dahlia offered gently.

"He didn't say anything?"

"Nothing about the sex. He just kept saying that you were a wonderful person. That you seemed to be a good mother, and that you were big on family. He said you both discussed your mothers."

"That's all he said?"

"I swear that's all he said. Oh, and that he loved your house. Did he tell you that he has three brownstones of his own?"

"Yes, he told me."

"Then what are we talking about here? Sounds to me like the perfect situation." Noreen raised both eyebrows in question.

"I didn't finish telling you everything that happened."

"Oh?"

Kat continued her story, slowly and painfully recounting the mortifying ending of her sexual adventure. Dahlia, feeling her friend's pain, held both hands over her mouth in shock and Noreen was holding her stomach laughing hysterically and trying to keep from peeing her pants. When Noreen's loud guffaws stopped, Kat spoke again.

"It's not funny. No. How can I see him again after what happened?"

"First of all, that shit is mad funny. He laughed, didn't he?"

"He kind of smiled after he got it out."

"Yeah, guys don't care about that kind of shit," Noreen responded.

"Are you sure?"

"I'm absolutely positive." Noreen looked to her other friend to support her position, but Kat had to ask.

"Dahlia…?" Dahlia fidgeted in her seat trying to find the right words.

"He likes you, that's what's important. Invite him over again. He likes to eat home-cooked meals." Dahlia leaned over and took Kat's hand in support; it made Kat smile.

"Just don't cook him corn, okay." Kat threw Dahlia's hand away from her and all three friends laughed at the joke.

Before the last gale of laughter died down, Noreen just blurted out her news.

"I have cancer."

CHAPTER EIGHT
MOMENT OF TRUTH

Dahlia and Kat sat stunned in their seats, mouths hanging slack. Noreen reached for the last of the Cristal. She poured the contents of the bottle into her flute and it only filled it two-thirds. It was going to be a long night. Noreen didn't have another bottle of Cristal so she would have to crack open a cheaper bottle if she was going to keep her buzz going.

"Anyone for more wine?" Noreen didn't wait for a response from her friends.

She got up from the couch and went into the kitchen. She had two bottles of Dom Perignon chilling in the refrigerator. They weren't cheap, but they were inexpensive compared to the Cristal. Noreen took one of the two bottles out of the fridge and contemplated bringing the second one with her, too. After a moment, she closed the refrigerator door and set the bottle of Dom on the kitchen counter. Noreen stood in the middle of the kitchen floor, hands limply at her side and stared at the bottle. Her mind wandered to and through the bottle to the other side of some other reality where she was not sick. Where she laughed and sang and enjoyed her friends. Some time passed; Noreen didn't know how much, when a hand rested on her shoulder.

"Are you all right, No?" The look of concern on Dahlia's face was heartbreaking. Kat looked on from just inside the kitchen doorway

Noreen woke from her reverie, not quite aware of her surroundings.

"Huh? Yeah, yeah, I'm fine. Just fine." She reached for the bottle, but her lack of focus sent it tumbling onto the counter.

Kat, who was already walking forward toward her two friends, lunged for the bottle and caught it before it toppled over the side of the terracotta counter top.

"Maybe we've had enough to drink, honey." Kat reached out to hold Noreen's hand with the hand that was not holding the Dom. Noreen took the hand and clasped onto it like a drowning woman who had just been thrown a life vest. She looked at Kat and then Dahlia and finally let the tears flow. Amidst the wracking sobs and guttural cries, the two friends helped Noreen back into the living room. They helped her into the white over-stuffed chair next to the sofa and each sat on one of the arms of the chair. The balancing act was no small feat for either of the women who could only fit a small part of their derrieres on it.

Kat held Noreen's head and occasionally pushed wisps of Noreen's hair away from her face, while Dahlia rubbed her back and cooed sympathetic inspiration in her ear.

"Cry all you want, baby, it's gonna be all right. We're here for you and we aren't going anywhere without you."

Kat was never good with this kind of girl stuff; she, like Noreen, had always been the tough one. Making jokes and talking big were her forte. Now, out of her element, she just paraphrased everything Dahlia said.

"Nowhere without you."

"We're going to beat this thing."

"Beat this thing."

"We'll find you the best doctors and best of care."

"Best of care."

"You're going to walk away from this and be better than ever."

"Better than ever."

It went on like that for ten minutes before Noreen's crying started to subside. Noreen sniffled one last time and picked her head up.

"I'm all right now."

"All right now."

For the last ten minutes, Dahlia listened to Kat repeat the last few words of every sentence she said, but after hearing her repeat after Noreen compounded by the shock and stress of finding out her dearest friend was sick, made her lose all of her normal composure.

"What are you, a goddamn parrot?"

"Wha..?"

"Can't you think of anything else to say? Do you have to repeat after everyone?"

"I'm sorry, I didn't…"

"I didn't, I didn't…see how it sounds stupid."

Kat knew fighting words when she heard them, and verbal pugilism was more her nature than sympathetic melodrama. She knew how to cut deep.

"Well, I would have said something else if you had stopped talking for more than a damn moment. It's like you nor your damn momma knows when to stop talking."

Fury welled up in Dahlia's eyes like a woman possessed.

"You don't even know my mother!"

"I know her enough," Kat retorted. "I heard weewee chew on the answering machine when I called you over there."

Dahlia stood up from the armrest.

"What did you call my mother?"

"Wee..wee…Chew!"

Dahlia started to go after Kat, but Noreen stood up between them in time, putting both hands on Dahlia to hold her back.

"Wait a minute now, both of you," she said, looking over her shoulder at Kat who had taken a defensive posture.

"Both of you must be out of your goddamn minds. I'm the one that's sick. This is supposed to be about me and you two are fighting about nothing."

Noreen wanted to let Dahlia go, but she still felt the fight in her and held her a little tighter afraid of what might happen if she did release her.

"Kat, apologize."

"I didn't start it. It was this hating heifer that started calling names."

Dahlia struggled against Noreen at the words.

"Hating! Please…I've kept hatin' bitches like you employed since nineteen seventy-five."

"That's right, I said it, *Hating!* If it was a disease, your ass would be hooked up to a life support unit right now."

Dahlia struggled against Noreen again and Kat started to bob and weave on the other side of the overstuffed chair like a shadow boxer.

"I said, stop it both of you and I mean it. Neither one of you looks like she knows how to fight, anyway."

After she said those words, Noreen felt Dahlia stop struggling in her arms. She looked over her shoulder to see that Kat had stopped her Apollo Creed imitation. Noreen let Dahlia go and plopped back down on the chair. Kat and Dahlia both stood looking at each other uneasily.

"I'm going to need both of you to get through this. You two are as good friends as any combination of us. Now make up."

Both women crossed their arms, neither giving an inch.

"Kat, you say sorry first."

"She started, let her say sorry first."

"Hmmph." Noreen blew breath out losing patience.

"Yeah, but you talked about her mother and you know mothers are off limits. Especially since you went and started making names up based on her oral sex habits…weewee chew."

Kat looked puzzled.

"Oral sex habit? I wasn't talking about any oral sex."

Dahlia's lips tightened trying to hold back another outburst, but she couldn't help herself.

"Kat! Take it back or we're not friends anymore."

Kat looked at Dahlia and so the hurt in her eyes. She knew it was more about Noreen than anything else and decided not to make matters worse.

"All right, I'm sorry. But I'm telling you I wasn't talking about any oral sex."

"Whatever…" Dahlia was trying to be the bigger person.

"Kat, this is serious, no mothers."

"I am being serious. She never let me finish when I called her mother Weewee Chew. I wasn't trying to say her mother gives blowjobs that leave teeth marks. I was referring to the Christmas carol message she was singing on the answering machine."

This time both Noreen and Dahlia were looking at her stupidly.

Kat didn't understand why neither of the women knew what she was talking about, so she sang it for them.

"Weewee chew a merry Christma, weewee chew a merry Christma, weewee chew a merry Christma and a hoppy new jeer."

Both the women were struck dumb when they heard Kat's rendition. It was a perfect imitation of Mrs. Ortega. Noreen started laughing first and very loudly. As much as she tried, Dahlia couldn't help laughing, either, although not as loud. Kat looked proud that she had made them both laugh at such a grave time. She left them in the living room recuperating from their hysterics and went back into the kitchen to get the bottle of Dom left on the counter. She found the corkscrew in the sink and was able to open the bottle without leaving cork shavings in it, the way she usually did. When she brought the bottle back into the living room, Dahlia was sitting on the couch and Noreen was still in the big chair. Both women looked relieved to see the bottle of champagne in her hand.

After pouring everyone liberal glasses of the golden fluid, Kat sat down in the wingback chair and got down to brass tacks. Problems were like business to her and she liked to handle them and solve them in that way.

"Tell us what you know."

"Kat, give her a chance. She may not be ready to talk about it."

Noreen downed the entire content of her glass and reached for the bottle again.

"No, Dahlia. Kat's right. I have talk about it, own it or not own it, and move on. That's the only way I'm going to be able to fight this thing."

Dahlia and Kat both took smalls sips of the champagne and listened.

"I have stomach cancer."

Dahlia and Kat both winced as if they were jabbed with a needle.

"Fortunately they think they caught it early. The endoscopy indicated that it was probably a small Helicobacter Pylori caused infection of the duodenum which invaded the lower intestine that caused the lymphocytic tumor."

Both women took another sip of their drink.

"Noreen, honey, neither one of us has a degree in nursing like you. Try telling us again…in layman's terms, please."

"My stomach hurts and there's a booboo! Hell, girl, there are no layman's terms; it is what it is."

"Does it really hurt?" Dahlia was concerned about the pain.

"No. I was just being an ass. It doesn't hurt. That's the good thing and the bad thing about stomach cancer. There aren't many symptoms. It usually doesn't start hurting until it's too late for them to do anything about it. By that time it has usually spread and you just waste away. I was lucky they caught it."

"How did they catch it?"

"I was helping the technicians test the new full-scan machine—one that can detect every small anomaly in your body. They told me to get in. I did. And they found the tumor. The doctor I work for took me straight downstairs to his buddy the gastroenterologist. They booked a room and in an hour they were doing an endoscopy."

"An endoscopy?"

"It's exactly what you think. They go in through the end."

Dahlia and Kat sipped and winced in unison again.

"They gave me some Vicodin for the pain. Between that and this champagne I'm barely feeling any discomfort at all."

Dahlia reached for Noreen's champagne flute, but Noreen held it out of reach.

"Noreen, you should know better than mixing narcotic drugs with alcohol." She reached for the glass again, but Noreen held up a fist.

"Ah, ah, ah. This is my last drink. Tomorrow I go under the knife. They told me nothing to eat or drink after twelve o'clock midnight." She downed what was left in her glass and reached for the bottle again. But Kat was too fast for her and was able to snatch the bottle of Dom from the table before Noreen could get to it.

"Well, that's no reason to be stupid, either."

Kat poured herself another drink and passed the bottle to Dahlia.

"And why tomorrow? Why are they moving so fast with this thing? I've never heard of anyone being diagnosed with cancer one day and being operated on the next day. What happened to a second opinion?" Kat was just being her usual businesslike self.

"I can go for a second opinion if I want, but it might take me another two weeks to get an appointment with another gastroenterologist that is this good. Then if it turns out that Dr. Lucas is right—that's his name by the way—then I would have to wait for an operating room to be open. That might be another two weeks."

"Why two weeks? They got tomorrow open easy enough."

"I got lucky...*Buuuurrrp*. Excuse me."

The cartoonish look on Noreen's face was evidence that the drugs had enhanced the effects of the alcohol. Kat waved the foul air that reached her from Noreen's mouth and turned her nose up.

"The lady that was supposed to get operated on tomorrow died just in time. I got her spot."

Kat couldn't think of any more questions that Noreen might be able to answer in her now intoxicated condition.

"What did your family say?" Dahlia wanted to know.

"Nothing."

"Nothing?"

"I didn't tell zem." Noreen was starting to slur her words.

"You know my mother, Dee. She's going to make a big deal."

"It is a big deal. She and your brother should know."

"I'm not going to tell zem until affer the operation."

"But you tell us?" Kat accused her.

Noreen looked hurt. "You're my friends. I love bofe of you." She smiled stupidly, then leaned over and threw up on the coffee table.

Kat and Dahlia both helped her up and into the bathroom. They helped her remove her clothes and stood outside of the shower stall listening to her sing a bad version of Amy Winehouse's *They're Trying to Make Me Go to Rehab*.

Dahlia found a nightgown in Noreen's bedroom and Kat tried to hold her still while Dahlia fought to get the thing over Noreen's head.

"I said no-no-no….heh-heh-heh." Noreen laughed at her own little joke. As soon as her head hit the pillow, she was snoring loudly.

Kat went into the living room and grabbed her coat. Dahlia almost called after her.

"I'm going to go pick up KJ from the babysitter and take him to my mother's house. I'll get a change of clothes and come back. Then you can go to your house and get some clothes and handle whatever you have to," Kat directed.

Kat reached the door and turned back.

"You thought I was leaving, didn't you?"

"The thought never crossed my mind. You're in the club now, and us big girls stick together."

"Great, the big girls club. We'll both be happy when we lose our membership."

Dahlia knew she was right. It was Noreen that always talked about the big girls club.

Kat left and Dahlia walked right over to Noreen's phone and hit the speed dial for Noreen's mother. She explained everything to her, then hung up the phone and waited. An hour later Noreen's brother and mother were sitting in the living room with Dahlia. Each lost in their own sea of worry for the woman they all loved and adored.

That night only Noreen slept.

CHAPTER NINE
BIG GIRLS DO CRY

Noreen was awakened by the smell of steaming hot coffee at approximately five thirty five in the morning and was not surprised to see four people sitting in the living room. Her brother Eric took up the whole couch. He lay in a fetal position with his socks off. She remembered how bad his feet smelled after a basketball game when they were teenagers and wrinkled her nose at the memory. When Eric saw her, he sat up, half expecting that she would tell him to put his sock back on when he saw her eye his feet on her new couch. Dahlia and Noreen's mother shared the overstuffed chair and were going through old photos in an album of Noreen and her brother at different stages of their youth. Eric's sudden movement made them both look up to see Noreen standing at the entrance of the living room. She looked as if she were about to say something, but the moment seemed to linger in the air too long, and Noreen's mother went back to the album ignoring Noreen. She pointed to a picture in the album bringing Dahlia's attention back to the book.

"She just had to have those sneakers. I told her that her feet were too big for those shoes, but she wouldn't listen. Here she was with them on again. You couldn't tell her she wasn't stylin'."

"I looked good," Noreen mumbled under her breath.

"Mmm-hmm" was her mother's only reply. She didn't bother looking up from the album again.

Noreen walked over to the couch and plopped down next to her brother. He put his large arm around her pulling her close and she let him. Kat who sat dozing in the wingback chair was startled awake by the vibration that Noreen's sitting caused.

"Is...is it time to go?"

"What time is it? I have to be at the hospital by seven."

Eric looked at his watch.

"We've got a little more than an hour to get there. I think we have time to get breakfast first."

"Noreen can't have anything to eat for ten hours before the operation." Dahlia looked up from the album.

"That ain't got nothing to do with me."

Noreen jabbed him playfully in the ribs.

"I've got to pack a bag for the hospital." Noreen got up from the couch.

"I've already packed it."

Noreen's mother pointed to the suitcase next to the wooden giraffe figurine in the corner.

"I'm sure there are a few things you forgot."

Eric, Kat, and Dahlia all shook their heads no simultaneously.

"I think I got everything." Her mother still hadn't looked up from the album.

"My nightgown."

"Three of them."

"My slippers."

"I got you pink ones and blue ones."

"New ones?"

"Mmm-hmm."

"What about my hair scarf."

"Four of them."

"My haircare products, my makeup, my iPod, my toothbrush, perfume."

"Mmm-hmm. And your robe, your warm socks, your reading glasses, and some underwear."

"And a bunch of other stuff I never would have thought of," Kat added.

"I didn't know you could fit that much stuff in a bag that small," Dahlia reported.

"Remember when I was getting my tonsils taken out?" Eric reminded Noreen.

"Like that?"

"Like that!"

Noreen looked to her mother, but her mother appeared to be concentrating on the album in her lap.

"I'm going to get dressed."

"You need some help," Dahlia offered.

"Since when?

"Just asking."

"I know."

Noreen was talking over her shoulder as she walked back into her bedroom. Thirty minutes later, the five of them were marching out of the apartment building. Noreen and her brother fought about who was going to carry her suitcase to the car. He won the argument, but she slapped him in the back of the head when he carelessly threw the suitcase into the trunk of his Denali truck.

At the hospital, the admissions team was very efficient. Within minutes they had taken all the information they needed from Noreen, and had her sign all of the paperwork that they needed. A nurse came out on cue and asked Noreen to follow her to the back. When the whole group started to walk behind the nurse, she stopped them in their tracks.

"You can have one person come with you to pre-op. The rest have to wait in the waiting room with all the other families."

Noreen turned back to the small group ready to choose the least stressful of her party, but it was not to be.

Mrs. Klein snatched the bag that her son was carrying.

"You all say your good-byes here. I'll meet you in the waiting room when she goes up."

Noreen knew it would do no good to argue. She hugged and kissed every-one, stopping to wipe the tears out of her brother's eyes.

"Punk."

He gripped her tightly around her waist and lifted her off of the ground in a bear hug. When he put her down, he quickly turned around and walked away toward the waiting area. The girls waved as Noreen and her mother walked away following the nurse through the swinging doors marked *Patients only.*

Clinging to the back of her dressing gown which threatened to expose her large and naked brown ass, Noreen sat in the wheelchair as she was directed by the nurse who was taking her to the operating room. Mrs. Klein stepped in front of the wheelchair before the nurse could push her daughter away. She wiped the tears from Noreen's eyes and put her short stout arms around her daughter.

"I'm going to be right there when you open your eyes again, you hear?"

"I'm going to be okay, Momma." It almost sounded like a question.

"Of course you're going to be okay. Now don't give the doctors any trouble and I'll bring you something nice from home, okay?"

"Okay, Momma."

Mrs. Klein turned to the nurse and gave her a look that said, *You better take good care of my girl.* The young nurse could feel a sermon coming and started to push Noreen away before it could begin. Mrs. Klein watched her baby until the nurse pushed her into the waiting elevator and the doors slid shut.

The short squat women waited a moment, then tried to take a step. She felt every bit of oxygen leave her body and trembled as the cold sweat squeezed through her pores. Mrs. Klein held onto the door to her right, sure that she was fainting. It took her a moment to recapture her equilibrium. Since her husband died, she was used to having to be strong. Her children had not seen her cry since the day that she buried her beloved husband, nearly twenty-five years ago. She gathered momentum as she walked through the hospital alone and remembered to wipe the tears from her eyes before walking into the waiting room to see her son and her daughter's friends. By the time she stood in front of them, she was fully composed again.

"Let's go get some breakfast."

"Shouldn't we wait until we hear something from the surgeon?" Dahlia asked.

"No baby, she's going to be in the operating room for at least four hours. There's no use all of us suffering."

"Amen." Eric was already out of his seat.

The four large people took up the entire hallway as they started out of the building.

"How was she?" Dahlia was wringing her hands nervously.

"Baby, you know Noreen. She was making jokes all the way to the elevator."

Kat heard and knew that Mrs. Klein was lying. She saw that Dahlia took comfort in the lie and even Eric smiled a little as he held the door open for the three ladies. Kat knew it was a lie and she and Mrs. Klein shared a look that each understood. *Only a mother knows this pain.* Both women said a quiet prayer as they passed beneath the hospital awning. The sun had barely come up, but the small warmth that each of them felt from it seemed to rejuvenate each one. They crossed the street to the diner facing the north end of the hospital and enjoyed one another's company before returning to the waiting room for two hours longer than the four hours they had all expected.

It was the epitome of the age-old adage: *If you want to make God laugh, tell him your plans.*

CHAPTER TEN
GETTING WELL

"Is that him?"

"I don't think so."

"That is him. I can't believe you told him about Noreen. First you told her mother when she didn't want you to, that one I understood. But why did you have to tell Dennis. They haven't been dating that long. You should have left that decision up to her."

"The man left twenty messages on the answering machine asking her to call him back in the last two weeks. The last message he left said that he was worried that she hadn't returned his phone calls and that he was going to come by the house to make sure that she was all right if she didn't call him back. What did you expect me to do?"

Dahlia and Kat made it a habit to meet up after work each day and come up to the hospital to visit Noreen together. It was Dennis whom they saw leaving the hospital now as they entered. Kat was glad he didn't see them. She didn't think much of him and she was not prone to small talk. The elevator came pretty quickly and Kat noticed how Dahlia never looked directly at anyone who appeared to be a patient. It was the cancer wing of the hospital and it was usually pretty easy to tell the patients from the visitors. A lot of the patients were missing hair, were unusually thin, or had some obvious deformity. Noreen was lucky. She only had a small scar to show for her debilitating disease as of the day of the operation.

"I can't believe you told him about Noreen's illness. When we get upstairs you're on your own. If Noreen gets out of that bed to whip your ass, you brought it on yourself. She'll probably pop her stitches going upside your head."

Dahlia knew Kat was right. She may have overstepped their friendship boundaries. When the two friends reached Noreen's hospital room door, Dahlia let Kat go in first. She stepped in a second after, prepared to face Noreen's wrath. When they entered Noreen was sitting up in the bed with several IV tubes sticking out of her arm. She didn't show any signs of being angry when they came in and Dahlia took it as a good sign.

"Was that Dennis we just saw leaving?"

Dahlia was a little taken aback that Kat brought up the subject of Dennis that quickly. She tried to look unaffected by the question and began to take her coat off and look around the small room acting as if she were distracted by the lack of space to put down her belongings.

"Yeah, that was him. Can you hand me that blanket at the foot of the bed." Noreen gathered the stark white sheet up under her chin and shivered.

Kat reached for the blanket, unfolded it and draped it over the thin sheet that covered Noreen.

"How's that? You want another one? There's one here on the chair."

Noreen trembled again and nodded yes to another blanket.

"The temperature keeps going up and down in this room. One minute I'm hot and the next I'm cold."

Dahlia still hadn't spoken and Noreen noticed.

"What's wrong with Ms. Mouth here?"

"Oh, she's scared you're going to try to whip her ass and open your stitches."

Dahlia put her things down in the seat that Kat took the blanket off of and went about straightening things in the room as if she were still not listening to her friends' conversation.

"Why? Because she told Dennis and everybody else that she wasn't supposed to tell that I was laying up here in this hospital?"

"Yeah, that's it."

"Well, I kind of knew that she would tell everybody. So I'm not too mad at her."

"I didn't tell everybody. I just told the people that I thought would be the most interested in your welfare." Dahlia took the bait and entered the conversation.

Noreen sat up in her bed and winced as she reached for a jug of water that was on the nightstand to her right. Dahlia saw the look of pain on her face and jumped to her feet to get the jug that she thought was just out of Noreen's reach. The tip of Dahlia's fingers just touched the jug when Noreen's hand deftly poked it with the purposefulness of a professional pool player making a bank shot. The mug went past Dahlia's outstretched fingers and the ice water that splashed onto her beige skirt spread quickly across her lap causing a stain that looked to Kat (social studies teacher) like the state of Rhode Island.

"Oh Dee, I'm sorry. Look, I ruined your skirt."

Dahlia felt the water soaking through to her underwear, but was consoled by the fact that it would dry and the stain wouldn't be permanent.

"It's okay. It's just water."

"No it's not. It's got lemon in it. Lemon water on a beige skirt might as well be Clorox, with all the acid it has in it. You better go try to wash that out now."

Dahlia's jaw dropped when she saw the smirk on Noreen's face.

"You knew! You did it on purpose."

Dahlia ran into the bathroom and the sound of her cursing was muffled by the jet spray of water that rushed into the sink.

"You didn't have to do her like that, No."

Noreen shrugged her shoulders indifferently.

"I'll buy her another skirt. You know she had it coming."

"That's between you and her, but you know she's only trying to look out for you."

"I don't see her telling all of her business. Did she tell you that she went back to that club the other night?"

"What club?"

"The S and M club where my brother bounces."

Kat's eyebrows raised in surprise, but she didn't want to comment about it with Dahlia just out of earshot.

"Yeah, she's not telling any of that."

Kat moved closer to Noreen and spoke in a whisper.

"Noreen, that is your best friend. She might have made some mistakes with telling your personal business, but you know she had only the best intentions. If she isn't ready to talk about the S and M club, you had better not bring it up just to embarrass her."

Kat could tell when someone was wallowing in self pity and Noreen had it in spades when she folded her arms like a child throwing a tantrum.

"I understand that you're sick, No, but so help me, if you do one more mean thing to Dahlia, I will not be your friend anymore."

Noreen turned her head toward Kat, but rolled her eyes up into her head in defiance.

"Okay, then I'll just call Dennis up and tell him that you never did like skinny men. I'll apologize to him for having tricked you into having to date him to begin with."

Noreen unfolded her arms.

"You wouldn't."

"Dare me."

The two friends' eyes met and they each knew that Kat was not bluffing.

"All right, all right, you win."

"When she comes back into the room, I want you to apologize for messing up her skirt. Don't make me pull that IV out of your butt and whip you with it. You know you're too sick to fight anyone now."

Noreen chuckled at the notion of being whipped by her friend, but that small gesture alone brought so much pain that she was instantly nauseated.

Kat saw the pain Noreen was in and grabbed her hand in an effort to show sympathy and support. She was surprised to feel how feeble Noreen's grip was when she attempted to squeeze her hand through the pain. Ten long seconds passed between the friends before Noreen was able to smile again.

"Thanks, Kat."

"Thanks? For what?"

"For being a friend. For just being here. For being there for Dahlia."

"You know us big girls have to stick together."

"Kat, you ain't no real big girl. You're going to lose that weight like you've been talking about, and you'll go back to being one of those stuck-up skinny bitches."

"You're right. I am going to lose this weight, but I have never been skinny." She patted her full hips for emphasis.

"And I have never been stuck up. The bitch part is arguable."

Both women laughed and another wave of pain engulfed Noreen. Dahlia came out of the bathroom with a bigger stain on her skirt than when she went in.

"I did all I could to save it."

She saw Noreen in pain and rushed to her side again.

"Are you okay?"

Dahlia picked up the hand that Kat was not holding and all three friends went through the pain together. After some moments, Noreen was able to exhale again and found her voice.

"I'm sorry about the skirt, Dee. I'll pay for it to be cleaned or I'll buy you a new one."

"Oh that's okay, you don't have to."

"No, I mean it. It was just childish of me to spill that lemon water on you."

"That's a nice way to apologize, but believe me when I tell you, you do not have to buy me a new skirt. This is your beige skirt. Remember about four months ago when we went to that party and I had to sleep over your house because Darrell didn't want to leave your building and you were going to go downstairs and stab him. This is the skirt you lent me to go to church in when your mother came over in the morning."

"My good Abby Z skirt? That is not it. Please don't tell me that's my Abby Z skirt."

"All right, I won't tell you, but it is."

Noreen was about to say something, but changed her mind when she felt the pressure of Kat squeezing her hand and what it meant. The girls settled down to a nice visit, each taking an opportunity to tell about her hectic day.

"Oh, I almost forgot to tell you, your mother visited me today."

"She did? I told her you might not want visitors. She wasn't a bother, was she?"

"No, as a matter of fact we had a nice visit. Of course it wouldn't be a real visit with your mother if she didn't leave me with the Puerto Rican word of the day."

It irritated Dahlia that Noreen always made fun of her mother, but she knew it was just Noreen's way of showing affection when she kidded with you. Noreen wouldn't make fun of anyone she didn't really like.

"What did my mother say today that tickled you so much?"

Noreen sat up in the bed, cleared her throat like a herald and announced, "The Puerto Rican word of today is *WHEELCHAIR!*"

"That is not a Puerto Rican word of the day. My mother knows what a wheelchair is."

Dahlia was happy to be able to defend her mother.

Noreen ignored Dahlia and spoke to Kat.

"Let me tell you what happened. Dahlia's mother came in right before lunch. So the nice nurse comes in and gives me a bowl of soup and my Jell-O. Migdalia's mom made such a to-do about how good the soup smelled that the nurse offered to bring her a bowl of her own. Of course she was only being kind about how good the soup smelled so she says to the nurse… *Don't jou worry if I get too hongri wheelchair.*"

Kat tried to keep the laughter in, but couldn't. Noreen laughed once and instantly doubled over in pain. Dahlia found the humor in it and chuckled. A few minutes later, the nurse came in and administered pain medication to Noreen. They said their good-byes and Noreen was unconscious before the door closed behind her old friend and her new friend.

CHAPTER ELEVEN
SHIFTING GROUND

Noreen looked in the mirror disgusted at what she saw. According to the scale at the doctor's office that she'd just left, she was six feet one inch and weighed one hundred and fifty-five pounds. The last time she weighed one hundred and fifty-five pounds was eighteen years ago, when she was fourteen years old. Nothing in her closet fit her anymore. Every time Dahlia came over she took one or two of Noreen's ensembles when she left. Noreen didn't mind. She was glad that someone was getting the benefit of using them.

Both Dahlia and Kat were there when the doctor explained how removing a large part of her stomach would cause her to eat less, which meant that her body would absorb fewer nutrients and cause her to lose weight. Although the surgery was a success and all of the cancer was now gone, Noreen felt that she lost a part of her self-esteem with each ounce of fat that left her body. Already three months after her cancer surgery, she'd lost more than a hundred pounds. She knew she was a little depressed, and Kat and Dahlia invited her out to a club to try to cheer her up.

Dennis was her only saving grace. He visited her in the hospital daily during her three-week hospital stay. When she was convalescing at home, he would bring her a different flavored soup every day so that she would not get bored with the only source of nourishment that she could tolerate. It was only a month ago that she'd started to eat solid foods again, and he took her to her El Quijote on 14th Street for steak and lobster. She was only able to get down a couple of bites of each entrée, but the thought he put into the restaurant he picked made her feel that he understood her needs—foodwise, that is.

On the sexual front they were not able to do much. They'd only had vaginal sex once since the time they met in Jamaica. The third night after they came home from vacation, he came to her house late one night at her behest. It took a whole lot of lubrication and was painful, but it was a good kind of pain. He had stretched her so wide with that massive appendage of his that it had given her a toothache. He came quickly and then attempted to finish her with his mouth. He wasn't very good and she faked her orgasm so that he would stop. It was the huge penis that excited her and she knew that if he could last a little longer, he would make her come harder than she had ever come before.

Noreen was also smart enough to know that her internal organs were not ready to be moved around the way sex with Dennis would likely do. Last week he suggested that he only put the head in and was angry when Noreen said no. He wouldn't admit that he was angry and Noreen placated him by going down on him. Today she had given him the same treatment and though no man complains about getting fellated, she knew that it wasn't satisfying to him anymore. Not wanting to seem like he had come over just for a blowjob, he was waiting in the living room while she got dressed. Noreen heard the doorbell ring and then the muffled laughter and greetings of her friends.

She walked out of her bedroom and into the living room to a round of whistles and clapping from her two partners in crime. She took notice that not one compliment about her appearance was uttered from Dennis' lips.

"That dress is gorgeous. I wish something like that came in my size."

Dahlia surmised that the dress Noreen wore was about a size ten or twelve.

Noreen looked to Dennis for his appraisal of her, but all she got was a lukewarm smile.

"Well, the gang is all here, so I guess I better be going now."

Dennis hugged Noreen awkwardly and attempted to kiss her on the cheek at the same time that she tried to kiss him on the mouth. It was an awful mess of a good-bye for two people who were supposed to have heat for each other. Dennis said an uncomfortable good-bye to Kat and Dahlia and closed the door to the apartment carefully behind him before walking to the elevator.

"Are you two breaking up?" Dahlia had become something of a callous person in the past few months. Kat nudged her to be quiet.

"What? All I'm saying is that good-bye was a little cold. A big dick is not worth all that is all I'm saying."

"We're doing all right." Noreen sounded unconvincing.

"Yeah, I can tell. You look like you're getting stretch marks around your lips."

Noreen's hand came quickly to her mouth in a tell-tale gesture before she realized that her friend was only kidding her. She smiled and blushed a little at the joke at her expense.

"Uh-huh. I knew it. You two were getting busy before we got here, weren't you?

"That is none of your business, Dee." Kat pretended to chastise Dahlia.

"No, you can tell us all about it in the car, with all of the juicy details and you better not skip one thing."

Kat and Dahlia slapped each other's palms remembering how their friend used to tell them about all of her bawdy sexual exploits.

In the car the girls begged Noreen to tell them what she had been doing with Dennis before they arrived at the apartment. They weren't so much interested in her sex life she knew, as much as they wanted her to be her old self again. The trouble was she didn't feel like her old self. She didn't know what she felt like, but whenever she looked at herself in a mirror, it was like she was living inside of someone else's body. She didn't know how to explain it to her two friends who were always talking about wanting to lose weight, but her weight had always dictated her personality. It allowed her to intimidate when she needed to. She was physically soft when it was appropriate, and weren't big people supposed to be jovial? For sure she was always ready with the first joke. Kat drove so Noreen didn't realize they were going to the S&M club where her brother worked until they drove past the front of the place in search of a parking spot.

Eric attempted to make conversation with Noreen at the door, but Kat ushered her through the doors while Dahlia ran interference, flirting and showing her cleavage off to the second bouncer and finally getting Eric's attention as she sashayed past him. She winked at him letting him know that she wasn't forgetting him. She was waiting for the kiss that he always blew her before making a grand entrance just past the person inside waiting to collect money from the clientele.

Dahlia was the toast of the place the minute she walked in.

"What are we drinking today, ladies?"

The handsome bartender behind the bar winked knowingly at Dahlia and pushed a long-stemmed Martini glass filled with a clear shimmering liquid and two olives toward her.

Noreen was glad to see the familiar face.

"The usual, Phil. But I think I'll have *three* olives."

"Pardon me, ma'am?"

Noreen attempted to keep her smile, but the nervous look on the face of the bartender who never forgot a regular customer's drink order made her feel uneasy.

"The usual, Phil. Don't tell me you're losing your memory."

"I'm sorry, Miss, I don't usually forget a customer. If you just give me your order, I promise to never forget it again."

"Phil, it's me, No."

The bartender looked her squarely in the face and still Noreen saw no recognition in his eyes.

A look of desperation came to her face.

"Noreen, Ms. Noreen! Don't tell me you don't remember me!" She was on the verge of becoming irate when Kat stepped in.

"You remember me, Phil?"

The bartender took a long look at her.

"Yes. Yes, I do you. A few months ago you came in with Ms. Dahlia and Ms… Oh shit!" He turned back to Noreen.

"I am so sorry, Ms. Noreen. My God, look at you. You're a whole new person. You look great."

"Fuck you."

"Noreen! That's not right." Kat pulled her by the arm.

The bartender smiled and went off to make Noreen's drink. Kat was talking to Noreen in hushed tones, trying to keep her calm.

The bartender came back with the drink a moment later, a smile still on his face.

"Here you go, Ms. Noreen. I'm sorry about the confusion. If you don't mind me saying so, you look really beautiful."

Noreen took the drink without looking at him. She took a sip of the drink, took one of the olives out of the glass and smoothly sucked it into her mouth. As she crushed it between her molars and felt the sour juice mingle with the alcohol in her mouth, she calmed herself and noticed that her two friends were staring at her. She swallowed the olive and was not surprised that it instantly soured her stomach.

"Should you even be drinking alcohol?"

The look on Noreen's face made Dahlia sorry that she asked the question.

"What are we doing here? Are we trying to have fun or not?"

The doctor warned her that her tolerance for alcohol would be almost non–existent, and when a moment later she felt the warm glow in her head heat her whole body, she ignored the signs and took another sip of her drink. The warm liquid did its job quickly and Noreen turned to look for a possible playmate in the throng of people that were milling about the place.

As the three women stood facing the crowded club with their backs to the bar, one by one the choicest of available men came by. Noreen noticed that none of them looked at her. They were all eyeing Dahlia. Kat noticed it, too.

"What the hell is that about?"

"I don't know. I guess they remember me from the last time we were here."

Noreen ignored the lie and eyed the next man who was passing them with his eyes down so that he made little eye contact. He hesitated in front of Noreen and then stopped in front of Dahlia.

He later regretted that decision.

✲✲✲

The ride home was loud. Noreen was the only one shouting. She was drunk in the backseat. It only took two drinks to totally inebriate her. It was the first time that she had any alcohol since the operation. Although she had been warned about how her body would have a hard time metabolizing the alcohol, she didn't know her tolerance would be so low. The events that transpired in the club would probably cause her to be blacklisted from coming back. Her brother would be lucky if he was able to keep his job, and she wouldn't realize any of this until tomorrow morning.

"I'm not drunk. I only had one drink."

"You had two drinks, No."

Kat was driving fast, weaving from one lane to another in a rush to get both of her friends home. She didn't like chastising her drunk friend, but she couldn't help herself. She hated the way that Noreen was feeling sorry for herself, and Dahlia wasn't helping matters any with her new aloof attitude.

"Why are you mad at me? It was Dahlia's fault that we got thrown out of the club."

"Don't blame me for getting us thrown out. If it weren't for me we would probably be in jail right now."

"We weren't going to jail and since when does a person get drunk on two drinks."

Kat was exasperated by Noreen's attitude.

"Since that person's whole GI tract got rewired and they absorb more alcohol than a normal person that is drinking does."

Noreen continued to argue that she wasn't drunk and Kat drove faster and argued even louder that she was. Dahlia wasn't about to get caught up in an argument with a drunk Noreen. She was bad enough when she was sober; now being belligerent on top of her normal arrogance was too much to deal with. She retreated into the memory of what happened at the club.

When Noreen grabbed the tiny man with the seersucker suit and bifocal glasses who stopped in front of Dahlia around the neck, it was a sure sign that something was wrong. Although she would never do it for money, her previous experiences at the club would definitely classify her as a professional dominatrix. What she did had no subtlety to it. In the dom world what Noreen did would be considered a rookie move.

"Didn't you see me here, Professor?"

Many people that were regulars at the club used pseudo names. The man with the bifocals was known only as *Professor*.

"Mistress?" He looked to Dahlia for help.

Dahlia opened her mouth to say something, but was shut down before she could intercede.

"Don't look to my friend for help, Professor. She can only help you if you want an ass kicking half as bad as the one I'm going to give you."

Noreen threw the man away from her and he landed on his ass next to a barstool.

"Meet me in the back next to the tables in ten minutes. I'll be there when I finish my drink. If you're not there you'll only make it worse on yourself."

Professor got up from the floor, dusted himself off and mumbled something under his breath before slinking off through the crowd of clubbers.

Kat, who knew nothing about the etiquette of an S&M clubber, was glad to see that Noreen had jumped right into the swing of things. After seeing her depressed for so many months, it was good to see her exert some authority and impose her will on someone. At the time she did not realize how much the alcohol had already affected her. The trio finished their drinks and ordered another round as Noreen became louder and more boisterous. They took their drinks with them as they made their way through the crowd to the back of the club where the S&M hardware was set up.

Unlike the last time they were there together, the crowd did not part for them as they walked among everyone. Kat did notice that the other obvious dominatrixes nodded to Dahlia as they passed through the crowd. Their male partners purposely lowered their eyes lest they raise the ire of their mistresses for daring to flirt.

Noreen still carried herself with certain aplomb, but it did not have the desired effect that it did the first time they walked the crowd together in this same club those few months ago. She didn't like the feeling of this new effect. It felt like disrespect to her, and with the firewater in her she started pushing people aside that did not get out of her path fast enough. The end result was that many people became angry and looked after the three women with disdain rather than respect as they passed.

Dahlia, who after a couple of months of attending this S&M club alone, was now familiar with its culture and worried about how her own reputation would be tarnished by Noreen's misbehavior. Dahlia had hoped that Professor did not obey Noreen's command at the bar. But as they arrived at the rear of the club, she saw that he was sitting near the strap-on section as he had been directed.

"You're not really going to do that are you, No?"

Kat was aghast that Noreen had bullied Professor into stripping from the waist down and had him bent over a chair. It was one thing to spank somebody who liked to be beaten, she rationalized, but to actually consider sodomizing a man was too much for her to absorb.

Noreen was tightening one of the harnesses that were kept available for clients who did not come with their own equipment. The equipment was constantly sanitized by club staff members that were perpetually cleaning up after the club's clientele. Club patrons couldn't put as much as a glass of water down for more than thirty seconds without someone coming around to pick it up. In the rear of the club where all the real action took place, there were dozens of club staff members designated to stand around and wait for spillage to occur. Bodily fluids were likely to be spilled and the club managers didn't want any excess of it laying around. Upon just one usage of any sex paraphernalia, a club employee would take the used equipment to the cleaning area in the basement and make sure it was cleaned in a mixture of water and Clorox. Other items were designated to be cleaned in a dish-washer that used water that was over 120 degrees to ensure its sanitation.

Dahlia was wringing her hands nervously as she watched Noreen prepare the phallus attached to her hips. She noticed Noreen wasn't using enough lubrication. She was barely wetting the tip. It would be just enough to allow Noreen quick entry into Professor's anus, but after that it would be a rough ride.

Noreen walked around to stand in front of Professor. She moved close and placed the phallus at his lips. Reluctantly, Professor allowed the object to part his lips. Noreen kept it there long enough for his saliva to drip from the head. Then she withdrew and walked back behind the man. Professor's eyes bulged when he felt the fat tip of the latex cock enter his ass. He didn't make a sound as he was well trained by other mistresses before this particular incident. He gritted his teeth and attempted to manage the terrible discomfort inside of him.

Within fifteen minutes of Noreen putting in work on his ass, he was crying and whimpering too afraid to tell Noreen to stop. One of the attendants, whose duty was to monitor such delicate situations, left the area amidst a slowly growing group of voyeurs to get the manager. Club rules allowed that only the manager could intervene in such situations.

The manager didn't run, but came quickly through the throng of onlookers as he knew that the attendant had been a good judge of misconduct on previous occasions.

The manager was allowed through to the inner part of the circle that formed and upon seeing Professor's face, he stepped immediately to his side, getting the attention of the tall woman who was connected to him via a large plastic penis. Noreen slowed the speed of her thrusts. Instead of the long focused thrusts, she lent short violent stabs into him keeping her eyes on the man who stood casually in front of her.

A moment of recognition passed between the two and the manager allowed a dangerous smile to play on his lips.

"Mistress Noreen. It's good to see you again."

Noreen acknowledged him with a nod, but continued her assault on Professor. The manager cleared his throat to get Noreen's attention again. Noreen looked up from her work again.

"I'm afraid, Mistress Noreen, that I'm going to have to ask you to desist in your endeavors this evening."

Noreen all but ignored him sending two quick thrusts into Professor in a show of defiance. Without any display of annoyance or even a hint of irritation, the manager snapped his fingers twice and two huge figures appeared at each of Noreen's sides. A sideways glance from the manager prompted the giants to grab Noreen one under each arm and pull her violently backward disengaging her from Professor. There was a loud sucking noise and then a popping sound as Professor's anus sucked air and attempted to reconstitute itself.

Dahlia held Kat back from interceding on Noreen's behalf. The manager's eyes caught hers and she was clear that he would not be tolerant of any further protocol disputations. The manager barely watched as his goons led Noreen none too gently to his office and then turned his attention back to Professor who was still silently bent over the chair. He looked down at the exposed anus of the man and almost lost his composure when the flesh in front of him reminded him of a freshly fucked virgin cunt. It was splayed and bleeding. The way it opened and closed might've made you think that Professor was actually using his asshole to draw breath. With a wave of his hand the manager of the club dispersed what was left of the voyeuristic crowd. Everyone went back to what they were doing.

The Professor was not moving. He stayed bent over the chair. It only took one word from the manager for Professor to lose it.

"Sir?"

Professor broke into back-wracking sobs and half-controlled weeping. The manager had a personal rule that he never touch the guests and he meant to keep that one rule at any cost. A glance to his left brought two attendants to Professor's side.

"Would you help this gentleman to the locker room and assist him in any way that he deems necessary." The manager gave both attendants a knowing look he knew they would both understand.

This boutique business was tenuous in the best of conditions. Situations such as this one had to be handled with kid gloves lest they land in the lap of the police department or even worse, the Department of Health. In order to keep attention away from the club, the manager had to placate dissatisfied members and guests. It was usually easy enough to do, as most people that frequented the club didn't want to draw any attention to themselves. He didn't think Professor would be a problem. The man was a member of the mayor's staff. He was a politically appointed special assistant, which amounted to little more than an administrative assistant, but still would not want his position in the government compromised by any sort of bad publicity.

"Anything he needs is to be charged to the house."

The attendants pulled Professor's pants up from his ankles in tandem and physically helped him upright. He gave them no help in buttoning his pants again and they led him down to the locker room still trying to control the gasps and convulsions that intermittently escaped him.

Before returning to his office, the manager turned on his heels checking to see that every club activity was in full swing again. He caught the eye of an attendant that appeared to be waiting for an assignment and waived one finger in a circle in the air. It was the signal for a round of drinks on the house. The bartenders would know to make the drinks strong ensuring that if anyone remembered the situation the next day it would not be as clear in their mind as it might be now. It was a costly maneuver, but damage control always was. He looked around one last time and then signaled to Dahlia and Kat who waited nervously just out of his reach to follow him. They reached his office without uttering a word to him or each other. They found Noreen sitting quietly with the two giants on each side of her in front of a huge oak desk that consumed most of the meager office.

It was obvious to everyone in the office that Noreen was inebriated beyond the point of reasoning. Her head lolled from side to side and her lips were pursed in defiance. The manager, who was always a man of few words, didn't bother wasting any of them on Noreen. He looked directly at Dahlia, calculating correctly from the look of her that Kat had no idea of the seriousness of the transgression Noreen had committed.

"Take her home down the back staircase. I don't want to see her in the club again."

"Ever?" Dahlia was nonplussed.

"If I need to talk to her in order to make restitution to the club member, I'll ask Eric for her information. If she shows up again within the next year, there'll be consequences and repercussions. Again, I'll speak to her brother about it."

Kat didn't bother to ask the repercussions. No matter what they were, they couldn't be good. Kat and Dahlia helped Noreen down the back staircase directly from the manager's office. Noreen's brother was waiting for them at the bottom of the stairs. When Noreen saw him, she broke into a huge smile. The night air seemed to stimulate her and she shook her two friends' arms off of her easily.

"Hey little Bro, you didn't have to come and see us off. We know our way out."

"Is she all right?" He was speaking to Dahlia.

"I don't know what happened to her. She only had two drinks."

"I heard what happened. Why didn't you stop her? You know the rules in there."

"Try and stop me. Who? Who's going to stop me?" Noreen looked at Dahlia, then at Kat.

"These two? They can't stop me. Nobody can stop me. I am large and in charge." Noreen stumbled and Kat caught her.

"There's a diner around the corner. They have some pretty strong coffee. You may want to take her to get some before you put her in the car. I'll talk to my boss and see if there is anything I can do to salvage our family name."

Noreen leaned to one side wretched letting loose a stream of viscous red fluid. It just missed Dahlia's shoe and she came up wiping her mouth and smiling again.

"Woowee, that's better. I think I could use some coffee."

She shrugged Kat's arm off her shoulder again and headed in the direction of the diner on her own. Kat went after her and Dahlia quickly caught up to them after giving Eric a quick kiss on the mouth. Neither Kat nor Noreen saw the show of affection.

Two cups of coffee later they were in the car and Noreen was begging her two friends' forgiveness. She was still loud and drunk but she was more aware of her surroundings than she was earlier. She didn't see the error of her ways yet and probably wouldn't until the next morning, possibly tomorrow afternoon.

"Why are we going home so early anyway? Let's find another club to go to. I've been thrown out of better places than that."

When they reached the front of Noreen's building, Noreen refused any help from Kat in getting out of the car.

"I'm good, I'm good. I'm not drunk anymore."

To prove it she broke away and ran up the stairs taking them two at a time.

Kat got out of the car in an attempt to catch her, but was too late. The two friends looked after her in awe. It was a long time since either of them had been able to run up a flight of stairs, two steps at a time. They were both jealous of their friend and scared for her. Her life was changing in ways that she didn't care for, and they felt helpless to do anything to make a difference.

"You can look after her. I'll park your car. I've had enough for tonight."

Kat would have argued, but Dahlia had already gotten into the driver's seat and put the car in drive. Kat walked quickly after her friend and was surprised to find Noreen waiting for her by the elevator.

"I messed up, didn't I?"

Kat shrugged. "It'll be all right." She felt genuinely calm.

In turn Noreen leaned over and threw up on Kat's powder-blue suede Manolos. The two friends stared at each other. They both looked sick. Kat pressed the elevator button and they waited for Dahlia to come. She took a long time and didn't look any happier to see them both leaning on the elevator door waiting for her to lend a hand.

CHAPTER TWELVE
LIVING IN A DREAM WITH A LITTLE BIT OF FANTASY

It was the fourth time that Dahlia was dropping Eric off at his home after the closing hours of the club when he finally got the nerve to invite her upstairs to his apartment.

"Would you like something to drink?"

"You did invite me up for a nightcap, right? Or was there something else you had in mind?"

Eric knew she was only teasing, but true things are always said in jest. Instead of answering her, he walked casually over to her and pulled her to him. The top of her head only reached the middle of his chest and she had to crane her neck up to look into his eyes. In Eric's eyes Dahlia could see the gentle soul of a would-be poet. What Eric saw when he looked into Dahlia's eyes was the salvation of his soul and the beginning of his life.

It was obvious that Dahlia knew that men were kinesthetic. She touched Eric everywhere that he liked to be touched. From the nape of his neck, to his hips, her hands roamed freely, finding all of his secret spots that were rarely found by his previous lovers.

Not wanting to push Dahlia to do anything before the appropriate time, he waited until she made her way to his belt buckle before he started to unbutton the top button of her blouse. It didn't take long before they were both naked and openly caressing each other in the middle of the small living room.

Dahlia attempted to go to her knees in front of Eric, but stopped her. She searched his face, trying to understanding why and was surprised when he not only lifted her back to her feet, but easily lifted her from under her hips until her vagina was directly in front of his face.

It was a first for Dahlia who had never been with a man that could lift her. Let alone doing it as easily as Eric did it. She thought of the time that she foolishly frequented Home Depot in hopes of coming across a man rugged enough to perform this same feat.

Now Eric stared into the depths of Dahlia's womanhood and could barely decide where to start. Just under her vagina he could see the extra skin in her ass that looked like the part of the balloon that you tie off after blowing it up. Dahlia's "balloon knot" became a private joke they would share for the rest of their lives together. He fought his instinct to start kissing there, not wanting Dahlia to think that he believed her to be anything less than a passionate woman.

He started by kissing slowly along her labia, but quickly found himself lapping at the freely flowing fluid that seeped from Dahlia's crevice. It wasn't long before she was grinding against his face, which he believed was his cue to enter her. Lowering her slowly he trailed kisses from the top of her pubic mound, to her navel, her breasts and then her neck, until he could feel the tip of his penis touch her pouting lips. Believing that it was what she wanted he entered her slowly and gently. When a soft mewl escaped her lips, Eric ground into Dahlia gently causing his pubic bone to press against her clitoris. Dahlia's spasms were involuntarily and Eric kissed her mouth tenderly feeling the staccato tremors that fanned from her tailbone to the top of her head.

They made love softly like that for more than two hours, but neither one of them reached a climax. Instead falling onto the couch wrapped in each other's arms and legs, both were physically spent; neither was satisfied.

They woke awkwardly a full two hours later and Eric walked Dahlia to her car. She settled into the driver's side and Eric leaned in and kissed her softly on her neck. This was the first time Dahlia had ever felt safe with a man. She was comfortable with her vulnerability and allowed herself to feel and receive Eric's love. It was warm, strong, and protective. Dahlia killed the ignition and got out of the car. Now, it was Eric's turn to be surprised. He took Dahlia's hand and led her back upstairs to his apartment.

CHAPTER THIRTEEN
TURN OFF THE LIGHTS, AND LIGHT A CANDLE

Kat's mother looked at her sideways when Librado came out of the bedroom smiling and offering his hand in salutation.

"Pleeze to meet *jou*, Meeses Davis. I am Librado."

Common courtesy indicated that Kat's mother take his extended hand, but the time it took her to do it and the look of disdain on her face made courtesy a strange and unlikely pleasantry in this first meeting.

"Lee who?"

"Librado, *Senora*."

The inflection in her voice and the slight at his name were subtly insulting, but Librado was raised too well to allow his annoyance at a parent or an elder to show on his face.

"That's Mexican, isn't it?"

Librado's smile never faltered as Kat's mother pulled her hand away and wiped it absentmindedly against the back of her pants leg.

"No, *Senora*. That ees a Spanish name. My family is from Puerto Rico."

"Well, they speak Spanish in Mexico, too, don't they?"

"Yes, they do, Senora. They speak Spanish. Not Mexican."

"Well, that's what I said, *they speak...*"

Mrs. Davis stopped in mid sentence when she realized how stupid she might have just sounded and looked suspiciously at Librado to see if there was any sign of triumph or of gloating in his eyes. When she found none, she went on choosing her words more carefully.

"What I meant to say was, it doesn't sound like any of the names of the Puerto Ricans or Dominicans that were raised around us."

"Oh I understand, Ms. Davis. *Jou* are more familiar weeth names like Juan and Jose and Jesus, maybe even Raul or Pablo."

Kat's mother nodded her agreement as if she had finally gotten her point across to a blind man in a game of charades.

"Yes, yes, now you understand."

Librado's smile didn't falter. Kat warned him before her mother came over that her mother may not respond as well to him as either of them would like.

Kat had been raised around Latinos when she was growing up in the projects, but the parents of her Latino friends were mostly first generation. They didn't talk much English and stayed to themselves or with others like them that were new to the country. Her mother and her mother's friends had taken the Latinos' fear of being in a new country to mean they thought they were better than the people whom they lived around.

The uneasy conversation was disrupted by a tiny voice.

"Nanna! Nanna!"

KJ came running into the kitchen from wherever he had been playing and leapt into his grandmother's arms. Clara Davis forgot her displeasure at the man in front of her for a moment and even forgot her failing back as she bent to scoop up her only grandchild.

"There's my baaaaby. Give Nanna some suga."

Clara turned her cheek for a big wet kiss and was not disappointed.

"MMuuuuaaahhh."

She kissed him back with all the love and affection that is reserved for a child that is endeared to a lonely old woman. She put him down because the pain in her lower back reminded her that she had not taken her pain medication before leaving the house.

"Did you pack an extra set of clothes for him?"

She reached down for his hand and KJ gladly grabbed for it. They were both unwilling to part with the other's show of affection that quickly. Kat was already going to the hall closet to get a coat for KJ when she heard her mother's voice call after her.

"I put two extra set of clothes in his bag just in case and some snacks."

"Snacks? What kind of snacks?"

Kat came back into the kitchen with KJ's coat and the little boy let go of his grandmother's hand and skipped toward his mother; anxious to put on his coat and leave the confines of the house.

"Just some apples and oranges and two Jell-O chocolate pudding cups."

"You don't have to pack any snacks. I have food in my house."

"Ma, I know you have food in your house, but you don't keep the kind of snacks that I want KJ to have."

Librado knew the tone of this discussion well. His grandmother had spoiled him rotten whenever his parents were not around, and his mother fought with his *abuela* to have him adhere to the same rules in both of their homes. He turned around and found a stool to sit down on well away from both women. Librado feared that if she showed any interest in their discussion he would be thought to be interfering by the slightest gesture or just by his mere presence. When Kat's mother started to raise her voice, he found some nonexistent dirt under his nails that he hadn't seen before and started working like hell to try to get it out. He put his head down and tried not to hear the conversation for fear that two black women would think that he might be trying to somehow interfere in their raising of a child. He remembered how his mother and *abuela* had almost come to blows over him, and it made him search even harder for the dirt that was not there.

"What do you mean, I don't have the kind of food you want KJ to have?

He eats the same things I gave you, when you were growing up in my house."

"Ma, last week KJ came back home asking for canned oysters in hot sauce."

"So?"

"So Ma, you never gave me any canned oysters in hot sauce when I was little. You never even let me eat candy until I got some from my friends in kindergarten. Now you give KJ anything he asks for."

Kat's mother looked guiltily at her daughter.

"I don't always give him what he likes. It was just that one time. Ms. Johnson, you know my neighbor. She came over with the groceries for our card game…"

Kat gave her a warning look.

"Don't worry, we didn't gamble while he was there. She opened up some of the canned oysters in hot sauce and when he saw us eating them he asked for some. I thought it would burn his mouth and he wouldn't ask for any more. I didn't know he was going to like it so much. Anyway, I didn't give him any more."

"Well, he came home and asked for oysters in hot sauce and got upset when we didn't have any."

"Got upset? What do you mean he got upset?"

"He started crying and throwing a tantrum."

"And what did you do?"

"I talked to him and tried to explain to him why he couldn't have canned oysters in hot sauce."

A look of disbelief came over Mrs. Davis's face.

"You talked to him?" The older woman paused for a moment and put her hands on her hips as she looked down at her grandson.

"He threw a tantrum!"

Like adults do, they had been talking about the little boy as if he weren't there and didn't understand what was going on. The little boy was used to this, but when his grandmother turned her attention to him, he put his head down in embarrassment. He did, after all, know right from wrong.

"Uh, uh. Nanna don't play that. He doesn't come over to my house with that nonsense. When Nanna says no, it no and that's all there is to it."

She looked sternly at the little boy willing his eyes up to meet hers. He looked up nervously at his nanna, but this time there was no mirth in his eyes.

"You giving your mama a hard time, boy?"

KJ answered slowly.

"No, Nanna."

"Good, 'cause Nanna doesn't want to have to tear that baby's behind up."

"No, Nanna."

Kat hoped it was an idle threat, but didn't put anything past her mother. Mrs. Davis's face softened again and she held her arms out to her grandson.

"Now come give Nanna some more suga."

KJ's face was happy again as he ran to his grandmother, glad not to have to face her wrath. Kat witnessed the entire interaction between her son and mother and decided that she would have a conversation with them both individually about the parameters of corporal punishment. She had never struck her son out of anger or to discipline him. She had never witnessed her mother to do it either. Although she remembered when she misbehaved as a child that her mother had no compulsions about *beating the black off of her or slapping the taste out her mouth* for her own good, that was not what she wanted for her son.

"Ma, just give him what I packed, okay."

"Mmm-hmm. I'll give him what you packed."

By the tone that she used, Kat knew that she would in fact not give him the snacks that she packed. It would be quite evident the next day when Kat unpacked KJ's bag and found smooshed apples and oranges underneath his dirty clothes. When she asked him about the Jell-O pudding snacks that were not among the fouled fruit, KJ explained that Nanna ate them, while he ate the peach cobbler that she made.

KJ slapped Librado five as they said good-bye at the door. Kat gave him a big hug and kiss and then watched him bound down the steps; not daring to go further than the bottom step without his grandmother, whom he thought was dawdling in her good-byes.

"I'll call you tomorrow after church."

Kat's mother hadn't gone to church in years and then only on holidays. Kat knew she was being nasty. What she meant was she would call Kat when she thought her daughter would be off of her knees after a night of repeatedly saying, *oh God, oh God.*

It was an old joke and Kat was glad that Librado was not familiar with it.

"Good night, Meeses Davis. Again, it was a pleasure meeting *jou.* Maybe next tine we maybe talk more. Maybe Kat will take me to church one day."

It was almost inaudible and under her breath, but Kat heard her mother.

"She'll be taking you to church, all right."

"Ma!"

"I'm leaving. Have a good night."

Librado and Kat didn't go inside the house until they saw Kat's mother and KJ turn the corner to go the few blocks up the street to the housing projects where Kat's mother still lived. Librado stepped back into the house first and Kat came behind him easing the door closed behind her. She turned the bottom lock and put the chain lock in place. Kat caught up to Librado who was heading directly toward the bedroom again and grabbed him around the middle, squeezing her face into his back.

"Mmm-hmm! I could hold you forever."

"I hope not forever. I have to go to work on Monday."

Kat loved how he took everything she said so literally. Sometimes she didn't know if he was joking or if he was serious. She was sure that his grasp of the English language was such that the jokes and seriousness in his delivery of unexpected phrases was about fifty percent mistake and fifty percent premeditated.

"Let's sit on the couch for a minute. I want to talk to you about something."

"Okay, but we should get dressed quickly. I do not want to *meese* any *of theese cho.* My tenant says that this *cho, Platanos and Collard Greens,* has been sold out for months now and I was lucky that he gave me the *teeckets.*"

"We have plenty of time. Come sit down for a minute."

Kat took him by the hand and led him to the living room couch.

"*Theese* sounds serious. Is it something that I did wrong?"

Librado sat down on the couch carefully without plopping. Kat took notice of it for the umpteenth time. She loved how deliberate he was about everything he did. As if he thought all of his actions through; taking a moment before doing anything. It was just the opposite of her ex-husband, Kenny, who couldn't care less where he plunked himself down and lived his life haphazardly without thinking about any repercussions.

Kat sat down next to him careful to keep enough distance between them so that she could see his entire body. She liked to think that she could read body language and this was a serious subject that she was about to introduce. She wanted him to speak his mind, but wanted to be able to read in his body the things that his mouth did not articulate.

"*Dirme querida.*" ("Tell me, my love.")

Kat felt the warmth of his words. After a few months of being with him, she had seen how his English was getting better and she was also starting to be able to understand some of the things that he would only utter in Spanish.

"It's about last night."

Librado reached over and grabbed one of Kat's legs and brought it to his lap. He played with her calf, running his hands up and in between the muscles near the back of her knee. Months of experience had taught Kat that it was not a sexual touch as much as it was a sensual one. Librado never sat next to her or even near her without touching her in some way. Early on the touching made her uncomfortable. Kenneth had never touched her in that way throughout all of their relationship. The sheer intimacy of it felt strange. It was only after she allowed herself to think of him as a real friend, and not just a lover, that she was able to relax totally when he touched her in this way.

Kat started to speak slowly, now unsure of the words that she practiced in her mind all morning.

"It's the light thing. I know how much you want to make love with the lights on. And I'm just sorry that I'm not ready to do that right now."

Kat reached over and grabbed the hand that was touching the back of her knee and held it in both of her hands.

"I know how frustrating it can be when you want to do something sexually with your partner and they don't want to."

Kat rolled her eyes up toward the ceiling.

"Boy, do I know how frustrating it can be."

Librado watched her intently as she struggled to work up to what she really wanted to say.

"The truth is that I've never had this problem before. I mean, I've never been fat before. I used to be comfortable showing my body. Forget comfortable, I used to show my body off."

When Librado just smiled at her, she continued, "You wouldn't know it to look at me now, but I used to be fine as hell."

"*Jou* are a beautiful woman, Kat…"

"Shh, shh. Let me say this."

Kat pulled her leg off of his lap, placed the hand that she was holding in its place and sat back again.

"I'm fat. I know I'm fat and I'm just not comfortable with it. I'm doing everything that I can to get it off, but it's just not that easy. I work out in the gym for two hours a day, eat salads three meals a day, every day, and it's just not coming off."

Kat could feel the unwelcome tears coming to her eyes and couldn't fight them back.

"I want to make you happy. But I can't do it with the light on. I'm just not comfortable yet. I know what you're going to say. That first time in the basement the lights were on, but that didn't count. I hadn't made love to anyone in close to a year and I didn't know what I was doing."

"I thought it was more than a *jear*."

"A year, eighteen months, whatever. The point is I don't want to lose you because of this. I don't want my insecurities to push you away from me. I just wanted to ask you to give me a little more time to get myself together. I know that I can lose this weight with just a little more time and then I won't have any problem leaving the light on. It's just that you look so good!"

Kat reached out to touch his face, but what she was really talking about was his body. In contrast to her large soft body, his was muscular and tight. Sometimes when she was alone in her bed at night, she could imagine the feel of his six-pack abs against her and it alternately turned her on and depressed her. Librado casually took Kat's leg again and put it on his lap. This time he leaned back and took her foot into his hands. He squeezed and massaged the foot forcing a groan from his throat.

"Ooohh…that feels so good."

"So what *jou* are saying is that *jou* want me to eat more and put on some weight?"

Kat gave him a look that said she thought he might be crazy.

"Uh-uh, that is not what I'm saying. Let's not get it twisted. You are fine and will stay fine. Understand?"

Librado smiled and nodded yes. Kat realized that this was one of those times that he was teasing her while feigning that he didn't understand her.

"May I speak my mind on this matter, *querida*?"

Kat gave her permission via her silence. The tears in her eyes still stung her cheeks and she was scared to open her mouth lest she start sobbing and boo-hooing like some stupid schoolgirl who couldn't hold down simple emotions.

"I have told *jou* many times, but maybe *jou* don't hear so good. It is not about how big *jou* are or how much *jou* weigh. It is about what is inside of *jou*. About how *jou* feel about *jou* and how *jou* make the people around *jou* feel about *jou*. The outside of *jou* is just a very small part of why I love *jou*."

Kat wiped the tears from her eyes as if that would make her hearing better. She made a mental note to spend a little time teaching him to say his "Y's" properly. Every time he said "you," it sounded like "Jew" and made her want to giggle.

However, it did not distract her from hearing the words that he actually spoke.

"Did you say you love me?"

Librado put her left foot down and picked up the right foot.

He looked Kat in the face and continued to massage her foot as if he had said nothing of any consequence.

"Why are *jou* asking me this question now? Last night *jou* told me that *jou* love me and I told *jou* that I love *jou.*"

"That was in the heat of passion, baby, that doesn't count."

"It counts for me."

"Then say it again. I loved hearing you say it."

Librado shook his head no. He massaged her even more deeply as if he were boring his essence into her, but he shook his head strongly and surely.

"Come on, say it again," Kat whined.

"If I tell *jou* theese thing over and over whenever or wherever *jou* want, then it will have no real meaning. It must come from my lips, how *jou* say... spontaneously."

It struck Kat as strange that Librado could say the biggest and hardest words perfectly, but pronounced the simplest words badly. It was another one of the things that endeared him to her.

"So you don't love me right now?"

"I did not say that, *jou* did."

"I'm not saying it, I'm asking it."

"Then no, right now I don't love *jou.* "

Kat pulled her foot away from him and before he could react, she jumped onto his lap. She put her arms around his neck and pulled his lips toward hers. Librado allowed her to handle him. Kat brought her lips so close to his that Librado was able to tell the flavor of lip gloss that she wore without their lips having touched. At the very last moment, she grabbed the long hair at the nape of his neck and pulled back hard, exposing his Adam's apple. She placed her lips gently on the protuberance at his neck and then let her lips glide from that area to the tip of his earlobe leaving a fresh trail of lip gloss and saliva in her wake. When she got to his earlobe, she licked gently and then bit just the slightest bit of the cartilage. It was a very sensitive spot for him she had learned while experimenting during their third lovemaking session. She repeated the maneuver two more times and the front part of Librado's pants where she was sitting seemed to take on a life of its own. She felt the hardness that had become familiar to her touch. It bumped against her mons and she immediately hopped off of his lap.

Kat stood over him for a second admiring her handiwork and then just walked off toward the bedroom.

"Where are you going, *querida*?"

"To take a shower," Kat said, talking over her shoulder. "I have to get ready to go to the show. We wouldn't want to be late for *Platanos and Collard Greens*."

Kat purposely sashayed her large backside so that Librado's eyes would be forced to follow its immense girth. She stopped for a second to undo the button to her jeans and allowed her hand to linger at the zipper before slowly pulling it down to its base. Kat air-kissed Librado from where she stood and then headed out of the room. Librado was further hypnotized with every bounce that the globes in the back of her jeans produced. He was shaken out of his trance when she went behind the door of the bedroom that was to the left of the kitchen.

"You don't love me right now, anyway," Kat said, peeking from behind the bedroom door."

Librado got up from the sofa slowly. The tent in his pants hindered him from moving as fast as he wanted to.

"Of course I love *jou*, *querida*. Come here."

Librado got to the bedroom door in time to see Kat go into the bathroom. He saw the jeans that she slipped off laying at the foot of the bed and was appropriately turned on by the prospect of what had been unleashed from their confines. He picked the jeans up and struggled with himself not to smell the crotch before folding them and putting them neatly on the chest at the foot of the bed. When he heard the shower jets hitting the newly tiled shower wall he had fixed the week before, he imagined how the water was cascading down the valley of her ass. The image that came to mind was overwhelming to him and he reached for the doorknob that led into the bathroom. When he found that the door was locked from the inside, he knocked on it gently.

"*Querida*, open the door," Librado whispered to Kat through the wooden door.

"Only if you say you love me right now," Kat teased him from the shower.

"*Jes, querida*, I love *jou* very much right now." He patted his own crotch, feeling a little relief when his engorged penis flexed and twitched under his hand.

He heard the click of the lock on the other side of the door and was not surprised when he opened the door and found that the lights in the bathroom were out. Kat was already back inside the shower and could see the silhouette of him reaching for the light switch against the back lighting coming from the bedroom.

"Don't turn on the light, just leave the door ajar a little." Kat thought that was a compromise that she could live with.

She watched Librado undress in front of the sparse light that entered through the doorway and felt her nipples harden when she saw the silhouette of his penis. Kat stepped backward and into the heat of shower jets to give Librado room to pass through the shower door. She was glad that she had taken the time to put on a shower cap when the force of the spray hit the errant hairs in the back of her neck. It reminded her that she could not afford to get too crazy in this shower or else her hair would look busted, when she finally did make it to the show. Librado's size filled the rest of the small shower stall. Kat tried very hard not to be aware of how much space she was taking up in the shower. The little light that entered the stall allowed the couple to make out arms, legs, and faces, but did little to help Librado remember the beautiful figure that he had only completely observed and enjoyed during the day of their first meeting. Since then it had been "lights out," whenever they made love.

Kat reached out and pulled Librado to her, afraid that there was enough light leaking into the bathroom for him to see the cellulite and stretch marks that she was so ashamed of. She knew he was lying when he told her how beautiful he thought her body was. She couldn't fathom how anyone could find her body to be beautiful, much less a gorgeous man like Librado. Kat couldn't help but feel self-conscious when he grabbed her ass in both his hands and bent to kiss the soft part of her neck between the line of her jaw and the carotid artery on her left side.

Can he feel the lumps in my ass? He is not going to want me if he feels these fucking lumps in my ass. The irrational thought that he had never felt the cellulite in her buttocks escaped her. Suddenly she was too embarrassed to have him touch her like that. Her vanity screamed for her to get out of the shower. The problem was that Librado was blocking her only exit and this little shower stall made it impossible for her to get past him. The struggle to get out would only show how big she had let herself get. She could just tell Librado to get out of the shower, but the hard penis that was pressing into her belly fat reminded her that it was she who had instigated this mishappened scenario.

There was only one thing that she could think of to get away from the probing hands of this man that she wanted so desperately to keep loving her. Kat pressed her hands against Librado's chest causing their bodies to part. She hated the feeling of Librado's lips leaving her neck, but couldn't bear his hands on her ass another second. She kissed the cleft in Librado's chest that separated his heavily striated pectoralis and then slowly allowed herself to trail kisses down his abdomen to his pubic area. Librado knew where she was headed and wanted to tell her to stop. He wanted to tell her to just make love to him, but his Puerto Rican machismo did not allow him to. He could hear his friends now, if he only dared to share how he truly enjoyed sharing his body with a woman. Not fucking and rutting like an animal, but truly sharing his spirit and love with a woman.

He suspected that was the reason his previous girlfriend left him. All she wanted to do was have sex. She didn't love him and he knew it, but that didn't keep her from just wanting to keep having sex. After some time his penis wouldn't get hard for her anymore. There had to be more than the physical to stimulate him. He needed the love, the passion, and the intellect. He felt he could have all of those things with Kat, if she just opened herself up to him.

Instead of lifting her off of her knees like he should have, he allowed himself to lean against the back wall of the shower stall. The shower sprayed against his chest and abdomen, and he sighed when he felt Kat's mouth totally engulf his manhood. Kat choked on the length of him and pulled her head back, drawing her lips to the edge of his dick head. She paused for a moment allowing herself to catch a breath and then jammed her face back down into Librado's crotch, causing his penis to lodge deeply in her throat. Kat continued this procedure, repeatedly impaling her gullet with Librado's penis until she felt her gag reflex produce tears in her eyes. The gagging tears mixed with tears of shame and were lost in the water that struck her head, flowed over her face and down the drain. She'd turned a loving and fulfilling sexual gesture that she always enjoyed, into a hurting and torturous punishment for herself. Swallowing Librado's seed, which was usually a prize to her, was a bitter and joyless act. Later the two barely looked at each other as they got dressed.

They made it to the theater to see the play *Platanos and Collard Greens.*

The play was intriguing in the way it showed the diversity of the Black American versus that of the Hispanic American. How the two could live together in harmony was obvious and not complex. How the fat and the skinny live together or side by side, that was the play that Kat wanted to see. Nobody was taking that to theater because nobody could feel her pain. Librado held her hand throughout the entire production, but his empathy was lost on her. She was lost inside of herself.

CHAPTER FOURTEEN
EXPOSED

After making what she thought was her one phone call to Kat and getting an answering machine, Dahlia unnecessarily begged the detective in front of her for another phone call.

"Please let me make just one more phone call. My friend wasn't home. I didn't want to call my family because my family would worry too much. My mother is going to have a heart attack when she finds out why I'm here. Please let me make just one more phone call," Dahlia pleaded.

The detective was tall and light-skinned, with dreads and bright greenish-gray eyes. He appeared to be in his late thirties and was in great shape, according to the muscles that rippled under his Armani suit. If Dahlia hadn't been so panicked, she would have found him very attractive. His name was Chemah Rivers and he was the lieutenant in charge of detectives in the precinct. Dahlia didn't know it and Detective Rivers could not tell her right away, but she was already in the clear. The forensic evidence had already corroborated the story that she had told the first detective. If they wanted to push it, they might've been able to charge her with reckless endangerment that caused death, but that would be up to the DA.

Chemah didn't see it happening. The DA's office already had enough on its plate. The victim had been a powerful business tycoon that had close ties to the governor's office. By the way that the DA had responded to his name,

Chemah guessed that a lot of phones would be ringing before anyone actually made a decision. No press is always good press during an election year.

"Ms. Ortega, as of right now, you can have as many phone calls as you need. My suggestion to you would be to call your lawyer."

"I don't have a lawyer. I'm trying to call one of my friends; they'll get me a lawyer."

Before she finished the sentence, she was already dialing Noreen's number. The phone rang three times before someone picked it up. It was a male voice that Dahlia didn't recognize, but she thought that maybe she was wrong.

"Dennis?"

"Sorry, I think you have the wrong number."

"Is this Noreen's house?"

"Hold on one second. Noreen, someone is on the phone."

Dahlia waited on the phone for approximately thirty seconds. The dread detective was watching her carefully. The way his eyes pierced hers made her nervous, but she didn't want to turn away and give the appearance that she was guilty of anything else. A sleepy Noreen came to the phone.

"Hello, who is this?"

"Noreen, it's me, Dahlia."

After a long pause, she responded, "Dee, it's two o'clock in the morning. Call me after nine."

"No, don't hang up, don't hang up, I'm in jail."

Another long pause.

"You're in jail! What did you do?"

"I can't explain it now, but I need a lawyer."

"Where the hell am I going to get a lawyer at this hour?"

"I don't know, I don't know, but please…"

"All right, all right. Don't break down. I'm gonna call Kat and see if she knows of anyone."

"I already called Kat. Her answering machine is on."

"You called Kat first?"

Dahlia heard the hurt in Noreen's voice and was immediately sorry.

"With everything going on for you right now, you know. I just didn't want to bother you."

"Okay, okay, no big deal. I get it. Don't worry about it. I'm gonna roll by her house real quick. She probably just turned the volume down on the machine. If we're lucky, she was just getting her freak on and forgot to turn the machine on again."

"Okay, but if you don't find her, then you come alone, okay?

"Don't worry, I'll be there. I'm not going to let you rot in jail."

There was another long pause on the phone and it worried Dahlia.

"No, you still there?"

"I'm still here. Dee, is it real bad? Like a body bad?"

Dahlia looked up into Detective Rivers' staring eyes again.

"Uh-huh."

"Damn! Dahlia, make sure you don't say anything until we get there with a lawyer, okay.

"Uh-huh."

There was a long pause again.

"You already talked to them, didn't you. You already gave yourself up."

"Uh-huh."

"Damn, damn, damn. Don't say another word. Don't say another fucking word. They're listening to you, aren't they?"

"Uh-huh."

"Right. I'll be there as fast as I can, just don't say anything else. What precinct are you in?"

"The first precinct, I think."

Dahlia looked up at Chemah.

"This is the first precinct, right?

Chemah nodded affirmatively.

"The first precinct, No. I'm in the first precinct."

"All right. Just hold on tight and I'll be there as fast as I can."

"Noreen?"

"What?"

"Don't tell your brother, all right."

"What?"

"Don't tell your brother!"

"Why not?"

"I just don't want him to know."

After a long silence.

"No, are you still there?"

"Yeah, I'm still here. I don't have time for this drama now, but you'd better come clean later. There's too much stuff you're not telling me."

"Okay, but later. Just please get me out of here."

"I'm coming."

Noreen hung up the phone, but Dahlia was afraid to put it down. She knew what was next.

"Detective Spencer. Miss Ortega is finished with her phone call. Put her in the holding pen. Let me know when her lawyer shows up."

Lieutenant Detective Rivers walked away leaving Dahlia to the older detective with the wrinkled suit jacket. She was unceremoniously put in holding cell three. It smelled of stale urine and mildew.

There were three other women in the holding cell with her. They were all sleeping on the one bench in the cell and not one of them seemed to be disturbed from their slumber when the door opened or closed with a dreadful, CLANK!

There was no room on the bench for Dahlia. She went to the farthest corner from the gate and found a spot that was no cleaner than any other part of the other cell and sat down. In talking to Noreen she realized that she made a huge mistake. They had tricked her into telling them everything without having a lawyer present. She'd told them everything and now wondered how much of her story they would use against her. She went over the story in her mind and it went a little something like this…

✠✠✠

Dahlia got out of the private elevator that went up to the penthouse of the Calloway Citadel towers which were situated on the corner of Florence and Hudson in the West Village. She wasn't stunned to see that the elevator let her off in the middle of an immense living room. What was a little scary, though, was the second elevator on the opposite side of the huge loft. It held two cars that faced the street through a large picture window. The Bentley coupe was red—she made a mental note that she had never seen that color before—and the white Volkswagen Beetle convertible looked as if a slip of the brakes and one good shove could send them both to the streets below.

Richard Ellington Sweeney III came from behind the bar where he was mixing drinks and walked toward Dahlia. He was a plain-looking black man with glasses. At approximately five feet ten with a full head of dyed black hair that was cut into a low fade, Richard was not unusual in his looks. He looked clean and well groomed. From his voice and his speech on the telephone, Dahlia had fully expected to be meeting a middle-aged or elderly white male. Now that she saw him in person, she recognized new money in him. It was the plight of the second generation of wealthy blacks that they didn't know what to do with themselves or their money anymore. They'd tried everything and everyone and were always looking for that one new thing that would put some spark back into their lives.

Dahlia didn't mind being that spark. She'd never had a black client before. Up until today they were all middle-aged or older white men. On the phone, he'd told her it was his first time. And now it was a first for her, too. Richard neglected to turn the blender that he was making the drinks with and was now annoyed that he had to try and talk over the noise that it made.

"Mistress Flowers, I presume. I…wait one minute, I'm sorry."

Richard Ellington Sweeney III walked back behind the bar and turned off the blender. He started walking back toward Dahlia and was talking a mile a minute. Dahlia thought it was nerves and decided that it was best to let him talk for a moment before they got started.

"I was just making Margaritas. They're the only things that calm me when I'm nervous. Not that I'm very nervous right now because you're here, it's just that I can't wait to get started because everyone says you're the best around now. I've always had the best and I'm just sick thinking of all the fun we're going to have and all the games we're going to play…"

He was going on and on for a full two minutes and Dahlia just took it all in. It took her that long before she realized that part of the game Richard wanted to play had already begun. He wanted to be told to shut up, that was why he was talking so much, so fast. Dahlia took the two steps that she required to get close enough to him. She then slapped away the glass that he put to his lips to sip from, out of his hands and watched it shatter against the brown oak floors. Richard gasped and held his chest secretly hoping that she would take this opportunity to strike him, too. The disappointment showed on his face when she didn't.

"Do you have your room ready?"

Dahlia stepped entirely into her role of dominatrix.

"Yes, Mistress."

Dahlia struck him in the face with her open hand, knowing full well that it was what he expected.

"You didn't use my complete title, did you, Richard?"

"No, Mistress Flowers."

"That is much better, Richard. Now show me to your room."

"Yes, Mistress Flowers."

Richard walked ahead of her to the back of the loft where there was a small room that may have once been a large walk-in closet. Now the room was a dungeon, complete with stockade, wall shackles, and a dangling rope which was strong enough to suspend a grown man twice the size of Mr. Richard Ellington Sweeney III. All of the walls were painted black and the floors were of a wood that was unpolished and untreated—better to cause discomfort for kneeling slaves. Dahlia put the shoulder bag she was carrying on the floor and gave a quick look around. Richard stood by the door waiting for her approval.

"Take your clothes off and go into the other room, but clean up the mess that you made. I'll use this room to get ready, and I'll call you when it's time for you to take your medicine. Do you understand?"

"Yes, Mistress Flowers."

Richard began to take his clothes off and Dahlia watched him. With every piece of clothing that he took off, Dahlia made a noise that told him he was being scrutinized, and not favorably. Richard had on no other clothing but his underwear when he tried to leave the room to perform the task of cleaning that Mistress Flowers had ordered.

"Haruummph!"

Richard turned back to face Dahlia.

"Yes, Mistress Flowers?"

Dahlia beckoned to him with the crook of his finger and he came to her slowly on visibly shaking legs. His fear was palpable now and Dahlia drank it in like an elixir that she needed to survive.

"These belong to me."

Dahlia put her four fingers inside the elastic of his underwear and made her hand into a fist. With one hard yank she showed the strength that her weight only hinted at. The Calvin Klein underwear was torn from his torso, now just a rag in Dahlia's hand. Richard stood there naked not knowing what to do next. Dahlia walked around him slowly. She turned him this way, then that way, examining first his genitals and then his buttock. Neither was disproportionate to the rest of him. Everything about him was about average, Dahlia thought. She was a little disappointed. There was something about fucking a man with a huge penis that turned her on. From her conversation with Richard on the phone, she knew that was part of his deal. He wanted to be treated badly and then tortured in the end. Dahlia smacked him on the ass really hard and he went up onto the balls of his feet.

"Get going. I'll call you when I'm ready."

Richard moved toward the door quickly, but Dahlia noticed the smile at the corner of his mouth just as he left the room. That was a good sign. He was scared, but he was still excited by the whole thing. Dahlia went to the door and closed it herself. She reached for her bag and pulled out the patent leather skirt, patent leather boots, and patent leather bodice that were the core of her costume. She took her time getting dressed, being careful not to break any of the delicate belts and clips that held the whole outfit together. The last part of the outfit for this particular customer would be the harness with the huge latex cock attached to it. She always carried two different dildos with her: the white flesh-colored one and the obsidian-looking one. They were both the same nine-inch size, but she had never had the inclination to use the white one until today. She imagined the contrast of the flesh-tone spike poking out of Richard's ass and knew that she was going to enjoy her part-time job today as much as any other day. She called Richard back into the room and when he saw her with the white phallus protruding from her pelvis, she knew she was right about him.

Richard's eyes bulged and his own penis became instantly rigid when he caught sight of the one Dahlia was sporting. Dahlia cleared her throat and held a pen up to get his attention away from her pelvis.

"Harrumph! Just one minor detail to be taken care of now, Richard."

Dahlia sauntered over to the too-small school desk and chair that were an obvious contrast to the rest of the décor. The desk and chair would have been more appropriate in a kindergarten classroom; Dahlia supposed that this was where Richard had first been disciplined and that he wanted to relive the experience. The paper that waited on the desk was a discipline contract. It was a standard document agreement between Mistress and Slave that simply stated that Dahlia would not be responsible for any physical or mental harm that Richard might sustain in the course of their time together. All acts that were to be performed were agreed upon previous to the contract. There was even a blank space on the contract where an agreed upon safety word was to be added by the submissive. It was to be initialed by both parties involved as acknowledgment that when that word was used by the submissive all previously agreed upon acts were to cease and desist.

The contract made no mention of money. Any mention of monetary gain in the description of a relationship between either party would make both of them volunteers in criminal behavior and would render the contract null and void. In their first phone conversation, Dahlia gave Richard the number to an account where he was to wire a prescribed amount of money. She would call him back when she saw that the money was in the account and give him the details of how the rest of their relationship would go. No further details would be necessary until the money was in place.

An hour after the first phone call, Dahlia's computer account notified her that a new deposit had been made to the account and she called Richard back. Dahlia thought it would be healthy to start their relationship by making Richard sit in the small chair while signing the contract.

"Sit right here, Richard, or shall I call you 'Dick.'"

"Just Richard, please."

"Dick it is then!"

Richard walked over to the desk and sat down as he was told. His knees didn't fit under the desk and he was forced to keep them pressed against the edge of the desk, causing indentations directly under his kneecaps. Standing over him Dahlia could see Richard's penis and testicles peeking out of the thick mass of hair between his legs, like a prematurely hatched chick awaiting two other eggs to hatch in a bird's nest. The sight looked absurd to her and she pressed her lips together to suppress a smile.

"Take your time and read everything carefully. It protects you and me in case of any misunderstandings. Also, as we discussed on the phone, you should have selected a safety word by now."

"Right. The word I picked is…"

"Just write it down in the space indicated. I'll initial that I understand it and we can get on with our session, Dick."

Richard filled in the blank as he was directed. He initialed next to the word and then signed the bottom of the contract and handed it up to Dahlia.

"Pen."

Richard handed the pen to Dahlia, who did not bother looking at him as he placed the pen in her open palm. Richard took notice of the meaty hands with the chubby fingers that held the pen and swooned with excitement. As a child he and his younger brother's nanny had been a big, beautiful black woman. So when his friend told him about the club's new dominatrix who everyone was talking about, he just had to experience her for himself.

Dahlia leaned all the way down and placed the contract back on the desk. She gave Richard a perfect view of the breasts that were swelling over the top of the patent leather bodice. She quickly jotted her initials on the paper next to the word *surrender* and then picked the paper up and folded it into four quarters. She then walked, or more precisely, glided (which is how Richard imagined her), over to where she had left her bag in the corner to put the contract away. Richard watched mesmerized by how the smooth and chocolaty flesh of her belly peeked out from under the bodice and jiggled as she walked. Her thick thighs had small amounts of cellulite on them, and he wished the tall boots that she had on did not come all the way up to her knees. He remembered that his nanny had some of the biggest sexiest calves that he ever remembered on a woman.

He watched a rivulet of sweat creep out from under the bottom of her skirt, make its way down the back of her knee and into the crevice of the lump of flesh that was pushed to the top of the boot. He felt a sweat break out over the top of his lip at the thought of her making him lick it out.

Dahlia ran him through what she thought of as the regular paces of a submissive. She sat on him for a while. Alternately sitting on his chest for thirty or forty seconds to keep his diaphragm from taking in another breath of air. Then she gave him a respite to catch his breath by sitting on his face, allowing the thick lips of her vulva to surround his lips while he desperately tried to suck in oxygen through the other crevices of her bare crotch underneath her skirt. Dahlia was going to spank him for a while. They'd talked about that on the phone. She was to use a brush to do it. Dahlia didn't know it, but that was how his nanny had meted out punishment. Dahlia sat on the wooden bench against the wall and called Richard over from where he lay gasping on the floor. He didn't come immediately as the lack of oxygen caused a ringing in his ear that took a moment to recuperate from.

"Dick!"

"Huh?

Richard turned from his back onto his side; his eyes searched and his rock-hard penis pointed in the direction where Dahlia was sitting. When he saw the stern look on her face and the brush in her hand, he got to his hands and knees and obediently crawled over to her. When he reached her, Richard raised himself up onto his knees and bowed his head not daring to look her directly in the face. If she had forced him to bark for her, he would've looked like a naughty puppy looking for praise.

Her knees were slightly parted and from Richard's vantage point, he could still see the residual mixture of saliva and vaginal secretions that he had left dangling dangerously from the inner lips of her vulva, threatening to fall to the wooden floor where he knew he would have to retrieve them with his mouth. Dahlia patted the thick meat of her sweaty thighs with two hands indicating where Richard should position himself.

"Right here, my little Dick."

To Dahlia's chagrin Richard raised himself up to his full height and stood by the side of her right leg without the help of his hands to steady himself, as Dahlia thought he would. She had warned him to keep his hands at his sides at all times and not to use his hands in any way. This was usually the cause of much of the disciplinary attention she gave her clients, as the average man found it hard to maneuver anything without the use of his hands.

Dahlia placed the handled brush down by her side on the bench and reached up to cup Richard's buttocks. She gave them a quick squeeze and then a sharp slap with the flat of her open palm. The force that she used made her feel the sting in her own hand, but Richard didn't even flinch. It was obvious that Richard had been with other dominatrix before her and would need more than just a firm hand from her.

Not a problem.

"Bend over onto my lap. That's the second time I've had to say it. If I have to say it again, it will only cause you more pain."

Richard's penis was almost at eye level with Dahlia. She noticed that it twitched at the mention of punishment and a clear drop of pre-seminal fluid appeared at the thin slit on the top of its crown. He started to bend down slowly clearly wanting to cause himself greater punishment by his tentative actions. When his head came down low enough, Dahlia grabbed what she could of the short curly hair on his head between her thumb and forefinger and twisted it hard, pulling downward the way her evil maternal grandmother would often do to her when she was little and visiting Puerto Rico.

Richard grimaced but didn't make a sound. He fell into her lap with a quick tug on his hair from Dahlia, and she caught him easily and pulled his side in to the softness of her overflowing belly. Dahlia felt for where the hardness of Richard's penis was pressing against her thighs, estimating how much she would have to open her thighs in a maneuver to trap his penis between them. In an instant, Dahlia spread her thighs approximately seven inches. The sweat trapped between them made a soft kissing sound as they parted. When she felt the head of Richard's penis touching the inner part of her left thigh, she adjusted her right leg slightly so that it raised Richard just enough to cause his penis to point downward. When she felt his penis start to slide down her left leg, she snapped both legs closed quickly causing Richard's penis to be trapped between the hot wet meat of Dahlia's thighs.

Richard tried not to make a sound, but the feeling that his penis was about to be snapped off at the root, replaced by the feeling of having his penis rammed between two hot and moist slabs of woman meat, proved to be too much for him.

"Aaaarrgh…!"

He quickly clamped his hand over his mouth, but it was too late. Dahlia already heard the gratification in his voice.

"Sshhhh…quiet, my pet. Quiet, quiet…"

She stroked his meaty-ass cheeks the way a parent may stroke the top of a child's head who was suffering after scraping his or her knee.

"Does it hurt, Dickie?"

"No, Mistress Flowers."

"Then you like the way it feels?"

"Yes, Mistress Flowers."

Dahlia adjusted her legs slightly and then started to slowly move her legs back and forth causing her thighs to gently rub together. She could feel the hard penis trapped between her legs rubbing against her begin to slip back and forth with the help of her sweat and the lubrication that came from his penis. She began to enjoy the massage that it afforded both of them. She did that for a moment before she started to hear Richard purr like a kitten. It was a mistake. She had momentarily gotten caught up in her own pleasure and had forgotten about the client. He was paying her for two hours of her time and so far only forty-five minutes had passed. It would not be useful to either of them if he came this quickly. Being the consummate professional meant that he was to climax very close to the end of the time that his money paid for. That was what her clients paid for. The discipline that it took for Dahlia to make that happen sometimes wore her out, but she also enjoyed it.

Richard's eye caught the movement of Dahlia's hand reaching for the wooden handle brush that he'd mentioned to her on the phone, and he immediately tensed up. Dahlia felt his penis move about an inch out from the sheath that her thighs had become when his buttocks clamped one against the other. Richard's breathing became labored as Dahlia held the brush only inches away from his face, showing him that she had purchased just the brush that he had described—a long-handled, dark-mahogany bristle brush.

In searching for the right brush, Dahlia learned that each one was made with hair from either boar, badger or a badger blend. The softest and most expensive brush was the badger-haired one, and Dahlia purchased it knowing that it was a good investment in professional equipment. When the first strike hit Richard's buttocks, tears came immediately to his eyes. Crying was one of the reasons that he enjoyed this typed of situation. When he was growing up in his parents' house, his father, a big construction worker of a man who made a wealth of money starting his own contracting firm, told he and his brothers that only women cried. Shedding any tears in front of the old man would get you ignored or sent to your room for the day with no food.

In contrast, his nanny, Ms. Onetta, would pay special attention to him if he cried. Although she was not one to spare the rod if he was doing anything that she thought a young boy should not be doing, she would always wipe his tears away afterward and rock him gently to sleep. When the second hit struck Richard, he yelped gleefully, glad to be able to shout and express his pain. The third strike came quickly thereafter and much more viciously. Richard trembled with the force of it and continued to shake even after Dahlia raised her hand to prepare to strike him again. Dahlia held her hand in midair gauging if a fourth strike should come so soon. She could feel

Richard was almost out of control by the way he was shaking and convulsing on her lap. She pulled him tightly into her stomach again using her left hand.

The white phallus that she had strapped on to her waist must have been sticking in Richard in the side the whole time because now as she adjusted and tried to pull him closer, she heard him groan from the pressure that it was exerting on his rib cage. It was another reason why she did not let the right hand descend to issue the fourth strike. Richard was squirming in her lap. Ten seconds now and still no fourth strike. He was so close to coming now, he knew that the next hit would cause him to spill his seed on her leg if not straight onto the floor.

Richard turned his head so that he could witness the final strike that would send him over the edge, and instead was faced with his new Mistress. She was smiling down at him. Not an evil smile, but a twisted one nonetheless. She was enjoying this as much as he was, and in the moment that he saw the twinkle in her eyes, he was sure that she would pay equally for the pleasure of performing this act on him as he had paid her if she had the financial ability.

"Not yet, Dickie. You don't want to come too fast, do you?"

But he did want to come fast. He wanted to come the first time she smacked the Margarita glass out of his hand. He was so close now that he started to pump his penis into the wet crease that her thighs had trapped his penis in. Dahlia could see the terrible need in his eyes but she would not give in to his pleading eyes. She kept the brush held high in an unmistakably threatening manner, but she wouldn't give him the satisfaction of letting it fall on his ass.

Richard continued to pump into her legs harder and faster, but as much as he tried, he could not bring himself to orgasm. He needed that last hit. He needed the brush on his ass. He needed his patent leather nanny to make him come. Dahlia allowed him to expend his energy sliding his cock back and forth, in and out of her pre-cum soaked thighs. When he stopped and just lay on her lap sobbing, she bent and kissed the dimple that his arced spine made at the small of his back. She watched as the goose bumps ran up from where she had kissed him all the way up to the back of his neck and then she stood up, letting Richard fall at her feet unceremoniously. Without even bothering to look at him Dahlia stepped over his body and walked over to the stockade twenty feet away.

Richard got on his hands and knees and followed Dahlia, without her telling him, the few paces to where she stood. The tears that were still in his eyes blurred his vision, and when he bumped the back of her patent leather boot, he stopped and looked up at her searching for but finding no mercy in her eyes. Richard felt a little winded; more than he thought he would after that short but wonderful performance with his new Mistress. He was eager to please her now. He wanted to show her that he could be a good boy.

The first time Dahlia saw a stockade was when she was in the eighth grade on a trip to Colonial Williamsburg. The tour guide said that people that committed crimes against the community when the pilgrims first landed in America were placed in the stockade in the center of town and were left there for days without food. Anyone who wanted to was allowed to strike the person in the stockade or throw rotted vegetables at them. At that young age she thought it was a vulgar punishment.

Dahlia undid the latch that kept the top part of the stockade from opening. After opening the hinge, she pulled the half of the stockade that would go on top of Richard's wrists and neck and beckoned for him to stand up.

"Get up, Dick. Now you're really starting to annoy me," she said when he didn't get up fast enough.

Richard got up slowly and started to wipe the tears from his eyes. His hand felt a little numb. He must have been leaning on it a little too much during the spanking.

"Thary Mithtres." He slurred his words and thought that maybe the Margaritas were now starting to take their full effect.

When Dahlia put the gag ball in his mouth and tied the straps it connected to behind his head, he didn't even try to object. He accepted his fate with quiet serenity. Dahlia guided him to put his neck and two wrists in the proper slots and then placed the top half of the stockade over his outstretched neck and hands. She got behind him and was disappointed that she could not see his face. Later before leaving, she would suggest to him that he have a mirror placed in front of the stockade so that both he and she could enjoy watching him while he was getting fucked.

Dahlia used the lube that she brought with her sparingly. She wanted him to feel her as she entered him. It was one quick thrust of her hips and she saw the brown eye that was once his asshole dilate and swallow the entire length of the flesh-colored phallus she wore connected to the harness. She reached around him and grabbed his hard penis with the hand that she lubricated the dildo with and allowed her hand to glide up and down its length in time with her thrusts.

This is how you like it, Martin. Huh? This is how you like it.

Dahlia always fantasized about abusing her ex-husband the way he had abused her and saw no reason why she couldn't indulge her little fantasy at the expense of the clients that liked to be sodomized.

Don't scream now, Martin. You know you love it. You know you love it.

Richard only struggled briefly. After a dozen or so strokes, she felt him relax and after a dozen or so more she was sure that he was going to come. His ass cheeks went rigid and his spine arched so much that she thought that his back would break. The cracking sound of his clenching toes startled her and then she felt the warm syrupy fluid that was his sperm coating her fingers as she continued to pump him in her fist.

A second later Richard's body went totally limp.

Shit, he's going to break his fucking neck.

Dahlia tried to hold his body up by the waist. She was still in his ass and was afraid that if she came from behind him she would lose her purchase on him and his neck would snap in the stockade.

She was strong, but she couldn't hold him much longer. Dahlia slapped

Richard's ass as hard as she could in an effort to wake him. She repeated the motion ten more times before finally giving up. She couldn't hold him anymore and was forced to pull the dildo out of him and try to hold him up. Just as she thought she would, she lost her grip on him and his body sagged behind the stockade. She hopped to where the latch held the hinge of the stockade together and slid the mechanism open. Dahlia pulled the top of the stockade open and tried to reach Richard before he hit the ground. She just wasn't fast enough. The THUD sound that Richard's head made when it hit the hardwood floor was deafening.

Dahlia scrambled to get down to where he lay, but her size and her costume made it difficult. She finally had to lay next to him, just to try and find a pulse. Her first thought when she realized that Richard was dead was to get dressed and run out the door. Her conscience and watching too many episodes of *CSI: Miami* had gotten the best of her. She knew that both her conscience and the police would entually catch up to her if she went with her first instinct.

First she called the police and then she started to get dressed. EMS arrived before the police. It took them twenty minutes or so.

When the police saw the bruises on Richard and the room where he was lying, the handcuffs went on Dahlia immediately. She thanked God that she'd had the sense to change back into her street clothes. In any case her secret was out. Now everyone would know.

✢✢✢

Noreen reached Kat's house and it was just as she suspected. Kat's phone was off and she was in bed with her new man. Noreen gave Kat a quick and brief account of what Dahlia had told her and Kat knew there was only one person she could go to acquire a lawyer at this time. Kat went into the bedroom to get dressed and to tell Librado that she had to step out.

Noreen still hadn't met him and even now, Kat told him to stay in the bedroom and wait for her while she ran an emergency errand with her friend. Librado argued with her for a moment, but realized there would be no winning and went back to bed. They would discuss it at a better time than three in the morning. Noreen heard the quick argument and had some words that she wanted to add to the discussion, but as the man had said, this was not the time for a major discussion.

Before they reached the car, Kat already had her good friend Margarita Smith on the phone. Margarita was relatively well off. Kat didn't know exactly how much money Margarita had, but she knew it was in the millions. Most importantly Margarita had connections to important people. She always had a lawyer on retainer for her own emergencies. Now Kat, who had been estranged from her for a short time, needed to ask her for a favor on behalf of someone else.

To Kat's surprise Margarita didn't ask a lot of questions. She put her on hold for two minutes. When she got back on the phone, she gave Kat an address to go where she was to pick her lawyer up. The address was in a well-to-do neighborhood near Gracie Mansion next door to where the mayor lived. The lawyer would meet her downstairs in front of his building in fifteen minutes. His name was Andrew Taylor.

"If there is anything else that you need, Kat, just give me a call."

"Thanks a lot, Margarita. I don't know if I'm going to be able to pay you back anytime soon…"

"Please, I still owe you. If you don't remember how many times you came to my rescue, I'm not going to remind you."

"Thanks all the same, Margarita. I'll call you tomorrow and tell you how it worked out. It's been too long since we talked. We have some catching up to do."

"All right, call me tomorrow. Try calling me before the sun goes down this time," Margarita joked.

Kat hung up the phone and told Noreen where to drive. The lawyer was indeed waiting in front of the building when they arrived. Kat recognized him as the lawyer who had handled Margarita's murder trial seven years ago. He was good. He had gotten Margarita off. Kat wondered if he would remember her. She was in the back of the courtroom for the entire trial. The lawyer got in the car and nodded to both women.

He doesn't remember me, but why would he. I wasn't the one on trial.

Noreen didn't know much, but she told him what Dahlia had told her. He grunted a few times annoyed that he would be unprepared for the case he was being forced to undertake.

Noreen and Kat walked up the steps of the police station with a lawyer that looked none too happy to be out of his bed at three in the morning. He wore his Burberry overcoat as comfortably as a doctor wore green scrubs. The wingtip shoes showed no creases, which meant either they were new shoes or that he had a bunch of them. He walked lightly with no hesitation in his step. His suit was immaculate for someone who must have gotten out of bed at a moment's notice. Both women were familiar with men's couture and without knowing each other's mind, they considered the suit's fabric in an attempt to identify its maker. Neither guessed that the suit was tailor made; a gift from Margarita on her last trip to Taiwan.

Noreen held the door open and Kat and the lawyer stepped through the door and went straight to the sargeant's desk. Noreen walked in behind them. She felt totally out of her element surrounded by all of the blue uniforms without the power of the nurse's uniform that they usually respected when they came into her territory. She just hung back. Kat seemed to have things under control for now.

"Warren Schwartz, Esquire. I'm Migdalia Ortega's lawyer."

Mr. Schwartz handed the sargeant his card.

"I'd like to see her right now, Sargeant."

You could see the instant recognition in the sargeant's eyes. He knew who Mr. Schwartz was. Warren Schwartz eyed the sargeant back with cool detachment. He was used to being recognized.

"I'll tell the lieutenant you're here."

The sargeant pressed three buttons on the phone and picked up the receiver.

"Sir? Yes, Migdalia Ortega's lawyer is here. A Mr. Warren Schwartz. Yes sir, I'll let him know."

The sargeant hung up the phone and smiled at the lawyer.

"The lieutenant will be right out, Mr. Schwartz."

It wasn't the fake kowtowing kind of smile that Warren Schwartz was used to when someone was trying to stay on his good side. His instincts told him something was wrong. Lieutenants didn't come out to greet lawyers.

Lieutenant Chemah Rivers came from his office on the second floor down the old wooden stairs of the century-old precinct. He walked down carefully, having fallen on a thoroughly worn step the previous week. The three people waiting for him at the bottom of the steps near the sargeant's desk all looked up at the same time. Each had a different reaction when they saw him.

"Fuck!" The lawyer didn't seem like the type that needed to use profanity, but there it was.

"Shit. It's Chemah," Kat said it in a whisper, but it caught Warren Schwartz's ear.

Damn! He is fine. Noreen didn't say it out loud, but her jaw was slack and she didn't see any reason to stop staring.

Lieutenant Rivers acknowledged Kat first. After all she was family.

"Kat? Is that you? I almost didn't recognize you."

Kat was Lieutenant Chemah Rivers' daughter's godmother. Chemah didn't like Kat just by her association with Margarita, his ex-wife. Kat didn't hold it against him. She knew he was a decent person. Before he and Margarita split, he and she had gotten along well enough. If Margarita wasn't part of the equation, she believed they would have been good friends. But Margarita was her friend first and foremost, no matter whatever her and Chemah's personal problems were.

It had been two, maybe three years, since they had seen each other.

Within the last few years, Kat only had seen her goddaughter, Hèro, when the little girl was visiting her mother.

"How are you, Chemah? It's been a long time."

"You're with Mr. Schwartz?" There was a tinge of disgust in his voice.

Kat was tempted to say no and to tell Warren Schwartz to leave. It was possible that today Dahlia had the shittiest luck in the world. Warren was the lawyer who got Margarita off when they charged her with attempted murder. Chemah was the man Margarita had attempted to murder. It was too late to go back now. She could only hope that Chemah was the same fair-minded person he had always been.

"He's here to represent my friend Migdalia Ortega."

"Ms. Ortega is a friend of yours?"

"Yes, she is."

Kat hoped that Chemah would not hold it against Dahlia in some way.

Chemah ignored the lawyer and looked over to Noreen. She had finally closed her mouth. Now she stepped forward.

"Hello. I'm Noreen Klein, also a friend of Ms. Ortega."

She offered her hand and Chemah took it and shook it formally.

Noreen didn't have a clue as to what was going on. Kat never had told her about Margarita.

Warren Schwartz grew tired of being ignored.

"I'd like to see my client now, Detective Rivers."

"Your client is on her way down right now. And it's Lieutenant Rivers. Counselor."

"On her way down to where? She hasn't waived her right to an attorney!"

Warren Schwartz lived for these moments. He fought tooth and nail, back to the wall for all of his clients, whether they were guilty or not. He didn't dislike Chemah, Chemah disliked him. There was nothing personal in it to him. It was only business.

"I demand to know the charges she's facing."

Lieutenant Rivers, who had already dismissed the irate lawyer to turn back to Kat, turned to face Schwartz again.

"Ms. Ortega is free to go, Mr. Schwartz. She has told us everything that we need to know. She signed a written statement of the entire account of the incident in which she was being held for. It turns out that not all of your clients are murderers. Some are just victims of circumstances. The DA already read my report and the coroner's report. All of the findings concur. She is free to go."

"But what was she charged with?"

Schwartz sounded like he was whining and it brought an ugly sneer to the lieutenant's face.

"As you well know, Warren..."

The lieutenant paused for effect making the lawyer's name sound like a joke.

"Now that your client is free, I'm not obligated to tell you anything. So please...and I do say this with all due respect, go fuck yourself!"

In all the years that Kat had known Chemah, and she had ample opportunities to see him upset, she'd never heard him use profanity in public. The past few years had taken a toll on him. He was changed. Warren Schwartz was infuriated, but attempted to keep some semblance of his dignity. He turned to Kat.

"Ms. Ortega is out for the night and I'm not needed anymore. Tell her to come to my office tomorrow afternoon. I want to go over her case."

"Wait a moment. As soon as she comes down, we'll take you home."

Schwartz waved her off.

"Don't worry about it. I'll catch a cab."

Warren Schwartz started to walk out of the precinct already thinking about how he would be billing Margarita extra for getting him out of bed so late at night. Add to the fact that it was all a waste of time he would throw on another five percent.

As an afterthought he turned back to Chemah who had pulled Kat to the side.

"Lieutenant, my office is going to be calling you for a copy of the written statement that Ms. Ortega was illegally asked to conjure for you. I'm going to want the tapes, too. If there was one impropriety during the interview, just a hint at coercion, then we will see each other sooner than you're going to like."

With that said, Warren Schwartz pulled the lapels of his coat toward one another and walked out of the precinct.

Chemah ignored the false bravado that came from the one lawyer he detested.

"Fucking idiot," Chemah said under his breath

Noreen, who had been hanging on to Chemah's every word, heard the remark and in trying to make an impression, she spoke out of turn.

"I don't like him much, either. You know how those Jewish lawyers are, he's probably chasing an ambulance down the street right now." Noreen said it low enough so that only Kat and Chemah could hear her.

Chemah found her words distasteful. He held no malice against Jews nor lawyers. His only qualm was with the word-twisting likes of Warren Schwartz. Chemah turned his back to Noreen and he motioned for Kat to step farther away from her friend.

"I heard about what happened between you and your husband."

"You heard what happened…?"

"You know the divorce. Margarita explained it to Hèro. Hèro came home and talked to me about it. I just want you to know that I consider you family. You've always been good to Hèro. If there is anything that you ever need, all you have to do is ask."

After all this time it was strange hearing these words from Chemah. He really did change, maybe not for the worse.

"I'm all right. Thank you, though, I really appreciate that."

In Chemah's eyes she was obviously not all right. After all, look at how she had let herself go. In all the years he'd known Kat, she was always into her looks. Now she was maybe sixty or seventy pounds overweight. He'd seen firsthand how losing a man could devastate a woman. The next thing after putting on all that weight was either homicide or suicide. Chemah never really had anything against Kat and his daughter loved her. He had few enough ties that bound him to his daughter and thought that befriending Kat now would be good for them both.

Kat was feeling a little uncomfortable. For whatever the reason, Chemah was feeling sorry for her although she didn't need anyone to. There was nothing wrong with her life.

"Despite that asshole Schwartz, your friend is going to be all right. The DA didn't want her. The coroner said that it was a heart attack. And I didn't find any evidence that indicated that she purposely caused the heart attack."

"How does one purposely cause a heart attack?"

"Just tell her to cool it for a while with her business. I'm sure that after the report goes to the deputy commissioner, she'll be getting a look from the vice squad."

"Prostitution?"

"Some people call it that. That's not what I would call it."

At this early morning hour, the quiet precinct allowed that you could hear a door closing upstairs. Chemah turned toward the stairs knowing who he expected to be coming downstairs.

"Your friend has to tell you about it, but if you need any help later, you can call me."

Chemah took a card out of his inside jacket pocket and handed it to Kat.

"It's a new number that Margarita doesn't have."

Kat felt guilty taking the number. She knew that Chemah meant for her not to give it to her friend. She would be in a bad position if Margarita ever asked her about it, and it made her hesitant to take it. Chemah read her mind and let her off the hook.

"Don't worry about it. You know your girl, if she really needed to get to me, she would find a way. Just don't offer it to her unless it's an emergency."

Kat took the card and put it in her coat pocket.

Chemah smiled kindly at her and then he seemed to remember something.

"When they called me in this evening, I never meant to stay this long. Hèro is with her mother tonight, but Tatsuya is home by himself. I've got to get out of here."

"My God, he must be so big by now."

"Yeah, he's fourteen now. He's growing up too fast."

"Fourteen? It was just yesterday that…"

She stopped herself from completing the sentence remembering what a sore point the past was for Chemah.

"It's okay." Chemah waved away the awkwardness.

Dahlia came down the same stairs that Chemah had come down minutes before. Now she was passing him as he went back up to his office to get his coat. Dahlia held a hand up in a half-wave and mouthed the words *thank you* as they crossed each other's path. Chemah smiled and nodded toward her. He hoped he didn't see her in this position again. She turned out to be a nice lady after all. He was on the job long enough that he could tell the good from the bad.

When he reached the top of the stairs, something else occurred to him. It didn't take Sherlock Holmes to see that Kat had found a friend that was close to her size. He remembered how his ex-wife and Kat would look at overweight women with disdain and joke at how they always traveled in packs. The stereotype almost fit if it weren't for the pretty slim woman that also claimed to be a good friend. He looked back at the beautiful slim woman at the bottom of the stairs and caught her staring up at him. *She's very beautiful,* he thought. He remembered when he was younger, his friends used to say that there was always one beautiful thin chick that hung out with the big girls. Something about how they had low self-esteem and hung out with the big girls so that they looked that much better in contrast.

They're all beautiful women in their own right.

Chemah gave the threesome one last look before going back into his office. He caught Noreen looking at him again and wrongly confirmed his previous thought.

Yeah, she thinks she looks good standing next to her two friends. Damn shame, too. A woman that fine should think more of herself. I'd sooner spank the crazy Latin woman…if I weren't afraid that she'd spank me back.

The embarrassment on Dahlia's face was evidence that her conscience was still hard at work. Noreen met her at the bottom of the stairs and hugged her tightly.

"You all right, girl."

Tears of shame streaked down Dahlia's face. Kat, who was standing behind Noreen's right shoulder, wiped the tears away with the back of her hand.

"Let's get out of here, guys. We can talk about all this in the car."

Noreen drove them all to her house. Dahlia started telling the whole story in the car and two hours later, they were sipping coffee in Noreen's living room and laughing at the whole ordeal.

"I know it's sad how the man died, girl, but are you going to keep doing this business?"

"I thought about it when I was in the cell. I prayed to God that if he let me out of this situation, I would walk the straight and narrow path."

"That's a shame, girl, because after this story gets out, your little side business would have probably tripled. You would have been able to call any price and the people that like this game that you've been playing would have gladly paid it."

Kat didn't get it and she said as much.

"No, she killed a man. I mean, she didn't kill him, but he died in the course of their intercourse. When people find out what happened, she was going to be out of business anyway."

Noreen looked at Kat gravely.

"Kat, you grew up in the pjs."

Kat nodded. "Yeah…and…"

"You've been around a few drug addicts, haven't you?"

"What's your point?"

"Do you remember what happens whenever someone dies of a heroin overdose?"

Kat shrugged her shoulders. "What?"

"All of the heroin addicts try to find out where the person that died got their dope."

Kats eyes widened finally understanding what Noreen was getting at.

"You see all those addicts want the strongest dope they can get. They want the dope that's going to get them higher than they've ever been before. None of them think that it's going to kill them. They think that one person that died was just weak…"

Kat finished Noreen's thought.

"…So when those crazy submissive people find out that Dahlia fucked a guy so good that it made him have a heart attack and killed him, they're going to want to have the same heavenly experience, except they don't think it's going to kill them."

"That's what I think."

Noreen sat back smiling at her own cleverness.

"If I were still a big girl, I'd consider going into business with you myself. That's a lot of money for very little work. The way you're doing them, you may need a nurse on your staff. I'd be willing to do consulting work if you go back into business. I'll show you how to use the paddles. That's the defibrillator paddles. Not the leather ones that got you into this trouble."

Dahlia started to cry again. Kat gave Noreen a dirty look.

"She was just joking, Dahlia."

"You know I was just joking, Dee, Besides, what are the chances that something like this is going to happen again?"

Dahlia wiped her tears away and sniffed twice before answering.

"They may be pretty good, because I'm sure I'm not going to give up this lifestyle."

She looked down at the floor afraid to see disapproval in her friend's eyes. Dahlia's two good friends looked at each other knowingly. The fact that Dahlia did not tell them about what she was up to before meant that she thought they would not approve. This was their time to be supportive of her decision if they wanted to remain a part of her life.

"I'm not allowed back in the club again so I can't have your back there. Besides that, I only liked the way that way everybody treated me when I looked intimidating. I don't do the skinny dom thing well."

Kat butted in again.

"I think what Noreen is trying to say is, if that's what you want to do, then it's fine. We're not supporting it, but we're not throwing you under the bus either. If you told us that you just realized that you are a lesbian, you wouldn't expect us to start eating pussy, too, would you?"

"Noo…"

The thought made Dahlia smile a little.

"Well, it's the same thing. When you're in that world, you're with those people and when you're with us…well, you're just with us, that's all."

That seemed to be an acceptable answer for everyone. After a moment of loud quiet, Noreen got up from the couch.

"I've got to use the bathroom again. Dee, pour me another cup of coffee."

When Noreen came back, Kat and Dahlia were talking about the next vacation they wanted to go on. Noreen plopped herself on the couch and interrupted the conversation. She laughed a little and paused to draw everyone's attention to her. It was the way she used to get ready to tell one of her stories, before the operation.

"I was just giving Virginia a good cleaning when I was reminded of what you said about lesbians."

Dahlia and Kat both took a sip of coffee prepared to listen.

"I know I didn't tell you this, Kat."

She paused for effect again.

"Please, you're not going to tell me that you're a lesbian."

"No, I'm not a lesbian, but I did let this girl go down on me once."

"Noreen, I just can't right now. I have had enough drama for one…"

"No…no…no, Kat. Let her tell it. Let her tell it. This is a good one. I heard her tell it before."

Kat acquiesced, sitting back casually on the couch and sipping her coffee.

Two minutes into the story Kat was laughing and trying to keep any more coffee from coming out of her nose. The laughter and stories continued for another hour before Kat's phone rang and her mother asked her when she would be picking up her son. Noreen called each of her friends a car from the car service run by the Africans a block away. They said their good-byes at the door and promised to call one another to announce when they reached home.

When her friends left, Noreen found that she was still too excited to sleep. Dahlia's accident, for lack of a better term, had made her come to a realization. She enjoyed the persona that she played as a big woman. She liked that people stared at her because she was big and beautiful. But to be true to herself she had to admit that for her whole life she only used her size as a tool to express the person that she really was inside. She made herself believe that if she were a small woman, that she would no longer have any worth and that people would discount her, the way that they had her petite grandmother (the only small person in her family), who worked her whole life as a servant to a colored family in Scarsdale. She didn't know her own thoughts concerning being accepted until she heard the words being said out of Kat's mouth.

In her epiphany she realized that there is a parallel experience that is shared by many women. The hatred of size is not really what it's all about. The truth is that the struggle with weight is really nothing but the struggle with self. And that if you can learn to love and accept who you really are deep inside, then it doesn't matter what size you are. She picked up the phone and called Dennis. She thought she might share the idea with him.

CHAPTER FIFTEEN
DEEP SECRETS

Noreen and Kat were sifting through blouses next to two manne-
quins with oversized breasts as they waited for Dahlia to come out
of the fitting room.

"I don't like this one," Dahlia was heard whining from behind the mir-
rored door.

"Come on out. Let us see it."

Noreen put the blouse she was admiring back on the rack and stepped
closer to the fitting room door. Dahlia came out of the fitting room adjust-
ing the jacket that she found to be too snug around the shoulders and too
big around the waist. Noreen stepped around her eyeing the whole outfit
suspiciously.

"Does the skirt fit?"

"It's a little long but it fits around the waist."

Kat came from around the rack she was searching in.

"Let me take a look at you."

She took the same walk around Dahlia that Noreen did, but stopped halfway when she was behind her and tried to adjust the jacket shoulders.

"Is this too big?"

"It feels tight!"

"It's hanging all wrong. Get rid of the skirt, too. It's making you look like
a runaway Jehovah's Witness."

Dahlia turned toward the mirror and looked at herself closely. It was a horrible outfit.

"I do look like a Jehovah's Witness." She turned to Noreen in a mocking tone.

"Good morning, Ma'am, I know it's six o'clock on a Saturday morning, but could I interest you in a *Watchtower* magazine."

Kat and Dahlia cracked up laughing.

"That's not funny. You shouldn't make fun of those people."

Dahlia stopped laughing when she saw the serious look on Noreen's face.

"What's wrong, No? I was only joking, girl. Look who all of a sudden wants to get serious. You joke about everything. I can't remember the last time you said something was off limits. Hmmm, oh yeah, I remember now, never!"

"Well, with religion it's different making fun of the way someone prays…"

"Wait a second… "

Kat jumped into the argument.

"Just the other night you were calling Warren Schwartz an ambulance-chasing Jew."

"Wait a minute, you know I didn't mean anything by that. I was just commenting on the greed of some lawyers."

"But you said *Jewish* lawyer, as if being a Jew was part of being greedy and chasing cars."

"I know that being Jewish is not relevant to being greedy. For God's sake, Kat, I work alongside Jewish doctors all day."

"Listen to yourself. "

Kat put her hands on her hips like Noreen did and mocked her.

"I work alongside Jewish doctors all day."

Noreen took her hands off of her hips and folded them across her chest.

"Why can't they just be doctors? Why do they have to be Jewish doctors? Do they heal people better because they're Jewish?"

"You know that's not what I mean."

"Yeah, but that's what you're saying."

Dahlia was taking the jacket off in front of the mirror. She knew that Noreen didn't mean any harm by the things that she said, but now she was glad that someone else besides her was confronting her on it.

"Kat, my last name is Klein. Get it? Klein is a Jewish name. As far as I know, one of my ancestors is probably Jewish."

"Noreen, you're missing the point. Judaism is a religion. It's not the way someone dresses, it's not the way someone looks, and it certainly isn't a name. Two of my married black friends are named Washington. They're both lawyers and have converted to Judaism. Would you call them ambulance-chasing Jews?"

"Why do they have to be your *black* friends?"

"What!"

"Why did you have to qualify them as your *black* friends?"

"I was trying to make a point…"

"And I'm trying to make one, too. You're taking this shit too far. I'm no bigot and I'm no racist. We just grew up saying shit like that because we heard our parents say it, and they probably heard their parents saying it. So I get it. You want me to watch what I say because it might hurt someone's feelings."

While the two women were going back and forth, Dahlia went back into the dressing room to change out of the skit suit that fit her badly. When she came out shortly, Noreen and Kat were laughing about how Noreen's wig was twisting to one side whenever she motioned with her head.

"You got a bobby pin, Dee? This girl doesn't wear wigs so I know she doesn't carry them."

Dahlia went into her bag and got out a hairpin. She gave it to Noreen and Noreen went to the mirror in front of the dressing room and adjusted her hair with the pin so that it wouldn't move again. She came back to the two women who were looking through the suit racks again.

"Are we still looking for a pants suit?"

Without looking away from the rack that she was rummaging through, Dahlia said, "If I'm going to stand a chance in getting that promotion, I'm going to have to at least look impressive."

"Those people at the bank don't care about what you look like, Dee. All they care about is that you make them more money or at the least don't let anything happen to the money they already have."

"I wish it were really that easy. If I get this job, I'll be flying all over the world. I won't be sitting behind some desk in the back offices of a bank. I'll be the face of the bank that I'm representing. There are a few other bank vice presidents in the company that could be going up for the job."

"A few other bank presidents? I was under the impression that there was a vice president and then a president. How many bank vice presidents are there?"

"In the state of New York, I'd say we have about eighty-five. That's just an estimate. I really haven't checked lately."

"Eighty-five! Damn. Here I am bragging all over the place, *my best friend is the vice president of a bank*, and there are eighty-five of you."

"You brag about me?"

Dahlia smiled showing all of her just whitened teeth.

"Well, I did before, but now that I know you're just one in a bunch, I'll just keep that little bit of info to myself."

Dahlia slashed at her with the skirt that she had in her hand and Noreen skipped out of the way to avoid the fabric. All three friends were laughing and tearing apart the last rack of Liz Claiborne suits in search of Dahlia's size when Kat asked, "So are you going to tell us why not make fun of Jehovah's Witnesses?"

Kat and Dahlia stopped their search through the racks and watched Noreen continue to look through the clothing; avoiding their eyes as she told the story.

"I had two cousins. My aunt's daughters, they were sisters. At that time I was what…? Seventeen, or so I think. That would have made them fourteen and fifteen years old. They were my little cousins. Skinny little things. Sweetest little girls that you would ever want to meet. Polite like your mother wanted you to be. Got good grades all the time. Never talked back."

"You mean they were the opposite of you."

Kat elbowed Dahlia in the arm for having interrupted Noreen's story. Noreen looked up and smiled sadly at them both.

"Yeah, they were the exact opposite of me." Noreen went back to searching through the clothes, obviously not really trying to find anything. She had been through the same clothes a few times already.

"Anywho, their father was a serious member of the Jehovah's Witnesses. He went to Kingdom Hall four times a week and his family, including my aunt, had to go with him every time. I used to make fun of them whenever they came over to the house. Rag on them for having to wear skirts all the time. Played them out for not being able to hang in the street. And I mocked them whenever I got the opportunity, *Watchtower...Watchtower!*"

Dahlia's blood ran cold when she heard the same mocking tone that she used to mock Jehovah's Witnesses.

"Every Saturday morning, like the mailman—rain or shine, sleet or hail—they were knocking on doors at seven o'clock in the morning. I'm talking about like the old-time mailman. The one with the full uniform on, at your house at the same time even if there was a monsoon outside. Not like *the raggedy-ass-wearing jean shorts, unlaced Timbs, a postal hat to the side, don't get your mail until six at night, sometimes eight at night person* that you have delivering now. I mean they were on it like they were going to meet God every day. Anyway, this one Saturday they get dressed as usual, but their mother, my Aunt Cleo, was too sick to get out of bed, so she can't go with them.

"Their father, being one of the staunch elders of the Kingdom Hall, decides that they should still meet their obligation to Jehovah and go on their regular route to deliver his message. So they go out. They go out and offer fellowship to the community. They offer the *Watchtower* booklet to anyone they come in contact with.

"And then… And then they get to this one apartment on One Hundred and Twenty-seventh Street between Adam Clayton Powell and Amsterdam, right near the chicken spot that burnt down last year."

"They just put up a dry cleaners in the same spot." Kat kept up.

"Yep, right there over that store."

The cracking in Noreen's voice was telltale and the rest of the story was told with tears streaming down her face.

"Some drunk motherfucker dragged them into his house and raped them. He tied the little one up and told her that if she screamed he would kill the older one. He killed her anyway and somehow after a whole afternoon of being raped, the fourteen–year-old escaped. She came running over to our house half dressed and her skirt ripped to shreds.

"The police arrested the man while he was still drunk and sleeping in his house. They said my little cousin's body was lying next to him on the floor while he lay on the bed."

"Damn!" Kat exclaimed.

Noreen stopped looking through the clothes again and glared at her two friends as she relived the sordid memory.

"Oh, that's not the crazy part. The next week, my little cousin, Robin, the one that *made it,* her father tells her that she has to keep fulfilling her obligation to Jehovah to show that *the Lord's soldiers will not be cast asunder.*"

"What!"

"Uh-huh!"

Noreen wiped away some of the tears with the palm of her hand. She would have to redo her eyeliner.

"Friday was the funeral, on Saturday he made my Aunt Cleo take her back out bright and early same as always. They knocked on door after door, gave out their literature same as always and then came back home.

"The next day Robin went up to the roof of her building and jumped over the side."

"Oh my God!'

"She left a note saying that she didn't want to work for Jehovah anymore, she'd do just as well to just go see him."

"Oh my God, that must have driven your Aunt Cleo insane."

"I don't know if it did, but you can ask her about it in another four months when she comes home."

"She didn't?"

"It's been seventeen years now."

All the tears were clear of Noreen's eyes now.

"Stabbed her husband eighteen times. Poked one of his eyes right out of his face. She probably could have gotten off with an insanity plea, but when the judge asked her what she had to say for herself, she just smiled and said, '*It was an act of God.*' She wouldn't take a plea or anything. I think she was punishing herself, too, for allowing that to happen to her daughters."

Noreen went into her purse and took out a compact mirror and a tissue. She cleaned the running eyeliner from under her eye and then put the compact away while her friends watched.

"And that, ladies, is why we shouldn't make fun of other people's religions. Any questions…?"

Her friends seemed to be too stunned to answer.

"Let's get out of here. They don't have anything nice in your size, Dee."

Noreen linked her now thin arms under the thick upper arms of her two friends and walked out of Macy's with them arm in arm. When they reached the parking garage where they'd left the car, Kat finally got her voice back.

"No, do you ever go to see your Aunt Cleo?"

"I don't go, but my mother goes to see her all the time. She and I were never that close. She didn't like my father and they say I looked like him."

Dahlia was driving today. She turned the ignition to the C45 Infiniti that she drove infrequently. Noreen was already in her usual spot in the shotgun seat. She pulled her seatbelt toward her left side and when it clicked into its proper position, she turned to Kat who was already settled in the backseat.

"Kat, what do you think you would do if someone did something to your son?"

"Something like what? Like what happened to your little cousin?"

"God forbid, but yeah, something like that."

"I'm sure I would try and kill anyone that harmed my son."

"I don't have any children yet, but that's what I thought, too. My aunt told my mother that someday she was going to find the man that did that to her daughters. She plans on living just long enough to get him."

"How does she think she's going to find him?"

"She already has. They've been communicating with each other on the internet for months. The guy has no idea who she is, but he told his story to someone else who knows how she got put in jail, and she was able to find him on one of those chat rooms. He's in one of those good behavior programs where you get special privileges. Imagine, prisoners on the net."

"What?"

Kat was in shock. And Dahlia, who had just started to move the car, pressed hard on the brakes causing all of their necks to whiplash when she heard Noreen.

"What the hell…? Are you trying to kill us?"

Dahlia turned to her friend.

"Noreen, tell me that you are not down with this, please."

"I don't have any part of it, but my mother says that she's not going to try to stop Aunt Cleo. She says if it were one of her kids, she would have gotten him killed in prison already. In any case they're all old. The chances are that one of the two will die before the man has a chance to get out."

Kat didn't want to hear anymore. She was sure that knowing any of this and not informing the authorities would make them all co-conspirators.

"No, listen to me."

She grabbed a hold of Noreen's shoulder.

"Do not tell anyone else about this."

"I didn't plan on telling you guys. I just thought it was something that you could appreciate."

"Well, I would appreciate it if you didn't tell me any more."

"Me too. I don't want to hear another damn thing."

"Hey, I'm not the killer in this car."

Noreen tried to make light of the changed mood in the car.

Dahlia stopped the car abruptly again.

"Do not go there, No."

"All right, all right."

Dahlia started the car again and they headed downtown to a new clothing store in SoHo that Kat had heard about. It allegedly designed unique styles that catered to the taste of highly fashionable plus-size women. They were quiet until Noreen set it off again.

"Do any of you know how I can go about getting a gun permit?"

CHAPTER SIXTEEN
LA GATA

Librado was returning from an emergency trip to Puerto Rico to see his ailing mother. It had been three weeks since Kat had seen him, and now standing by the gate waiting for him next to the luggage pickup area, she was feeling a little anxiety. At the last minute she had to ask Noreen for a ride to the airport to pick up Librado. Her mother had borrowed the car earlier to take KJ to a children's breakfast birthday party in Brooklyn being given by one of her cronies.

"Who the hell gives breakfast birthday parties?" Kat had asked her mother.

"Never mind. I bet it's Mrs. Frasier."

Her mother didn't bother to say whether Kat had made an accurate guess. Kat knew for sure it was one of the five old ladies she liked to call *The Drac Pack*. She claimed they would suck the life out of you if you stayed around them long enough to hear all of their embellished stories.

She gave her mother the car keys and made her promise to be back by eleven. Five minutes before Kat was due to leave for Kennedy International Airport, her mother called to say that there was traffic on the Brooklyn Bridge and they were going to be at least an hour late. Dahlia was working on this Saturday and Noreen was the only other person she could think to call that would lend her a car.

"No problem, I'll go with you. Dennis just called me to say he wouldn't be able to come over this afternoon, so I have nothing to do."

Kat hesitated too long with a response.

"You're not still hiding him, are you? I already met the man, Kat. If you don't remember, let me refresh your memory. I met him before you did."

"I'm not hiding him."

"Well, you haven't brought him along to any parties that we go to and you hide out with him in your house and don't invite us over when he's there."

"I know. He doesn't want to be around his cousin when we're together."

"Did he tell you that?"

"He doesn't have to."

"Yeah and he hasn't been around me because…"

"Because you two have nothing in common."

"I breathe, he breathes, he eats, I eat. What don't we have in common?"

"You don't understand."

"Maybe I don't. But I only make fun of Dahlia's family because I like them. Maybe it's you that has the problem with race."

"Are you going to lend me the car or not?"

"Yeah, I'm lending it to you, but I'm coming along. These walls are closing in on me."

Kat didn't have any more time to argue. She'd promised Librado she would be at the airport when the plane landed at twelve o'clock sharp.

"All right, pick me up in fifteen minutes."

"Give me twenty. I have to fix my face."

"No, I'm already late. Fifteen minutes."

"I'll do my best."

Noreen actually made it to Kat's house in twelve minutes. She quickly applied some eyeliner and some lipstick. She drove on Adam Clayton Powell Boulevard where there was no traffic at this hour. The lights were synchronized so she never had to stop until she turned down Kat's street.

Kat was already waiting outside the house when she got there. She hopped off her stoop and damn near ripped the door hinge from the car in her haste to get in.

"Was that fast enough?"

"I was about to call a cab."

Noreen looked at her watch.

"That was less than fifteen minutes."

"Yeah, but you sounded like you were going to take your time."

Kat fastened her seatbelt.

"Come on, let's go, let's go."

Noreen pulled away from the curb and headed for the Triborough Bridge.

"LaGuardia Airport?"

"Kennedy."

"Oh, that's going to take at least an hour at this time of day."

"I know."

"Well, why didn't you call me earlier?"

"I didn't know I wasn't going to have my car."

"What time is he supposed to get in?"

Noreen was already doing forty-five miles an hour in a thirty-mile-an-hour speed zone. She made a right and was now speeding along 125th Street.

"Twelve o'clock."

"Twelve o'clock?"

"Tssk!" Kat sucked her teeth annoyed at herself for having waited so long before leaving. She thought she would never lend her mother the car again.

"Dang girl, don't worry, we'll make it."

Noreen reached the ramp that would put her on the Triborough Bridge and gave the gas pedal an extra nudge. It made Kat's head lean back into the headrest, and she gripped the side of the door for support thinking that maybe being late wasn't such a bad thing after all. When they reached the airport, it was two minutes to twelve.

"Don't bother parking. Just drop me off at arrivals and go around the airport once. His plane should have gotten here already. We'll probably be out in five minutes."

"All right. Just don't have me waiting out here all day."

Kat took her seatbelt off and opened the car door before turning back to her friend.

"You've got somewhere to go?"

"Upside your head if you don't hurry up."

Kat had already gotten out of the car and was walking toward the automatic doors. Kennedy Airport was crowded. There was an air traffic jam and planes that were supposed to have landed half an hour earlier were still in the air. The rain in Boston made it too dangerous to land there and all of their international flights were diverted to JFK this afternoon.

Kat had already waited twenty-five minutes by the luggage retrieval exit before she heard the news. The monitor that showed the schedule for arriving flights was directly behind her, and she found that flight seven sixty-two arriving from San Juan Puerto Rico would now be arriving at one o'clock. She sighed with relief. After twenty minutes of waiting by this exit, she thought that she had somehow missed him.

There was one seat available at the end of the bench next to the concession stand that was selling soup and sandwiches. Kat saw the seat at the same time as a Pakistani woman who wore a veil. Fortunately, Kat's legs were longer and she beat the lady to the seat. The five extra pounds she had somehow put on since she last saw Librado was slowing her down, she thought as she barely made it to the seat before the lady who pulled a suitcase behind her. Kat smiled at the woman sweetly, but was not about to give up the seat. She was happy to have another moment to think about her future hus… *well, whatever he is.*

During the three weeks that they were apart, they had talked for many hours over the phone, sharing history and reviewing details of previous conversations that they shared when they were in New York together. From those conversations came the intimate details of parts of their lives that neither pressed the other about when they talked to each other in the dark and after hours of their passionate lovemaking. Somehow they had become even closer over this long time and distance than they were when they had easy access to each other. Not that they didn't appreciate each other when they were in close proximity. But the distance afforded them a better perspective of just what they meant to each other and what they could never have imagined to have developed in their previous relationships. Kat finally asked him about the deep scar tissue on his back that she could only feel in the dark. Except for their first encounter, they still had not made love with any lights on.

That was when Librado told her about his father: the man who beat him for everything from not tying his shoelaces properly; for looking directly into his father's eyes while being admonished for a poorly done chore and for speaking to his mother with too much bass in his voice. He even recounted with glee in his voice how at sixteen years old and a full head taller than his father he had stood up to the old man and told him how he wasn't going to take his shit anymore. It was the first time his father knocked him out. Kat was disturbed at how casually Librado talked about awakening the next day with almost no memory of how he'd ended up in bed with his mother sitting next to him replacing the ice pack that covered the bump on his head. In her mind she saw his face and the slightly misshaped nose and knew that it was his father who had ensured that his face was just less than perfect.

"*Oh, I deserved it,*" she remembered him telling her. "*I was talking back and trying to be a man before my time. He did what a father was supposed to do.*"

For the life of her, Kat could not see how anything that he told her equaled his father knocking him out on several occasions. When she tried to sympathize with him, he just shrugged off her words.

"*It made me a man.*"

He couldn't understand why she felt sorry for him, but they agreed to disagree chalking it up to cultural differences.

"*Now that the old man is dead, I am the man of the house. On his deathbed he told me to take care of my mother. I loved him and am grateful to him for making a man out of me. I honor his house by taking care of my mother.*"

Kat remembered the conversation fondly. He spoke to her about how his mother always pushed for him to go to school. How she insisted that his father allow him to come to New York every summer for the world culture that her sister in New York was giving to her own daughter, Migdahlia. She taught him poetry and although she had a limited education she gave him books to read. She also taught him how to eat properly as she had learned from watching the people at the hotel where she worked as a maid and his father worked as a maintenance worker. Librado gave his father all of the accolades for teaching him how to repair almost anything and as he put it, for making him a man.

Kat was sensitive enough not to mention that he was nothing like his father. He was a gentle man, a caring and forgiving man. He was a person who looked for and found culture simply for the sake of it. He was the man who his mother made him into and although he did not see it that way, he honored her by living the way she taught him.

"Move over!"

"Huh?" Kat almost jumped out of her skin.

"How long were you planning on leaving me out there? I made my way around this airport twenty-two times. The price of gas the way it is and I'm out there driving in circles."

"I'm sorry the flight was delayed.'

"I saw that! You could have picked up the cell phone and told me to park."

"I was rushing around the house so much I forgot it. Sorry…"

Noreen wasn't as upset as she was making out to be. She had been working extra hard at the hospital all week and looked forward to going out with Dennis. When he cancelled, she was glad that anybody at all called her. At this point a trip to the airport was as good as a picnic.

"Move over."

Noreen pushed Kat, forcing her to sit forward and make room for her on the cushioned seat.

"You don't fit."

The man sitting next to Kat turned slightly to his left and away from them, hoping that they would be content with sharing a seat. Normally chivalry would have made him give up his seat, but he had now been in the airport two hours longer than he thought he would be and he was tired. Maybe if he pretended that he didn't see them, the situation would right itself.

"I don't need that much room."

Kat sat on the corner of her seat. One of her large buttocks was touching the thigh of the man she was sitting next to. He moved a little, but all it did was make more room for her buttock. It still made contact with his thigh.

"I'm sorry."

She looked over her shoulder at the man whose seat she was impinging on.

He merely smiled at her indicating that he understood. He was glad that he didn't have to get up to make room for her.

"These seats are kind of comfortable, aren't they? I can fit two of me in here."

"Yeah, or just one and a half of us."

Kat wriggled closer to Noreen again in an effort to get her butt off of the nice man. Fifteen minutes later they were in full shoe fashion conversation mode. Both of them and the kind man to their left were happy to have any seat as the airport became more congested with each passing minute. The two women whispered to each other back and forth discussing the footwear of one woman or another as they passed. Noreen paused in her conversation noticing a man and a woman who were standing approximately twenty feet away.

"You see that guy over there."

"Yeah, what about him?"

"When I first walked in, he was over by the coffee stand trying to kick it to the sister over there with the red mini-skirt on."

"So, do you know him?"

"I don't know him, but I was just thinking that he's probably one of those good-looking guys that you see around, talks to a lot of girls and probably gets laid a lot."

"You can tell all of that by just looking at him."

"Kat…"

"You could be right. He's nice looking. He probably gets his fair share and somebody else's too."

"So why is it that if a guy gets laid a lot, he's a player and if a girl gets laid a lot, she's a slut."

"Are you hatin'?"

"Yeah, I'm hatin' right about now. I'm sittin' here in an airport with you because I'm trying to be monogamous when the truth is that there is more than enough of me to go around than just for Dennis."

They were already talking in whispers, but Kat spoke even softer, inching closer so that even the man sitting next to her couldn't hear.

"I thought Dennis was you know…packing."

Noreen still whispered, but didn't bother with the effort that Kat put into it.

"He can be packing like FedEx, but it doesn't matter because he hasn't been delivering from Jersey to New York."

Kat covered her mouth to stifle the laughter that still escaped between her fingers. After a moment she stopped and looked at her friend.

"Is it that bad?"

"'I'm here hanging with you at the airport, aren't I?"

"You've got a point there."

"Don't worry, I'm not going to cock block you."

"Ssshhhh…"

"I'm sayin'… When I drop you off at the house, I'll just take my butt home. I know you haven't been getting any since he left for Puerto Rico. I'm going to let you do your thing."

She nudged Kat knowingly and gave her a sly smile.

"Please…by the time I get home, my mother will be there waiting with KJ. I won't be seeing any until way past his bedtime."

"You want me to take Kenny home with me?"

"Can't. His father said he might come by to pick him up."

"Call him and tell him to pick him up at my house."

"And tell him what? That I wanted to fuck, so I sent my son over to my friend's house? He's going to call me a tramp."

"See, that's what I'm talking about. Wasn't Kenny supposed to pick the baby up last night?"

"Yup."

"And why didn't he?"

"He said he was going to have to work late."

"And you believed him?"

"Hell no, I didn't believe him. He was probably out all night chasing some ass."

"And nobody is calling him a tramp, but the minute a woman does it, she's the town Skunt."

"Skunt?"

"That's right a combination Skeezer with a you know what…"

"Who came up with that?" Kat wrinkled her face in disgust.

"The same men that want us to think that what's right for them is wrong for us."

"Librado is definitely not one of those men."

Kat folded her arms, obstinately denying in her own mind that a man that she loved would ever think like that.

"Maybe not him, but I'd dare say the majority of men in New York— barring race color, creed, or education—has the same mentality."

"I don't think it's the majority of men, No."

"You don't, do you? Want to try a quick experiment? Watch this."

Before Kat could stop her, Noreen reached past her and tapped the man sitting next to Kat on the shoulder. The man appeared to be in his late thirties or early forties. He wore a neat gray suit with a white shirt and red-and-white tie. *Very fashionable for a white man*, Noreen thought before she touched him.

"Excuse me, but my friend and I were having a discussion over here and we thought you might help us with a little social experiment."

The man who had earlier turned away from the two women who might threaten to remove him from his seat now took an interest and turned toward them. He had already taken stock of the two women out of the corner of his eye. They were both beautiful, and although the one sitting next to him was thicker than he normally found attractive, she was still breathtaking. He was sorry that he hadn't given up his seat to them earlier. It would have given him an opening to start a conversation. Given the opportunity now, he smiled at them enthusiastically.

"Anything I can do to help."

"If you don't mind, can you tell us what you do for a living?"

The man shrugged, happy and proud to say, "I'm a dentist. I'm on my way to a convention in L.A."

"That's nice. Would you say that you're an average man?"

"In what way?"

"It's just for the sake of argument, but would you say that you're of about average intelligence for a man."

The man smiled and although he truly believed he was of above average intelligence he nodded yes.

"I'd say I have about average intellect for a man."

"Good, then this question will be easy for you. What is the term used to describe a person that indiscriminately takes on many lovers and is also the name of a gardening tool?"

Without taking a second to think, the man answered, "A hoe."

Noreen smiled at him and reached past Kat and patted his leg.

"Thank you. You've been a great help. You've just proven my point."

Then she looked to Kat.

"See, I told you."

"That doesn't prove anything. Half of the women we know would have said the same thing."

"That's not the point. The point is that men think like that of women all of the time. No one thinks of men sleeping with women indiscriminately. They're supposed to be that way."

Noreen noticed that the man was still turned to them and looked puzzled that there might be another answer to her question.

"Just for future reference, Mr…."

"John. You can call me John."

"John, okay John, the English dictionary defines a man who is a philanderer and womanizer as a rake."

"Oooohh!"

John slapped his palm to his forehead in frustration of his slow wit.

"I knew that one, that was so stupid of me."

"Don't beat yourself up too badly, John. It just proves my point. You're educated enough to know both of those answers, but you're conditioned like most men to think that women that sleep around are for lack of a better term…garden tools."

‡‡‡

Librado saw Kat first. He moved his one suitcase from his left hand to his right and lingered for a moment, dwelling on how much he had missed her. Their long conversations on the phone were the only thing that kept him from rushing back to her. His mother had insisted that he didn't have to come out to Puerto Rico to help her convalesce after another hip replacement. But Kat had agreed that she would probably heal faster with someone there who would pay special attention to her.

Librado never believed in the old adage, *absence makes the heart grow fonder,* but now that he was a victim of it, he truly felt closer to Kat now than before he'd left for his trip. Before he left, he was about to talk to her about how annoying it was to have to make love to her in the dark all the time. Now he thought maybe it wasn't so important.

After an unusually long phone call with Kat one day, his mother broached the subject of the special woman in his life. She didn't speak any English, but when she heard Kat's name she recognized it as *cat*. Librado explained to her that it was spelled with a K, not a C. but after that day every time they talked about Kat, Mrs. Anglero referred to her as *La Gata*, which translated from any Spanish dictionary meant *The Cat*.

"Was that The Cat you were talking to again?"

"She's not The Cat, Mama, just Kat."

"It's the same thing, son, it's the same thing."

Librado knew better than to continue trying to explain to her. Once she set her mind to thinking one way, his mother had a hard time deviating from it. Besides, she was just getting over the hip surgery and was still pretty weak.

"I'm sorry that I was listening to your conversation, but you were speaking a little loud and I am a nosey old lady."

Librado smiled at her kindly and sat on the edge of her bed.

"It's all right, old lady, just get better so that I can go back to New York and stop worrying about you."

"After the conversation I just heard, maybe it's me that should be worrying about you."

Librado wondered just how much his mother had overheard.

"Why is it that you tell this woman all about your father and how he was so mean, but you don't tell her how good he was to you? But you don't talk to her about loving her. You don't talk to her about building a family. All this time that I hear you talking to her, I never hear you tell her that you love her and you never speak to her in Spanish."

Librado grimaced a little at the question that hung in the air. He came close to asking Kat to come to Puerto Rico with him for a few weeks, but was unsure of how his mother would have responded to a woman that did not speak Spanish. His mother didn't have any color issues. His father was a very dark-skinned man with hair so nappy that the man had to give himself a haircut every week to keep it neat, because he refused to bother combing it. His father was a very modest man; not good looking in any sense of the word. When his parents were teenagers, the people in town wondered what a beautiful young woman like Gladys ever saw in the dark and sullen Librado, Sr. His mother was blonde with green eyes. Everyone loved her. She was always happy and she always had a kind word for anyone that crossed her path. Neither one of their families had money, but for sure, with Gladys's good looks she could do much better than Librado. Even Librado's family wondered why she had chosen him.

Now that Gladys Anglero was alone in her bed and heard her son talking to someone on the phone the way that her husband talked to her when they were courting, she remembered why she'd picked her husband. It was the way that he made his voice softer than when he spoke to anyone else. Without seeing him she could hear Librado smiling into the phone, the same way she used to hear his father when he spoke to her from outside of her bedroom window.

"I speak to her in English, because she doesn't speak Spanish, Mama."

"Her parents didn't teach her Spanish? I hear that a lot of the people that leave here don't teach their children Spanish when they're born in America."

"She doesn't speak Spanish because she's not Puerto Rican, Mama."

"Mother of God in Heaven, please don't tell me she's Dominican!"

Librado never understood the hatred that elder Puerto Ricans held for Dominicans, but he was sure it was rooted in something stupid and archaic. Whenever he asked his father why he hated Dominicans so much, he always said something different. And always something totally ridiculous. *"They wear white socks with a full dress suit." "They speak Spanish too fast and are always making up words."* Or Librado's favorite, *"They think they're better than us."*

"No, Mama, she's not Dominican."

Librado's mother performed the sign of the cross on herself, and then she grabbed her son by the head forcing him to lay his head again her bosom.

"Thank you, Lord, for not allowing my son to stray from your righteous path."

Librado didn't know what the Lord had to do with Dominicans, but he didn't want to contradict his mother at this time. Gladys Anglero let her son up, but held him by the shoulders.

"So what is she? Colombian, Venezuelan, Guatemalan?"

Librado never knew his mother to be a racist and briefly wondered why she didn't think that he would be with an American woman.

"She's an American woman, Mama."

"An American woman?"

His mother looked incredulous. She let go of his shoulders and he was able to lean back and take in all of the awe that he saw in her face.

"A Black American woman."

"An American woman?"

His mother repeated her question, but this time she had a huge smile on her face.

"Yes, Mama, an American."

His mother didn't seem to think that the color of the woman he was seeing was an issue.

"So tell me, what does this American woman do?"

Strangely, Gladys seemed to have become energized at the mention of Kat's citizenship.

"She is a schoolteacher."

Gladys's face seemed to be glowing now.

"Aahhh, a schoolteacher. She is a college graduate. A woman with brains.

I always knew you would marry a smart woman, but an American, you are so lucky, my son."

Gladys grabbed his head again, but this time she planted a big wet kiss on his forehead. Librado couldn't believe how happy she was. It was only when she said, "You just have to make sure that her friends don't get too involved in your affairs."

That was when Librado realized why his mother was so happy. Since *Sex in the City* started being translated into Spanish, it had been his mother's favorite show. Now all of her views about American women were based upon episodes that she watched on her twenty-inch television. According to the show, she now believed that all American women ran in packs of four until they found a good man. Of course only an American woman's friends would be able to talk her into and out of a relationship. It was an ignorant thing to believe, and he did not like to believe it of his mother, but at seventy years old now, she was liable to believe anything on television. Librado's mother had reduced any of the problems he may have been having with Kat to the most rudimentary theme of *Sex in the City*. Clearly each character's problems were exacerbated by another character's input. Ergo, his mother was happy that her son's problems could be diminished by her simple advice. (*Don't let her friends get involved in your affairs.*) In the Spanish novellas, which are equivalent to the American soap operas on television that his mother watched, whether they were based in Colombia, Mexico, or Puerto Rico, the bride-to-be could and would only be influenced by her parents. As she knew this to be true in Spanish cultures, it only made sense to her that *Sex in the City* was the model for how women behaved in America.

What Librado found sort of insulting even coming from his own mother was that she apparently hadn't had any faith that he could attract an American woman, much less an educated American woman. It was sad that this type of self loathing was prevalent in so many cultures. It was his mother who had shown him to be proud of his own culture. She also gave him a taste of other cultures, so that he would not feel awkward when he finally left Puerto Rico, like she always knew he would.

"So this woman loves you very much, doesn't she?"

Now his mother sounded proud, as if she were the one that had hand-picked his future wife.

"I don't know if she does, Mama, we've only been together a short time."

"Bah! Of course she loves you. Why else would she spend such a long time on the phone? She calls you every day. Do you know what her phone bill must be?"

His mother's logic was that of another era, but it almost made sense to him, too. Five days after that conversation his mother was so anxious for him to go home to his Kat that she started getting out of bed on her own just to show him that she was getting well.

Now as Librado stared at Kat from across the crowded airport he was glad that his mother forced him to come back home. As he walked toward her, he noticed that his cousin's other friend was with her. The woman had lost weight, but her face was unmistakable. She was beautiful with or without the extra weight. As Librado walked toward her, Kat caught his movement out of the corner of her right eye. She turned and saw the man whom she loved walking toward her. She jumped out of her seat and Noreen turned to see where she was going.

Noreen watched as her friend fell into her man's arms. For a split second she was jealous of her. She wished she were as happy as her friend was. Noreen felt a tap on her leg and turned back to face her new acquaintance John.

He handed her a card and paid her compliments that she was used to hearing when she was a bigger woman. On second thought it wasn't when she was a bigger woman, but when she was a *confident* woman. She was realizing that her anger at Dennis for standing her up was contributing to her swagger coming back. She was feeling in control of her life again, now that she was open enough to know that she was going to confront Dennis. If he didn't want to be with her, he would have to come out and say it, because now she didn't know if she wanted him anymore. Truth be told, the only reason that she even felt any loyalty to him up to this point was because he had been there for her throughout her illness.

"Jesus Christ, are you two going to stay there kissing all day?"

The couple broke their embrace and faced Noreen holding hands.

"Is that the only bag you have?"

"This is it."

Librado lifted the bag up to his hip.

"You were gone for almost a month and that's all the luggage you have?"

"What can I tell you, Noreen, I travel light."

"You remember my name?"

"How can I forget you, Noreen. You are an unforgettable woman."

Noreen blushed not knowing how to take the compliment.

Kat felt good for her friend. It had been a long time since she had seen that fire in her eyes.

True to her nature Noreen couldn't just let the compliment stand.

"Who's going to pay for the parking?"

"I will pay for it," Librado volunteered.

Noreen and the couple made their way toward the airport exit. When they got into the car, Librado sat in the backseat.

"You can sit in the back with him if you want, Kat."

"You don't mind?"

"I was just kidding; no, you can't sit in the back. Keep your ass right here with me. Damn, you a flat leaver. I swear it's like you never had a man before… Hey, want to hear the Puerto Rican word of the day?"

"Save it for Dahlia, No."

"The Puerto Rican word of the day is *chick*…"

Kat's voice rose a couple of decibels above Noreen's.

"I said, save it, No!"

"All right, you don't have to get nasty."

Before Noreen could start the car, Kat opened her door and got out. She slammed the door closed and opened the rear door and got in beside Librado.

"All right, you can go now."

Noreen laughed her old genuine laugh again. She started the car and took off toward the parking toll. The only time she addressed the couple again for the rest of the ride was for parking money and toll money. She looked in the rearview mirror a few times during the ride and enjoyed the feeling of jealousy she felt at seeing her friend with a man. It was the kind of feeling that made her want to make moves.

CHAPTER SEVENTEEN
SLOPPY SECONDS

It was lust at first sight for Dennis when Noreen first appeared around the makeshift *Dating Game* partition in Hedonism. This vivacious and voluptuous Amazon clad only in an emerald-green bathing suit, a sheer pink sarong, and high heels, was a perfect size twenty-four. Dennis persisted through the initial lukewarm start and it paid off in spades. Noreen Klein was the first woman who boldly took Dennis on in bed like a true heavyweight champ. Dennis was more than pleased to have her as his prize and eager to make her his bride.

As any good man would do, Dennis stayed by Noreen's side and helped her battle the cancer. Through several tumultuous months, he dried her tears and kissed her pain away. He knew Noreen would kick the cancer in the ass, and in her customary "take no prisoners" style, she did. Dennis was relieved with Noreen's victory, but at six feet one and one hundred and fifty-five pounds, Noreen was a shadow of her former self. As much as Dennis fought it, the more weight that Noreen lost the less physically attractive she was to him. Dennis was angry that the disease thief had stolen the flesh of his woman and left him with nothing except a bony shell.

Dennis derided his friends who were stepping out or leaving their women when there was a change in their weight. "Pretty in the face, thin in the waist" was the creed they lived by. He judged them to be shallow and self-absorbed, only interested in who could make their dick twitch. Dennis just couldn't get with it and he didn't want to. In college, he tried fucking thin women; it was uncomfortable and even painful, pelvic bones grinding against each other. Dennis was a genuine lover of healthy women. Big, strong girls were warm and soft, confident and kind. They loved him deeply and hungrily received his love. It was built into his DNA; he couldn't fight it. Now, he couldn't believe he was stepping out on Noreen, disturbed that he had fallen in love with a beautiful woman that he could not get an erection for now.

Standing under the shower, Dennis tried to scrub away the guilt and disgust he felt. The sultry voice coming from his kitchen brought him crashing back into his current reality.

"Babyboy, do you have another jar of mayonnaise in your cupboard?"

"It's in the back next to the tuna fish!" he yelled over the sound of the shower water cascading onto his head and over his ears.

"Got it! C'mon, baby, hurry out of the shower. I'm fixin' us a little snack to keep our energy up for later."

The woman in his kitchen was making a sandwich out of everything that was available in his refrigerator. The woman wasn't Noreen, by any stretch of the imagination. Just another random body accepting temporary love, Dennis knew he would be moving on to someone new before the end of the week. She was neither particularly smart nor particularly pretty. The only thing definite was that she was every inch a size twenty-four. And twenty-four was a sexy number.

When she first met him, she told him that she was on the Weight Watchers point diet. It was information that he thought was useless to a man that loved big women. But he changed his mind when in the middle of their lovemaking she asked him if he knew how many points he thought she should take off for swallowing a mouthful of warm cum.

Her vulgarity turned him off and he looked for some other redeeming quality in the woman, but found none other than her immense proportions.

Dennis dried off and went into the kitchen with the towel around his waist. Watching the woman in his kitchen, fussing over him while preparing a meal, left him with a dick that was harder than twelfth-grade math. Why did it always have to come to this? The flesh wants what the flesh wants, and he felt helpless to do anything other than satisfy it.

CHAPTER EIGHTEEN
PRYING EYES

Noreen banged at the bathroom door in Eric's small apartment. After dropping Kat off at her house, she decided it was as good a day as any to suffer her mother's attitude. When she called her and invited her out to dinner, her mother told her that she should pick her brother at his apartment first as he had already offered to take her out. She immediately regretted her decision, but when she got off the phone she got dressed and went to Eric's apartment. If nothing else, it would be a family affair. Without any doubt, Mrs. Klein had enough misery to distribute evenly to each of her grown children. Noreen, the eldest, developed a sharp wit and even sharper tongue to deal with it. Eric, her little brother, appeared not to have a coping mechanism and consistently acquiesced to his mother's disposition and demands. Noreen often stepped in to rescue her six-foot-four, two hundred-fifty-pound so-called little brother, but many times, Eric had to fend off both of them—like today.

Bang, bang, bang. The dilapidated bathroom door shook each time she struck it.

"Hurry up, Eric, I called you an hour ago. You should have been ready when I got here."

Eric raised his voice over the sound of the shower. "I'm almost finished."

"Sit down and chillax, Noreen. I swear you need to be easy already."

Noreen wouldn't sit down. She had more energy than she knew what to do with after being stood up for three nights straight by Dennis. She paced around the small living room, picking up one knick-knack and then another before becoming irritated and bored. Eric's bedroom door was open so she decided to be nosey.

The room had very little in it. There was a tall dresser, a king-sized bed, and a desk that held Eric's computer along with a messy array of papers, magazines, and books.

Noreen noticed an open email displayed on the monitor and out of pure boredom she peered into the lit screen. The very first line she read told her that it was not the type of email that a sister should be reading from her brother's computer, but her recent bout with celibacy made her push on and read the rest.

Eric, our earlier conversation has kept me hot and hungry all day. After nearly six months you continue to keep me intrigued and off balance. When I hear your voice, I imagine what it will be like when next we make love—which needs to be very, very soon.

There is something smoldering and dangerous about you, Eric. I sensed it when I put it out there that I wanted you to take me. You said you couldn't, but I knew you weren't being truthful. Your truth lies just beneath the surface. I've gradually come to realize that your touch isn't gentle, it's restrained—and there's a very subtle, but important difference between the two. All it would take is a look, a submissive sigh or permissive pose to give you the green light that you need to handle me; to fuck me any and every way that you really want.

I feel your desire for danger in the heat of your kiss. How much restraint you employ to keep from ripping off my panties? Or from biting my nipples? From pulling my hair so that it snaps my neck back and arches my ass? How much control do you call upon when I bow before you and offer my ass? You do fuck me hard in my ass and I love it. It's a thrill knowing how much control you're calling on when you're fucking me. You really want to haul off and slap the shit outta me, fuck me hard, then kiss me gently. You whisper to me I'm beautiful when my head is thrown back, hair stuck to my sweaty face, and my lips parted? Is it hard for you to decide whether you want to put your tongue or your dick between them?

I'd like to push you just to the edge of danger and we can play somewhere between rough and rape, kissing your lips neck and chest with hunger and heat—moist with desire. Will you push me slowly to my knees and feed your dick to me? Cup my head in your hands and control the tempo and rhythm as I lick and suck from tip to base to balls. I love the feel of your dick in my mouth— and yes, I want to go to sleep sucking on it…but, you knew that, didn't you? What are you thinking when you see your dick disappearing between my full and unpainted lips? Your stroke is sure and urgent. Do you love me more when you're fucking my ass or when you're getting your dick sucked, baby?

I want you to suck my tits, lave my pussy, eat my ass and then fuck it. My asshole always expands wide enough to accommodate your brick, you oblige, pushing in—slowly but steadily.

The first time you told me you loved me I didn't dare think it could be true— so quickly, so real. I feel, and have always felt, the same way. I can't wait until you hold me again so that I can tell you over and over again that you are the only man for me.

Please miss me.

In Joy,

Migdahlia

It was probably the sexiest letter that Noreen had ever read. In the midst of reading she contemplated printing a copy of it. That was before she saw who it was signed by.

She was willing to concede that maybe it was another Migdahlia that was loving and doing her little brother. But her Dahlia was the only person in the world whom she knew ended all of her emails with *In Joy* before signing her name.

Oh hell no, not my little brother! I will read that fucking bi...

Noreen didn't hear Eric coming into the bedroom. He had a towel around his waist and had to hold it with his right hand to keep it from falling off as he rushed toward the desk and Noreen.

"What the hell do you think you're doing, No?"

Noreen jumped away from the computer startled by the bass in her little brother's voice.

"I can't believe you're reading my personal emails."

Noreen gave him the look that he was used to getting all his life when he said something stupid.

"I take that back. I can't believe the thought that you were invading my privacy never dawned on you. Don't you remember how you felt the time Momma eavesdropped on your telephone conversation when you were a junior in high school? You still have feelings about that shit, No. You cried for three days after she whupped your ass and put you on punishment for a month because she found out you weren't a virgin anymore and actively fucking ole what's-his-name? Momma don't have a key to your apartment today behind that. And now you, of all people, are reading my personal email—clearly you knew you should have walked away after the first sentence."

"Eric...it wasn't the same and don't try to divert this conversation. Tell me you're not fucking Dahlia. Please tell me you're not fucking Dahlia."

Eric reached past Noreen and hit the power button on the monitor, temporarily clearing all evidence of his and Dahlia's affair.

"I don't need a lecture, No. I'm old enough and grown enough to decide who I want to have a relationship with."

"Yeah, you're old enough to decide who you want to have a relationship with, but you're only grown enough when you know everything about the person that you're having a relationship with and you still want to be in one with them."

"I think I know Miggy well enough."

"Miggy? Who the hell...?"

"That's what I call her."

Noreen took a deep breath and composed herself. She knew her brother would not listen to her if she got over excited.

"I get it, I get it."

"Do you, No? Because you don't really sound like you do."

Eric shifted the towel around so that he could hold it together with his other hand.

"Well, maybe you don't know everything you need to know about Dahlia."

"You think there's something important that you know about Miggy that I don't know about?"

For a second Noreen considered to whom her loyalties belonged to in this particular instance. There was no question that blood trumped friendship in this case.

"Did you know that Dahlia is heavily into the S and M scene?"

"I work security at the club, No; of course I know she enjoys the S and M thing."

"Do you know that she takes side jobs outside of the club?"

Eric looked at his sister carefully, gauging to see if she were lying or telling a half-truth.

"I know that she doesn't have sex with anyone that she does the S and M thing with. It's just a mechanism that she's found to help her work out excess aggression. I don't have a problem with that."

Noreen recognized that her brother was an intelligent man. He had completed his bachelors degree in psychology at Pace University with honors while playing football all four years. She wished that he had continued his education in psychology; then he'd know that the philosophy of releasing aggression in order to empty the reservoir of hostility was as out of date as Freud's cocaine-influenced dream interpretation theory. Everyone in the medical profession in the last ten years was trained or retrained to know that *violence only begets violence.* As far as Noreen was concerned, Dahlia was the perfect model for the person that practices violence, continuing to get better at committing violence with each violent act that she engaged in.

It only now dawned on Noreen why on the night that Dahlia called her from the precinct she asked her not to tell Eric that she was in jail.

"I guess you don't classify sodomizing a man until he dies as being dangerous."

Eric had the look of a man who had been caught in a lie.

"That was a one-time thing. You can't judge her based on that."

"You know about that?"

"It's a very small community of people that are involved in that scene, people at the club talk, No."

"Then she didn't tell you?"

Eric shook his head no and then tried to explain.

"She thinks I don't know about it. She probably hasn't mentioned it because she thinks that I'll judge her."

"She thinks you'll judge her because you're supposed to judge her. She's fucking men in the ass, Eric."

A crazy idea crossed Noreen's mind.

"Eric, don't tell me you…"

Eric almost laughed as he half read his sister's mind. His broad chest pushed out a little more and he strutted to his sock drawer, letting his sister dangle in her own assumptions. He let the air around them become a little uncomfortable as he looked for a matching pair of socks. He found a pair quickly, then turned to his sister.

"You read the email, No, was there anything in there that would give you the suspicion that I was going to be her next victim?"

Eric puffed out his chest even more. He looked exactly like the peacocks that men became when they expound on their sexual prowess. It was an even more unbecoming look on her brother because after all the years she knew him, she could clearly see through the masquerade. He was hiding some sort of insecurity.

Eric thumped his chest twice with his fist. "I'm the one doing the ass-fucking in this relationship."

"Eric, who do you think you're talking to?"

Eric didn't allow his chest to deflate, but he clearly understood to whom he was speaking. His sister knew him better than anyone else and would not let him forget it.

"I'm the one that changed your diaper when Momma was at work, and unless Jesus has come back and performed another miracle on that little thing under your towel you are not breaking anyone's back."

Eric tried to hold his head up, but when Noreen tried to snatch the towel from him, he lost a little of his swagger.

"Stop playing, Noreen." He only used her full name when he was upset with her.

"Yeah, that's what I thought."

Eric gathered his towel against his waist more securely and walked to the other side of the bed steering well clear of his sister. "Are you going to get out and let me get dressed?"

"The email said that you told her that you loved her. Is that true?"

"I just told her what she wanted to hear."

Noreen knew her brother. She saw the way he looked up to his left when he spoke and heard how his voice lowered just an octave. He was lying and she decided to call him on it.

"Look at you, you can't even lie straight."

"What are you talking about?"

"You do love her, don't you?"

Eric couldn't meet Noreen's eyes anymore. He went to the closet and pretended to be sorting through some of his suits.

"Why don't you just tell her to stop going to the club? You've obviously told her how you really feel."

Eric didn't turn back to her. He continued to go through the closet. "She's a big-time executive, Noreen. She's got a bad crib, drives a phat car, makes what, two hundred thousand a year. I made fifty thousand last year. Who am I to tell her to stop anything?"

"Well, according to the email, you're the fucking man. You're the one she's been waiting for. I know Dahlia. Eric, she's not bowing to any man, but she told you that she loves you. She's waiting for you to tell her to stop. You've got to read between the lines of that email."

Eric came away from the closet and faced his sister again. "If that's true, then why didn't she tell you that she and I were seeing each other?"

"Probably because she's just as insecure as you are. You know she's never been comfortable with herself, especially her weight."

"Weight?"

Noreen forgot who she was talking to. Her brother was raised by big women. He didn't see women that weighed more than three hundred pounds as having a weight problem. For him, "normal" and "sexy" was in the 200 to 250 range. He would tell his friends, "Only a dog wants a bone." Noreen was always sure that he would marry someone big like their mother.

"She's very uncomfortable with her weight, Eric. She doesn't need her ex-husband or other losers anymore. She beats herself in the ground about her weight…and everything else that's not Halle Berry-like. She doesn't see the powerful, professional, smart, caring woman that we see. She tunes into the negative and instead of kicking Martin's ass and telling him where to get off, she's perfected the prejudice. The S and M thing is a way to step outside of herself. It's her way of getting in touch with being sexy, and powerful. She's doing the fucking instead of being fucked. She's allowed you to glimpse who she really is—beautiful, soft, and vulnerable. She's even going so far as being submissive for you. She hasn't deferred to anyone since that asshole husband of hers."

Eric plopped down on his bed, holding his head in his gigantic hands.

"First, you sound like you don't want me to be with her; now you're saying I should wifey her up."

Noreen thought for a second before she responded.

"Dahlia is my best friend, Eric. I know she's a good person and I think you two would be good for one another. That is providing that you are really okay with the S and M thing. And since you already know that she was involved in someone's death and don't have a problem with it, I guess that point is moot, too."

"You think she'll really stop if I ask her to?"

"Nothing beats a try. And your soft ass better not give in if she says no. If you guys ever have a baby together, I'm not trying to see my baby nieces and nephews in leather diapers."

Eric laughed at his sister's joke. She usually had a wry sense of humor. She was changing, too.

"And there's one more thing you need to know, because of course, you know I don't like to lecture."

"Of course not, No, you never lecture," he said, rolling his eyes and getting up from the bed again.

"Whatever, but listen to this for one second because it's probably the information that Momma should have given to you instead of me when I first started dating." Noreen let a few seconds of suspense go by to make sure she had his attention before she dropped pearls of wisdom on him. The time lapse in her words did what it was supposed to; he inched closer and listened.

"It's just as easy to fall in love with a rich woman as it is to fall in love with a poor woman, but living with a poor woman is much harder."

Eric let that sink in for a moment. "Momma said that to you?"

"She substituted man for woman, but yeah, that was it."

"But you never dated any rich guys."

"Yeah, but I never let myself fall in love with any poor men, either."

"So you're saying I should live off of Miggy?"

"I'm not saying any such thing. All I'm saying is don't make it an issue that she makes more money than you. Enjoy the little extra things that she can afford. She's not going to think you're any less of a man because you make less money."

Eric didn't look convinced.

"Fifty thousand dollars a year is a decent amount of money for a man your age to make, Eric. And next week you start working for NYC sanitation. What's the top salary there, seventy, maybe eighty thousand a year plus the best medical benefits you can get working for the city? That's worth at least another twenty thousand. With some overtime, by next year, you'll be making six figures."

"I'll still just be a blue collar worker, No. Her father is a doctor and she's still the vice president of a bank."

"So it's not the money?"

"Not so much."

"Then baby, I feel for you, but I can't quite reach you. If everything that Momma taught you about respect and pride is not enough anymore, then you're on your own."

"No, I do care about her."

"Then man up, punk. Pull your panties up and your skirt down, you're going to make me throw up with all your whining."

"That's the sensitive Noreen I know." Eric went back to his dresser and pulled out a pair of underwear. "Can you go to the living room so that I can get dressed in private?"

"Don't get an attitude with me, little man. I'm not the one that can't handle my women making more money than me." Noreen turned her back on her brother before he could get another word out. The huge man knew better than to continue a fight that he could not win. He let Noreen walk out of his bedroom, closing the door behind her.

Noreen walked into the living room and pulled out her pink Blackberry Pearl and sent a text message to Dahlia.

Gotta talk to you. Come to my house after nine o'clock tonight.

She didn't receive a response until she was at dinner with her brother and mother.

Can't make it until nine-thirty. See you later.

"Something important?" Noreen's mother asked.

"Just something I have to take care of later."

"Anything I can do to help?" her mother asked her.

"No, Mom, you've done enough."

Noreen mulled over in her mind, what she would say to Dahlia when they were alone later.

CHAPTER NINETEEN
TRUTH OR DARE

I t was already ten p.m. when Dahlia rang the bell to Noreen's apartment building. Noreen was in a bathrobe already. Her mood was foul after having dinner with her mother. The woman never let up about Noreen not having a man and children so late in life. It took all of her strength not to be disrespectful. Eric even took some of the weight off of her by starting to talk about how her mother had to stop spending the money that he gave her on gambling. When the argument started between those two, Noreen was able to eat the small salad she was capable of digesting with her sad excuse for a stomach. It also gave her time to think of the good times and secrets that she and Dahlia shared. Although Dahlia and Kat became quick friends, there was still the bond that secrets and lies build between comrades in arms that can never be touched. Those that Noreen and Dahlia had were forged in fire and would probably never be broken. By the time she finished her salad, she knew what she would say to Dahlia.

When Noreen buzzed Dahlia up, she didn't bother waiting for her behind the apartment door. She left the door ajar and went back to the kitchen where two chilled glasses waited in the freezer. She and Dahlia always had their most open and vulnerable conversations when they had a little wine in them.

There were two sharp knocks on the door before Noreen heard the hinges of the apartment door squeak open.

"Noooo, it's meeee."

"I'm in the kitchen!"

Noreen heard her apartment door close and heard Dahlia fumble with the two locks and then the chain on the police lock. She never used it herself, but it was just like Dahlia to be extra careful. Dahlia came into the kitchen with all the aplomb of a Broadway diva. She had on a long black dress and the diamonds fixed on her ears and about her neck gave her the appearance of an heiress attending the king's ball.

"What do you think?"

Dahlia gave a twirl that sent the bottom of the dress floating about her calves. She personified the meaning of "beautiful Black Queen." Noreen thought that maybe she didn't need to move forward with her game plan. Maybe a simple talk would do, but when she didn't answer Dahlia immediately and she saw the doubt in Dahlia's eyes, she knew she had to go forward with her plan. Either Dahlia had changed or Noreen could not allow her to be with Eric.

"What the hell are you supposed to be? Did you borrow that tent from Ringling Brothers or from the Big Apple Circus?"

Dahlia stopped twirling. She put her head down and bit her lip as if trying to keep from saying something. It wasn't like Noreen to say something mean about her weight. When she lifted her head again, she had a forced smile on her face.

"I was at an evening gala with my company. Guess what…"

POP!

The cork from the wine bottle that Noreen opened hit the ceiling and ricocheted against the refrigerator door. The smile on Dahlia's face became genuine.

"How did you know?"

Noreen began pouring the wine into the chilled glasses.

"How did I know what?"

"The promotion. I got the promotion. They announced it at the black-tie affair tonight. I'm the new senior vice president of acquisitions."

Noreen new how important this promotion was to her friend. In the last year whenever Dahlia talked about her job, all she ever said was how good it would be for her if she could ever get promoted to that position, Although she had another agenda tonight, Noreen knew she had to put it to the side for a moment to celebrate her friend's success.

In the midst of pouring, Noreen stopped and put her thumb over the top of the bottle top. She shook the bottle vigorously and then moved her thumb. The volcanic bottle of wine sprayed over Dahlia, wetting her hair and her face. Dahlia was close enough to grab the bottle, then covered the top of it with her free hand and shook it herself before pointing it toward Noreen. The champagne erupted in foam and spray again, this time catching Noreen in the face even as she tried to shield herself with her hands. When the jet spray dwindled, the two women were soaked with champagne. They were both laughing at how the other looked.

Dahlia tipped the remnants from the bottle into the chilled glasses, and there was barely enough fluid left to make a toast. Noreen raised her glass in the air.

"To Dahlia. May she prosper and flourish in all of her endeavors."

Dahlia raised her glass and touched its rim to Noreen's glass. It made a sharp CLINK sound that only good crystal made. Both women took a small sip from their respective glasses.

Dahlia took a moment to examine her wine glass carefully and then took another sip before speaking.

"Is that the good crystal that I gave you last Christmas?"

Noreen took another sip and then put her glass down on the counter.

"Mmm-hmm." She nodded her head up and down as she reached into the refrigerator to get another bottle of wine. Noreen closed the refrigerator door and started to take the foil from around the top of the fresh bottle of champagne.

"After my operation, I decided I'm not saving anything for a special occasion. Every day that I have left on this earth is a special occasion now."

Dahlia tilted what was left of the golden liquid to her lips and then put her glass on the counter.

"Amen to that."

Noreen was having trouble twisting the cork out of the bottle and Dahlia took the bottle from her without even thinking. Noreen watched as her friend easily pulled out the cork. It was something that she had always found easy to do. The extra strength was a perk of being a big girl.

"I bought a party dress last month, you know, for a special occasion."

Dahlia nodded while pouring them another glass of wine.

"I wore that thing to go to the bodega yesterday."

"To go to the bodega?"

"That's right. I felt like looking pretty and I just put it on to go down the street. Bought myself a ginger ale and a box of tampons and came right back upstairs and sat on the sofa watching *American Idol*, just me and my red dress."

Dahlia handed Noreen the filled wine glass and then raised the crystal goblet toward the ceiling for another toast.

"To me!"

Noreen touched her glass to Dahlia's, but barely allowed any champagne to pass her lips. Her small intestine was no longer able to absorb alcohol the way that it used to, and it now took very little alcohol to cause her to become inebriated. She was already feeling a little buzzed. If she drank any more, she might forget the reason that she'd invited Dahlia over.

She was responsible for her brother having met Dahlia, and she would take responsibility for making sure that Dahlia was not trying to put something over on him. Dahlia was already high. She had obviously had a few drinks at the event that her job hosted, but she was always careful not to drink enough to get drunk. She only sipped wine at these events knowing that it was not savvy to get drunk in front of the bosses. After the announcement of her promotion, she may have had one more than she would have normally had, but the wine she was enjoying now brought her over the top.

Noreen did not mean to give Dahlia enough alcohol to make her giddy. She just wanted it to act as a lubricant to get Dahlia going. Now that she realized that Dahlia was as lubricated as she wanted her to be, she tried to find a way to ease into the inevitable conversation. Finding no easy way to say what she had asked Dahlia over to discuss, she got right to the point.

"Dahlia, why didn't you tell me that you and my brother Eric had something going on?"

Dahlia's jaw went slack and her eyeballs bulged. She looked like a deer caught in someone's headlights.

"Huh…? I…I…I…I…Huh?"

A second ago she was feeling a nice buzz, but now the adrenaline and fear coursing through her sobered her up quickly.

"Yeah, I know about you and Eric."

Dahlia was swallowing saliva and gulping at a rate. Her mouth seemed to go completely dry, but she didn't want to take another drink of the wine.

"Eric told you?"

"Not right away. I read the email that you sent him while I was in his apartment today. He didn't really have any choice but to admit to it after that."

"The email…?"

"Yeah, the email. *'I love the way you fuck me in the ass'*…blah, blah, blah, blah."

Noreen could see the embarrassment on Dahlia's face, but she wouldn't let up. If Dahlia were serious about her brother and not just leading him on, she would have to tell Noreen now.

"I really called you over to tell you to stop seeing him. Then I changed my mind. I thought maybe you were really serious about being in a relationship with him. Maybe you were finished with the S and M bullshit."

Dahlia didn't know how to respond. She knew how protective Noreen was over her family. That was the reason she didn't want Noreen to know.

She knew that for Noreen it was one thing to have a friend with a proclivity for causing pain, but another thing to have someone like her dating her little brother. She had already decided that she would give up the S and M gigs if Eric asked her to. She didn't want to be the one to bring it up. He had to ask or it wouldn't mean anything. He had to say that he loved her enough to want her to stop.

"But you're not going to stop, are you? You can't stop hurting the people you want to be most like. The people that hold all the power. The beautiful people that make you feel like you're nothing."

"I was going to stop, Noreen."

"Bullshit. You were never going to stop. You hate yourself too much. Look at you. You're the same fat bitch who couldn't hold on to your husband. "

"Don't say that, Noreen. You know that's not true. I've changed."

"Changed into what? Someone that hates herself so much that she doesn't know how to do anything else but hurt other people behind closed doors? Someone who can't even stand up for herself unless she wears leather and has a whip in her hand?"

"I do stand up for myself."

"But do you love yourself, Dee? Do you really love yourself?"

Noreen was unprepared for the avalanche of emotion that she pried loose from Dahlia's precariously tilted psyche.

In a rush of anger and frustration Dahlia swung her arm in a sweeping motion over the kitchen counter, clearing and shattering all of the glassware that had been previously set on its flat surface—the vase holding a beautiful display of orchids, the fine crystal, and two empty bottles of wine that they'd indulged themselves in.

"Who the fuck do you think you are telling me who I love and who I don't love? I have changed who I am. I do love myself and I do love your brother. Eric is the only man in years that has ever made me feel like I can be myself. The only one I have ever been able to be soft with, without fear-ing that he was going to shatter my spirit. He lets me feel vulnerable knowing that he isn't going to hurt me any more than he can kiss away the pain. And yes, when he hurts me I love it. I love how gently he hurts me and how softly he hurts me. He kisses away my tears when I can't stand to bear the pain of what I may have become."

Noreen hadn't bargained on all the emotions coming from Dahlia, and she certainly hadn't wanted to relive all of the things that she'd read in the email in her brother's computer.

"But why my brother, Dahlia? Why him? There are thousands of men out there just like him."

Dahlia was raving now.

"Your brother! I don't care if he's your brother! I wouldn't care if he were the devil's brother. How dare you make this about you again. That man showed me that I am worth something. He showed me that I can be and am worthy to be loved like anybody else. He thinks I'm beautiful and he showed me just how beautiful I am. He showed me how to love myself."

The look on Dahlia's face made Noreen think that she was about to physically attack her. Instead the emotional catharsis took all of Dahlia's strength and she crumpled to the floor in a heap. She was sobbing uncontrollably when Noreen knelt next to her and took her head into her lap.

Noreen stroked her hair and soothed her.

"It's all right, Dee. Everything is going to be all right."

Noreen pulled Dahlia's wet hair away from her tear-stained cheeks, while Dahlia continued to moan softly. "Let me tell you something, Dee. That brother of mine, he's something special, all right. But it was you, Dee. It was you who showed him how to love. It was you who showed him that you deserve to be treated like a lady, because my mother only taught him how to respect a real woman. Until you he never knew that someone could love just for the sake of loving.

"You're the one who's been on this journey to discovering the person that you truly are since the day we met in that bar with your ex-husband. You're the one who has shown me every day and in every way since I got out of that hospital bed that I needed to love myself whether I was big or I was small. And I've learned it, Dee. I've learned it from you.

"I've never been the type of person that let anybody tell me what to do or stopped me from saying what I wanted to say, but you still stood up to me. You showed your strength through silent courage sometimes. And other times you said your piece and put me in my place. I've never told you how much I appreciated you in all of those times.

"And Dee, I don't ever want you to give anybody that power to belittle you again. Don't ever let someone make you believe what we both know is the truth: *Ain't nothin' wrong with a big strong girl!*"

CHAPTER TWENTY
BUSTED

Noreen called in sick on Monday morning. She wasn't feeling ill, but she needed a mental health day. The emotional roller coaster ride she'd gone through over the weekend left her feeling out of sorts. She thought only two things could make her feel better—having sex with Dennis or breaking up with him. She knew he would be home today, as it was his day off.

Noreen knew his address and intended to drive over and surprise him. It wasn't the sort of thing that she normally did, but she wasn't feeling "normal" these days. She needed closure on this relationship if she were going to move on with her life.

The loyalty that she felt for Dennis stemmed from him having been there for her throughout her ordeal with cancer. Otherwise, with the way he was making moves without her, she would have moved on long ago.

Noreen had to make one stop at the bank before she made her way to Jersey City. Her mother had petitioned her for a few dollars while they were at dinner yesterday. Noreen knew that she was going to gamble it away with her friends from the senior citizens center on their next trip to Atlantic City. However, she knew she was saving her brother the few dollars that she would get from him if she didn't produce some funds.

Noreen had on what she deemed to be her sexiest outfit. She would either be enticing Dennis into having sex or leaving him wishing that he had done the right thing.

The stilettos that she wore made her walk carefully over the grating that she had to pass over to get to her car. When she reached the other side of the street, there was an older woman at the corner that seemed to be confused as she waited for the light to change.

They were at 125th Street and St. Nicholas Avenue, so it was apropos that Noreen took a closer look at the woman to make sure that she wasn't just out there faking a disability for begging purposes. Noreen took notice that although the woman was not dressed in what anyone would call their Sunday best, she was immaculately clean and neat.

"Excuse me, Miss, are you okay?"

The elder woman turned in Noreen's direction, but Noreen's nursing instincts immediately told her that something was not right.

The woman pursed her lips as if she were tasting the air before she spoke.

"I'll be okay, if maybe you can tell me when that light turns green. I'm blind in one eye."

The elder woman pointed to her right eye and Noreen was clearly able to see the milky white cataract on the pupil through the woman's glasses.

"And my other eye doesn't work so good anymore, either. I got a little lost a minute ago. That's the bank right across right there, though, isn't it?"

"Yes, ma'am, it is."

Noreen reached out and hooked her arm under the women's arm, feeling very little muscle in the frail woman.

"Let me help you across the street, Ma'am."

"Oh, thank you, young lady."

Even though she didn't appear to be able to see, the older woman still turned her head both ways as if looking up and down the street before allowing Noreen to lead her across.

Noreen decided to take the woman into the bank and when the woman still appeared to be a bit disoriented, Noreen decided to stay with her a while longer.

"What is it you want to do, Ma'am?"

"Call me Pearl, dearie."

Noreen smiled. Pearl was her grandmother's name. You hardly ever heard that name being given to babies anymore.

"What did you need to come to the bank for, Miss Pearl?"

"I need to put some rent money into my account."

Miss Pearl reached into her pocket and took out a wad of bills, mostly hundreds.

Self-preservation lessons from her mother immediately kicked in and Noreen looked around and even peered out of the banks store window to see who might have been following this old lady with all the money. When she was sure that no one was interested in Miss Pearl's business, she turned her body toward her in an attempt to shield the cash from any prying eyes.

"Okay, put it away, Miss Pearl."

Miss Pearl heard the concern in Noreen's voice and realized her error.

"Oh my, baby, you right. Sometimes I forget where we are."

She put the money back in her coat pocket and allowed Noreen to take her by the arm again. Noreen led her to the teller line that only consisted of two waiting people.

Although there were only two tellers on this Monday morning, they were quick and Miss Pearl was able to complete her transaction in no time.

"I can make it from here now, baby. You go on, I know how to get myself home."

Noreen still had her arm linked under Miss Pearl's arm and she held the door to the bank's side exit door while leading her out. It was obvious to Noreen that she was not okay and needed a bit more assistance.

"Where do you live, Miss Pearl?"

"Not far. Just down Morningside Park."

"What street?"

"A Hundred and Eleventh."

Three blocks down and fourteen blocks over. That was seventeen blocks away, Noreen quickly figured.

"Did you walk all the way here?"

"How else was I going to get here?"

You might have spent some of that money that you put in the bank on a cab, Noreen thought, remembering the six-digit figure she glimpsed when the teller gave Miss Pearl a copy of her bank statement.

"Let me take you home, Miss Pearl. My car is right over there."

"Well, if it isn't too much trouble. I don't want to be a bother to anyone."

Miss Pearl's tone was one that Noreen was quite familiar with. Her grandmother used it on her mother all of the time, and now her mother always tried to use it on her, except she never let her mother get away with. She wouldn't accept her mother guilting her into anything. That's why later that night she sat in her bed wondering why she had allowed Miss Pearl to do it.

"It's no problem at all, Miss Pearl, come on."

Noreen helped her across the street again and then led her to where her car was parked. It was a bit of a chore loading Miss Pearl into the car.

She complained that the seat was a little too low. She was used to just slipping into her grandson's Lexus. Miss Pearl mentioned that she was the one who had bought it for him and that once a month, he came around and took her grocery shopping.

Noreen smiled through the whole ordeal, promising herself that this was her last good deed for the year.

As they slipped away from the curb and onto St. Nicholas Boulevard, Miss Pearl became very talkative.

"Baby, I didn't even ask you your name. That's not like me. I'm getting on in age now. Startin' to forget things."

"My name is Noreen Klein. Pleased to meet you, Miss Pearl."

Noreen kept her eyes on the road, but used her peripheral vision to watch Miss Pearl take a pen and a piece of paper out of her bag and write down her name.

"What's your sign, Noreen?"

"Huh, pardon me?"

Noreen was taken aback. No one had asked her what her sign was since she got out of high school.

"Your horoscope, baby. Anyway, you might as well tell me your date of birth now."

"Virgo, September thirteenth."

Noreen wasn't moved when Miss Pearl wrote that on the paper, too.

"You were born on Friday the thirteenth! That's a good luck day."

"I was always told it was a bad luck day."

"Shoot, that's only a bad luck day for the people that were born on the twelfth. Everybody knows that."

Noreen winced as she heard Miss Pearl speak casually about the unknown, with the authority in her tone of a crazy person.

Miss Pearl slipped the piece of paper with Noreen's information into her bag and closed her eyes for a second. At a stoplight Noreen looked over at her, watching the old lady breathe deeply. When her eyes snapped open, the light changed and Noreen took off into traffic again.

"Do you want a man in your life?"

"A man. You mean like a boyfriend?"

"A male friend. Do you want one?"

Noreen was now only a half-mile away from Miss Pearl's home and didn't see the harm in humoring the old woman.

"Well, I have Dennis right now. I guess you could call him a male friend."

"Not him, baby, he already got somebody. You know that."

Noreen ignored what the woman said, already having decided that she was dealing with someone that was three cards short of a full deck.

"You're right, Miss Pearl, you are certainly right. Yes, I guess I'm going to want my own man one day."

Miss Pearl closed her eyes again and Noreen heard her deep breathing in the seat next to her. Noreen chanced another look at the old woman and her curiosity almost caused an accident. At the last possible moment she had to swerve away from a car that came so close that she was able to see the fear in the other driver's eyes.

By the time Noreen brought the car back under her full control, Pearl's eyes were open again.

"I see a man that could be for you. But he is hidden in light. That means that he is being protected by someone that is like me."

"Like you?"

"Yes, someone in the path of the light. But the other person is too strong. Must be much stronger than me. I only read cards and throw bones sometimes."

Pearl shrugged her shoulders to indicate that it was no big deal.

"But I can tell you this. He has grayish-green eyes. The color of the ocean right before the sun sets. And he has the hair like…what do you call those boys, Achristofarahs?"

"You mean Rastafarians?"

"Yes'm, hair like that."

"Hmm, I don't think so. Me with a Rastafarian? What else do you see?"

"Nothing. It's like I told you, I can usually see more but…"

"…Right, I got you. He's being protected by the light."

Miss Pearl smiled and sat back in the car seat content in the knowledge that Noreen understood the state of her affairs.

With only five blocks left before they reached Morningside Park Boulevard and One Hundred and Eleventh Street, Miss Pearl started talking again. She told Noreen information about her mother that only her family members knew. And she told her that her brother was going to have children soon. It would be twins, a boy and a girl.

When they reached their destination, Noreen was half convinced that Miss Pearl did know something about her family. It gave her the creeps and suddenly she wanted to be far away from Miss Pearl.

"Which house is yours, Miss Pearl?"

"Oh, I'm right inside the block right there. I'll just get out right here."

Before Noreen could move the car up to the house where Miss Pearl pointed, the old lady had already popped the door open and gotten out.

Before walking away Miss Pearl popped her head back down into the car window to say good-bye. Noreen got a clear look at her face. She watched as the woman's good eye turned from a gray color back to the original brown that she had first seen before she helped Miss Pearl cross the street toward the bank. Suddenly the old lady didn't seem so blind or disoriented anymore.

"Thanks again, baby." She waved. "We'll see each other again. I'm sure of it."

Noreen nodded politely, but didn't say a word. She was already unsure of what she had witnessed.

Miss Pearl stepped away from the car and Noreen didn't bother seeing that she got to her door. She left the curb in a flurry of dust and was already three blocks away when she stopped shaking enough to realize she was headed downtown toward the Holland Tunnel. It was the quickest way to get to New Jersey.

‡‡‡

Noreen had only been to Dennis's house once, but she had the address and all she had to do was program it into her GPS and it guided her right to the front of his doorway.

She looked back and saw his car in the driveway, glad that she had not wasted the effort of this surprise visit. When Noreen rang the bell to his house, it took a few moments before she heard the footsteps that meant someone was coming to the door. She saw someone peering through the peephole and then the door began to open. Noreen didn't know what she expected him to say, but she definitely did not expect this.

"Yes, how can I help you?"

The woman who answered the door was very pretty. She was tall; approximately six feet, Noreen guessed, given that she was about half an inch shorter than her. She couldn't be more than twenty-five years old and she weighed about 260 pounds. *Give or take an ounce,* Noreen thought, feeling a little jealous.

"Maybe I have the wrong house."

Noreen knew that she didn't have the wrong house even before she saw through the door and past the younger woman to where Dennis was coming in from the backyard.

"You're looking for Dennis?"

"I was, but I guess I'm not anymore."

The young woman looked Noreen up and down with an attitude that she herself might give to a woman knocking on her door looking for a man she already called hers.

"Excuse you?"

"Can you just tell him that Noreen came by and that there's no need for him to come knocking or calling anymore?"

Being the older and hopefully wiser person in this small confrontation, Noreen believed that taking the high road was the better course of action. She turned to leave, but felt the younger woman grab her upper arm.

Noreen turned to face the woman again and the look on her face alone made the younger woman release her.

"I just want to know, how you know Dennis?"

"We were friends…intimate friends."

The younger woman looked annoyed at Noreen's answer, but didn't see it as any more than a vague lie.

"Hmm, I don't think so, Miss. DENNIS!!"

The young woman screamed over her shoulder for Dennis not knowing that he was already just a few feet away.

"What's the problem? Who's at the do…?"

When he saw Noreen on the other side of the threshold, his face froze with rigor mortis that could have rivaled a three-day-old corpse.

"Hello, Dennis?"

"Noreen? Noreen, what are you doing here?"

Noreen shrugged her shoulders, amused at the look on the younger woman's face.

"I don't know. I thought I'd come by and find out why you weren't coming by my apartment anymore. I guess this is why."

Noreen gesticulated toward the younger and bigger woman as if she were Vanna White unveiling a prize that Dennis had won.

"Noreen, I can explain…"

He looked from Noreen and then to the younger woman blocking the door in front of him. She in turn stared back at him.

"…Explain what? I know you are not standing here about to tell me that you've been fucking this skinny bitch behind my back!"

Under any other circumstances, those might have been fighting words for Noreen, but today she did feel like a *Skinny Bitch*. And having known the pain of having a man pick a thinner woman over you despite being smarter, funnier, and prettier, she could not fault the woman for her behavior.

"It's not like that Bridgette…"

When the first punch hit Dennis squarely in the nose, Noreen was fully satisfied that he was getting his just desserts. She turned on her heel and headed toward her car. She didn't bother looking back. She heard the door slam and then she heard furniture moving. And it was heavy furniture.

On the way back to New York she started to think it was time for another vacation. She wondered if she could convince Kat and Dahlia to come with her.

CHAPTER TWENTY ONE
THE NEW MRS.

Kenny was already two hours late dropping Little Kenny off from their weekend visit. He showed up at the door carrying the little boy who was dead asleep in his arms.

"Where do you want him?"

"Take him downstairs to his room."

Kat led the way to the next landing. She opened the door to Little Kenny's room and turned on the lights. When Kenny put his son down on the bed, the boy barely stirred. His father took his son's shoes off and then stepped to the side as Kat proceeded to undress him and then fit him with pajamas. When it was all said and done the whole putting the baby to bed process took a total of five minutes.

The parents made their way upstairs to the front door and were both ready to say good night when they heard a car horn sound.

PAAAMP! PAAAMP!

The sound of the horn in his E Class Mercedes was distinctive and they both recognized it.

"You have somebody waiting for you in the car?"

"Yeah, I've got somebody waiting."

Kat wasn't mad. The man was entitled to have a life, but she thought it was strange that Kenny didn't mention he had somebody waiting in the car.

"Who have you been keeping company with around Little Kenny?"

PAAAMP! PAAAMP!

"Seems like she's a little impatient."

Kat turned the doorknob she was holding onto and opened the door to look out at Kenny's car. There was a woman standing next to the car on the passenger side waving a garment bag.

"Is that Harriet Washington?"

"Yeah, I meant to tell you about her."

Harriet was one of the drivers that worked for Kenny's limousine business. When Kat was helping to run the business, she thought it was a good idea of Kenny's to hire a few beautiful women that wanted to be drivers. Then the men who hired limousines in an attempt to give the appearance of being rich playboys, could have the full effect of their fantasies with a beautiful woman at the helm.

"It's your business. I don't think it's a smart idea dating someone that works for you, but I'm not gonna hate."

Kat waved back to the woman and astonishingly the woman took that as a signal that she should come up to the house. Kat watched her close the car door and joyously run across the street carrying the garment bag. She still had the same gorgeous body that she had when she was first hired. She ran so quickly up the stairs Kat guessed she was probably still working part time as a trainer at the New York Sports Club. Kat couldn't get over the huge smile on her face. The woman was already beautiful, even without makeup. The big smile just made her seem sexier somehow.

Kat stepped over the doorway saddle at the threshold of her home to greet the woman. She didn't want to give the woman the wrong impression, that she was somehow welcome in her home.

The woman came running up the stairs laughing. It wasn't a mischievous or even malicious laugh; she seemed genuinely happy about something.

"Oh my God! Hi, Kat. I just looked into the backseat on a whim and I saw that Kenny forgot to bring Little Kenny's tuxedo in the house with him."

Harriet attempted to hand the garment bag to Kat, but Kat made no attempt to take it from her.

Kat's face was stone cold as she stared into her former employee's face. Out of her element in the presence of her former employer, Harriet looked uncomfortably back at Kenny, but when his face showed a defeated look, she had nowhere else to look but back at Kat's deadpan stare.

"Why would a little boy need a tuxedo?" Kat asked Harriet, forcing the woman to look at her again.

"It's for the wedding. It's next Saturday. He's going to be the ring boy." Harriet was talking as if it was a done deal and it had already been arranged.

"Who is getting married?"

Kat asked not entirely wanting to know the answer.

Harriet looked questioningly at Kenny.

"Didn't you tell her? I thought you said you already spoke to her."

Kenny made his way past Kat to his fiancée.

"Harriet, wait for me in the car."

"You two are getting married. Oh hell no. I can't believe this shit. I hired her."

She yelled at no one in particular.

Kenny walked Harriet halfway back to the car with his arm around her shoulder as if he were shielding her from something that might come flying from the direction of the house. Kat could hear him attempting to smooth things over with her. *She must be very easy to live with,* Kat thought with some resentment. She knew that she could not be talked off of a ledge as easily.

Kenny walked back toward the house, but Kat had already gone inside. She was pacing the living room floor wringing her hands.

Kenny came inside and closed the door behind him.

"I wanted to tell you, Kat, but it never seemed to be the right time."

"The right time? The right time for what? You're not my husband anymore. You don't owe me any explanations. I think that you owe me just a little bit of respect, that's all. She's the one you were sleeping with all along, isn't she? She's the one you left me for."

Kenny shook his head.

"No, she's not. She and I didn't start seeing each other until after the separation. It was after the divorce that we began to think about marriage."

"If that's true then why now after a whole year."

Kenny couldn't look her in the face when he said, "We're having a baby."

Kat couldn't believe what she was hearing.

"You're having a baby?"

"Harriet's three months' pregnant."

Kat didn't know whether she was madder because Kenny had kept his wedding plans from her for so long or because Harriet's stomach was still flat and she was able to run up steps being three months' pregnant.

It had to be a matter of genetics. When she was three months' pregnant, people that guessed how many months along she was always guessed six months.

"I don't want Little Kenny in your wedding."

She knew she was being childish, but she didn't care.

"He's my son, too, Kat. I have a right to have him in my wedding." Kenny continued, "You can take me to court. I'm sure you'll win. In three months.

"I know you have someone in your life. Little Kenny told me you have a friend that comes over. His name is Lee, right? Little Kenny likes him and he told me he spends the night sometimes."

"Little Kenny has never seen him in my bed. He leaves before Little Kenny ever gets up."

"But still, you have somebody. You're happy. Why is it that I can't be happy, too? You got the house. You have our son and you get all the money you want."

"And I better keep getting it, too. That bitch and your bastard aren't going to get one single cent of anything that I worked hard for."

Kenny had had enough. He was going to leave while he still had some control over his anger. He headed for the door and almost made it without breaking.

But all it really took was for Kat to say, "You sorry excuse for a man," for Kenny to lose his cool.

It's not what he ever felt, but it came out mean between his clenched teeth, anyway. "You fucking fat bitch!"

He wished he could take it back as soon as he said it. He stopped walking toward the door and turned back to Kat intending to say sorry.

The words he uttered hurt Kat deeply, but she didn't show it.

"I know that's how you always felt. You've said as much before. But nothing has changed, has it. And it probably never will so I've learned to accept myself this way."

It wasn't until she said it at that moment that she knew the words to be true. She had finally accepted her weight problem and now she realized that it was never really a problem.

"Kat, I have never thought of you as a fat anything."

"Of course you did, Kenny. And you told me it wasn't your fault that I put on forty extra pounds."

"I remember what I said, Kat. My excuse for cheating on you was that you wouldn't make love to me anymore. At least not the way you used to before Little Kenny was born. You blamed the extra weight as the reason why you didn't feel sexy anymore. My rationale was *why should I have to suffer because you don't feel good about yourself. It's not my fault you put on forty extra pounds.* All you ever heard was, it's not my fault you put on an extra forty pounds. As if all I cared about was that you were not slim anymore. It may not make a difference to you now, and I'm sure that it would sound like a lame excuse to most women, but the reason I cheated was because I wasn't getting any sex at home. It had nothing to do with your weight. I'm sorry, Kat. As any real man would attest, after those nine months of no punany, I would have had sex with you if you grew a hump on your back."

"That makes me feel a lot better, Kenny."

Kat tried to sound sarcastic, but the truth was that it did make her feel better.

And now that the truth had set them both free, she realized that she had to get him out of the house. She'd forgotten that Librado was on his way.

"Okay, Kenny. Is the practice wedding dinner on Friday?"

"Yep."

"Come and pick him up on Thursday night. He can miss a day of school."

"What about you? Are you coming to the wedding?"

"Let's not get crazy now."

Kenny raised his hand in mock surrender.

"You're right. Too much, too fast."

Kenny reached the door and opened it quickly thinking that maybe she would change her mind. He almost left without saying anything else, but thought better of it and lingered long enough to say a soft, "Thanks, Kat."

Kat waved him off and he walked down the steps in just enough time to see Librado coming up the walkway.

The two men passed each other with only the acknowledgment that a head nod provided to each of their egos. Nothing more was required.

✠✠✠

When Librado went to bed that night, he slipped into Kat's bed and turned off the nightstand light. He was taken aback when Kat reached over and past him and turned it back on. He thought that maybe they wouldn't be making love tonight, and that he would possibly have to endure having another conversation and lecture like the time that he had dared to leave the toilet seat up.

Looking at her closely now for a hint of what he might have done wrong, he was surprised that he had not noticed the silky lingerie that was loosely draped about her shoulder. He hoped that he wasn't misconstruing the look in her eyes. When he reached out to slip the lingerie the rest of the way off of her shoulder and she slapped his hand away, he thought that he was definitely reading her wrong.

Then Kat did the most improbable thing. She pushed him back against the headboard of the bed and slowly got up to stand on her mattress. She walked backward two steps until she was in between Librado's feet. Then she allowed the left shoulder strap of the silk gown to slip off. The gesture barely allowed the top of her left breast to show, but that was enough to make Librado's lips go dry. Librado licked his lips, careful not to carelessly make them crack, his gaze never leaving the cleavage of the woman standing over him. When Kat shrugged her right shoulder and the strap that was barely clinging to it raced down her arm, Librado bit his bottom lip unintentionally drawing his own blood.

Kat was only nude from the waist up, but it was a beautiful sight to behold. Her breasts were so full and hung so delicately that it made Librado fantasize that they may still house some nourishing moisture that he could devour during their lovemaking. Kat saw the look in his eyes and was amused. She knew what he was thinking and was glad later when he suckled against her in the afterglow of their lovemaking.

Kat closed her eyes and pushed the rest of her robe down her hips letting it fall to her feet. She didn't want to see a look of disgust in Librado's eyes if he did not approve of the soft loose flesh around her thighs and the stretch marks that her child left her as a memento of the body they had once shared.

When she noticed that Librado didn't run from the bed screaming, Kat opened her eyes and looked down at Librado. He was smiling lasciviously up at her still licking his lower lip.

"*Mamita*, you are so beautiful," he cooed to her.

Kat let her eyes blaze a trail down to Librado's pajama-covered groin and his eyes followed hers. He already knew how hard his penis was. It was going to be hard getting his pajamas down over it. As it turned out, that was to be his last worry. Kat dropped down to her knees in between his legs and steadied herself by briefly holding onto the back of his knees. Taking a part of the open flap in Librado's pajamas normally used to slip your penis through when using the bathroom in each of her hands, she pulled hard in opposite directions and rent the cotton pants apart from the waist to the inner seam. Librado's large dark penis was two shades darker than the skin on the rest of his body. The purple head stared up at Kat and she fought the urge to take it in her mouth. Instead she slid over his body, allowing her breasts to drag over his knees, his thighs, his penis, and last against his abdomen. They were finally chest to chest.

"Tell me you love me," Kat demanded of him as their loins touched and the breath from their lips mingled.

"I love you, *Mamita*. More now than…"

His breath caught in his throat, as he felt the velvet mouth of Kat's vagina envelope his cock in one movement.

Librado took hold of her hips and forced them to stay put. He was afraid that any other movement would cause him to come inside her before having any chance to enjoy in the way that he hadn't since the one day that they'd made love in the light.

Kat felt no need to move again. She had him where she wanted him, deep inside of her rubbing against her G spot with every contraction of her cervix. By the time Librado realized what she was doing, it was too late. He was the one that had forced her down on him hard, and now he didn't have the strength to lift her off of him when she was viciously grinding down on him.

He finally gave in to the sensation of her milking vagina and let go of her hips. To his surprise, letting go of her hips lessened the sensation of her sucking pussy and he was able to stop himself from cumming.

Librado reached for Kat's face and gently brought it down to his. He kissed her tenderly at first and then each took turns devouring the mouth of the other. They stayed in that position for more time than either of them thought they could and then Librado couldn't hold it anymore. He thrust into her just the once when he felt the cum racing out of him and that was enough to bring about her orgasm.

"Oooh fuuuuck! I'm cummmmmiiinggggggggg."

Her vagina fluttered around the shaft of his cock uncontrollably for a full twenty seconds and then clamped down on him hard enough to make him grunt.

"Uuuuugh!"

They squirmed and convulsed against each other for long moments before either of them was spent.

It was the best lovemaking that either of them had experienced in their entire lives. And it only took them thirty minutes to realize that they could duplicate the experience over and over again.

CHAPTER TWENTY TWO
MOVING FORWARD

Honolulu in June was as hot as any other June day in New York, but without the mugginess.

It took Noreen no time to convince her two friends that Hawaii was the place they ought to be. Neither of the three women had ever been here before and each felt that the other two friends were in need of some new scenery.

When the plane landed and Kat looked out the window, she could see the rows of pineapples in the distant field. The way they stood so small and sturdy in neat rows reminded her of yesterday when she'd left Little Kenny at his first day at summer camp. Her mother convinced her that he would be all right and when she saw how easily her son assimilated into the sea of little people, it comforted her.

At least one of the men in her life wouldn't be too disappointed that she was going on vacation without her.

Librado had said that he didn't mind her going without him, but she saw the concern in his eyes. Culturally speaking, she was not following the modus of his people. After he hinted that maybe they should think about living together, she thought it prudent to set a precedent for what he could expect from her if he were going to be a part of her life. There was no use in making him think that she would turn into someone that would remind him of his mother. This trip was just a reminder that she would always be true to herself.

Noreen nudged Dahlia awake. Somehow Dahlia was able to sleep most of the way to Hawaii and now that they were at their destination, Noreen was a little anxious that they all experience every part of their trip to the fullest. They had all promised one another that men would not be a concern on this trip. That was easy for her two friends to say; they had men waiting at home.

Dennis still left messages on her phone. She didn't know why. Maybe he felt guilty for leading her on, or maybe as his messages indicated, he was just looking for a friend now. Whichever one of those lame reasons it was, she was not interested. She had already moved on and if things went the way she planned on this trip, her love life would be twice as interesting when she got back home.

Dahlia woke slowly when Noreen poked her in the ribs. She was glad that Noreen talked her into coming. Due to the country's economic woes, twenty of the bank's branches had been forced to close and her promotion quickly went out the window. She was lucky that the original branch that she worked in was still running and the company let her resume her responsibilities as vice president.

After an afternoon of sightseeing in a crowded bus with couples from the Midwest, the three women were glad to be sitting poolside at their resort.

Noreen took a sip of her drink and pulled her pink sunhat further down on her head. It was an attempt to escape the bit of sun that was sneaking past the rim of the huge umbrella attached to the chaise she was sitting on.

"My God, do you see the size of the women on this island?"

Kat turned to see the woman that Noreen was referring to. The woman was wearing a Hawaiian print kimono that could serve as a pup tent, and she was serving a fruity drink concoction to a frail-looking man sitting just fifteen yards away from them. She was indeed an immense woman by the standards of anyone living in New York, but to the people in Hawaii she wasn't anything more than the average middle-age woman.

In her own mind Kat compared the Hawaiian woman to the size she was now. The woman was at least four sizes away from what she was, but it didn't make her feel any better. She reconciled that she was meant to be a big woman, but to be the size of the woman behind her would probably be unhealthy for her. Now that she had taken on the plight of the big woman she couldn't let anyone say anything negative against one of her big sisters. Even if that person was once one of them.

"Don't forget when you were that big, Noreen."

"I was never that big, was I?"

"Maybe never that beautiful, but you were pretty close to that size."

"Ouch! Was that necessary?"

"Maybe not, but I didn't want you thinking you were any different from us now."

"I wasn't thinking that. I was just thinking how nobody seems to mind how big the women here are. Nobody looks at them funny like they would in the States."

"This is one of the states."

"You know what I mean."

"Yeah, I know what you mean. I was listening to someone on Oprah's show talking about it on one of the reruns. They called it *The Last Prejudice*. It's all of the negative things that you think about when you see a person that you think is overweight. Like when people don't like blacks just because they're black or say they won't hire Puerto Ricans because they're lazy."

"That's just racism."

"Well, this is worse because there are fat women of all races and it seems like everyone is entitled to be prejudiced against us."

Dahlia turned onto her side to face her friends.

"Did you say *us*, because I am not fat."

"Oh?"

"At least not here, I'm not. Here, I'm just another big-boned girl."

Dahlia put her hand on her hip and struck a Marilyn Monroe-like pose.

The three women laughed at Dahlia's little joke. The other guests that lay poolside looked over at them and whispered to one another, probably saying unkind things about the big black women and their skinny friend.

The larger-than-life Hawaiian waitress came over to them and offered them an afternoon cocktail.

"Three Tiki punches with an extra shot of rum in each. And don't move too far away from us because we're going to be drinking all afternoon." Noreen, whose tolerance for alcohol had changed since her operation, was obviously planning on getting wrecked while on vacation.

"Coming right up."

The woman hadn't made a half-turn away from them when Dahlia reached out and grabbed her wrist stopping her in her tracks.

"I'm sorry, miss, can you make that two Tiki punches and one pineapple juice."

"No problem. Anything else?"

She looked from Dahlia to Noreen and then to Kat and found nothing but awe in the two women's faces.

"All right then, I'll be right back."

Kat and Noreen waited until the waitress was out of earshot before they said anything to Dahlia. The look on their faces before they spoke already told her that she had some explaining to do. After all, if you didn't drink on vacation where would the fun start?

The friends spoke in unison.

"Pineapple juice?"

"Let me explain."

"My tolerance is nil and I'm still having something stronger than pineapple juice."

"Well, maybe if you were pregnant…"

Kat popped up out of her chaise.

"I knew it, I knew it."

"What do you mean you knew it? You didn't know."

"You've gotten bigger. I didn't want to mention it because you know...
You can be a little sensitive."

"*Moi*, sensitive?"

"A whole lotta sensitive."

Noreen agreed.

"Does Eric know?"

"Of course he knows. I told him not to tell your mom until I went on
vacation. I didn't want her making a fuss."

"You didn't want to face the wrath of mom, that's what."

"That too."

The waitress came back with their drinks and Kat made them all raise
their glasses.

"To babies and big girls."

"BABIES AND BIG GIRLS!" they all shouted at the same time.

The girls chatted about babies and baby names for some time before the
conversation turned to men.

Without being asked the waitress was back with fresh drinks for the trio
and they toasted again. This time it was Dahlia who raised her glass first.

"To us. May we prosper and live long."

Kat turned to Noreen.

"She's a *Star Trek* fan?"

"Big time."

They all raised their glasses in time.

"LIVE LONG AND PROSPER!"

They were all on their fourth drink when Noreen popped the big question.

She put her drink down feeling that the rum was already giving her the
courage she needed to ask.

"Kat?"

Kat was caught in mid sip.

"Hmm?"

"I need that detective's phone number. The one with the dreadlocks. I want to ask him out."

Kat tried to swallow the small sip she was taking at the time, but it went down the wrong pipe and she started to choke.

When the choking didn't seem to be subsiding, Noreen got up from her chaise and came to Kat's side. She patted her on the back a few times in an attempt to get the extra fluid to leave her lungs.

Kat finally recuperated and was able to say something.

"Are you fucking crazy?"

"What?"

"You want me to give you Chemah's number? Do you know who his ex-wife is?"

"I don't know. Nor do I care to know."

"Well, I'm going to tell you, anyway. His ex-wife is my best friend. Or *was* my best friend until a little while ago."

"I'm not telling you to stab her in the back or anything; I'm just asking for his phone number."

"I'm not worried about her getting stabbed in the back; I'm worried about you getting stabbed. The last two women that Chemah was in love with that Margarita knew anything about have both died. And not mysteriously, either. And if I tell you that she can wield more power in just one well-placed phone call than the mayor of New York, I would not be exaggerating."

"C'mon, Kat, she's just another woman. She can't be that bad."

"She's the one I called to get Dahlia out of jail, No. You think it was a coincidence that the DA didn't want to press charges? The lawyer she sent with us was just for show. She's the one that made sure that there was no case. And if she can do that, do you really want to be on her bad side?"

Noreen took a big swig of her drink. It was obvious she wasn't going to get anywhere with her friend. The drink was making her paranoid.

"All right, I guess you've made your point."

She thought it best that she drop the subject, but she knew that she would go back to that precinct in New York and look Lieutenant Rivers up.

The old lady that she met coming out of the bank came to her mind and she felt suddenly that the woman was absolutely right about where she might find the man that would be hers.

"Have you thought about names for the baby, Dahlia?" Kat asked.

Dahlia looked tired. She had been listening to her two friends and she knew that neither believed that the other was going to leave the subject of Lieutenant Chemah Rivers alone. She didn't care either way. The baby was making her tired already. She wanted to go back to her room.

"London, if it's a boy, and Paris, if it's a girl. Those are the two places we're going for our honeymoon."

"You're getting married?" Kat felt as if she were out of the loop again.

"As soon as I get back. Nothing big. Just city hall and a get-together with some friends. Corporate America is still unforgiving to unwed mothers and I can't afford to lose my job in this climate. It's already looking up now that Barack has taken office, but it's going to be a long time before any of us should feel so comfortable in our jobs that we forget that this country still has built-in conditions and rules."

"You mean you could lose your job for being pregnant?"

"No, they won't call it that, but still they'll find a way of getting me out if I don't conform to their way of thinking. It's all about appearances."

Dahlia tapped her stomach and then rubbed it gently. She talked about getting married as if it were a necessary evil, but she was actually happy that her situation gave her a valid excuse to go through a ceremony that she'd vowed to never be a part of again. She was sure that it would be years before Obama or any other president would make a dent in the country's general prejudice toward giving gays and lesbians the right to get married. When she thought about it, she felt hypocritical about going through with it for reasons other than love. She hoped that by the time her unborn child was of an age to make the same decisions she was now making, it would not be an issue.

She looked at Kat and remembered how in January during the inauguration ceremony they had watched on television together, she had pointed to the television and told her son that if he studied hard, he could be president one day, too. It was the first time Dahlia had heard a black woman ever say that to their child. After all of the success that President Obama had in changing policy over the past few months, she was sure that she would be saying the same thing to her own child, no matter what it's sex was.

Dahlia was feeling dreamy until Noreen snapped her out of her revelry.

Noreen remembered what the old lady had said about her brother having two children, one of each sex.

"You think maybe you might have twins in there?"

"Noreen, please, don't even wish that on me, girl."

Noreen took another sip of her drink and looked up in time to see John, the man whom she met in the airport with Kat on the day that they went to pick Librado up.

She didn't tell her friends that she'd made arrangements to meet him here. They already had men of their own and right now all she wanted was to have fun.

When Kat spotted him, she looked at Noreen and saw the mischievous look in her eyes.

"You'd better not even think of leaving us here by ourselves."

"He's going to take us to dinner."

"And then what?"

"And then we'll see..."

About the Author

David Rivera, Jr. has been writing short stories for many years and has been inspired by the writings of the contemporary black male writers who have emerged during the past few years. His first book, *Harlem's Dragon*, was received with great enthusiasm by other writers as well as literary critics. David lives in Harlem, U.S.A. with his family and aspires to reignite the literary flame that Harlem had been renowned for with his novels *Harlem's Dragon, The Street Sweeper, Playing in the Dark*, and now *The Last Prejudice*. He received a bachelor's degree in sociology and a master's degree in public administration. David Rivera, Jr. can be contacted at setodavid@aol.com. Visit his web site at www.davidriverajr.com.

IF YOU ENJOYED "THE LAST PREJUDICE," GET
STARTED ON THE AUTHOR'S TRILOGY WITH
THIS EXCERPT FROM

Harlem's Dragon

THE LOVE YOU CAN'T FIGHT

David Rivera, Jr.

WE KNOW YOU'LL LOVE IT!

Chapter 5
WHO STOLE THE COOKIE FROM THE COOKIE JAR?

"Two-Ninety Central Park West," Chemah announced. "Last stop." He and Nairobi were still making silly jokes with each other.

"Would you like to come upstairs?" Nairobi asked, her face turning serious again. Chemah wanted to say yes, but tried to play it cool again. "I'll never find a parking space out here, I'd better just go," he said.

"Is it because I'm white?" she asked plainly.

"Because you're white?" Chemah repeated.

"Yeah, because I'm white, you think we shouldn't be together," Nairobi said genuinely.

"I never even thought about the color situation, Nairobi," Chemah said honestly. "I just move cautiously whenever I deal with women. We just met an hour ago and I thought maybe we were moving too fast."

"Too fast for what?" she snapped.

"Too fast to get to know each other better. Too fast for two people that obviously have chemistry to have a glass of wine?"

"Listen, Chemah, I keep my life very simple. If I don't like you, I stay away from you. If I like you, then I want you around me. Life is too short, and I plan to enjoy every minute that I can. I know you like me, so stop fronting."

Chemah laughed at her attempt to use slang.

"Yes, stop fronting," she repeated.

"Nairobi, are you trying to say frontin'?"

"That's what I said," she repeated, "fronting."

Chemah laughed again. "Your ebonics are terrible," he said. "Who's been teaching you this awful slang?"

"My students teach me sometimes," she said proudly.

"Then by all means…We had better spend more time together, you really ought to practice more. Your pronunciation is deplorable." They both laughed.

"I'll tell you what," she said. "You go around the block a few times, and look for a parking spot; that'll give me some time to tidy the place up. I wasn't expecting any company, and I left the place a mess this morning."

"OK," Chemah said this time. "I'll bring your box upstairs."

"I'll let the doorman know I'm expecting you. Don't take too long."

"What apartment?" Chemah screamed after her.

"Fifteen A," she called over her shoulder.

Twenty minutes later Chemah was in the elevator on his way up to Nairobi's apartment. The doorman had been expecting him and attempted to take the box from his arms. "Thank you. I'll take it up myself," he assured him.

"Yes, sir," the doorman said, being accommodating.

Chemah looked up and down the hall as he stepped off the elevator and stood in the middle of the hall. He saw the apartment number 15A approximately ten feet away to his left. He walked to the door, but as he reached to touch the doorbell, the door swung inward.

Nairobi stood at the threshold to the door and smiled. "Come in, the coast is clear." She had changed her clothes. She wore gray sweat pants and a T-shirt. Chemah looked at her from head to toe and saw that she was barefoot. Her feet were well pedicured. Chemah and his friends always discussed how important it was for a woman to have nice feet. Chemah crossed the doorway and walked down a hallway littered with pictures on the wall. Chemah noticed that Nairobi was in most of the pictures; the other people he guessed were family members. The living room was immense. It housed two huge bookcases opposite each other; they ran wall to wall, and floor to ceiling. Neither one looked as if it could house another book.

"Make yourself comfortable," Nairobi said. "I'll get us some wine."

Chemah sat on a couch that he thought he had seen in an IKEA catalog, and Nairobi came into the living room with two glasses of wine. "You haven't read all of these books, have you?" he asked.

"No, I inherited them from my family," she said as she handed Chemah a glass and sat close to him. "Ninety-five percent of them were already here when I got here."

"So this is your family's apartment?" he asked.

"No, it's my apartment. It used to belong to my grandmother, and she put me on the lease. When she died I took it over. It's rent stabilized so they can't raise the rent any more than when my grandmother was alive. She and my grandfather lived here for over fifty years. On a teacher's salary that's the only way I can afford to live on Central Park West."

"I was going to ask you how you could afford to live here, but I thought it would be rude," Chemah said.

"You'd be surprised how many people inherit their apartments from parents and grandparents out here. I know some families who damn near go to war over who gets their grandparents' apartment."

A silence subtly settled between Nairobi and Chemah as they looked at each other. Nairobi inched closer to him. "Chemah, can I be totally honest with you?" Chemah nodded yes not knowing what she would say next. She began, "Like I told you in the car, when I meet someone whose vibe is on an even keel with mine, I make it my business to spend time with them. I don't want this to come out sounding like some line that I give every man I meet because I really don't. I mean I haven't been in a relationship in a long time. What I'm trying to say is I find myself very attracted to you. I feel a warmth from you that I don't normally feel from anyone when I first meet them. I'm not trying to scare you; I know we just met one hour ago, but I believe in love at first sight."

Chemah was startled by what she said, but he kept his composure. "I'm feeling you too, Nairobi; I just don't know if it's love right now." In actuality, Chemah knew it was love the moment she got into his car. He was fighting it with every bit of his mother's anti-white rationale. She had told him on more than one occasion, there's only one thing a white woman wants a black man for. Nairobi took his hand in hers. He could feel the softness and firmness of them.

"I'm not telling you my feelings to obligate you, Chemah," she said. "I just felt that some part of you was not allowing you to pursue me; and I just wanted you to know that I'm yours if you want me."

"Just like that, if I want you I can have you?" Chemah felt a wave of pleasure wash over him like the first time he'd held a girl's hand. He felt those unusual butterflies he got when he was twelve years old and he'd first told a girl he loved her. His mother had called it puppy love. "Nairobi, I haven't even kissed you yet."

"If you kiss me do you think it will change the way, you feel about me?"

"I don't know."

"Then kiss me and find out."

"That won't prove anything," he said. "How can you know in so short a period of time that you're in love in with someone?"

Nairobi leaned back, and away from him putting her hand behind the couch for support. "I know because I've been waiting to feel like this for a long time. I've never felt it before so it must be love," she answered.

Chemah thought he'd throw her a curve ball when he asked, "How many Black men have you been with?" It was always a possibility that she just had jungle fever.

"I've never been with a Black man," she said matter-of-factly. "Chemah, maybe I've taken the wrong approach. Why don't we just relax and drink our wine, and you can tell me more about yourself." This line of conversation was easier for him to get into, but immediately left him wanting that feeling he felt when she was expressing her feelings for him.

Chemah started by telling her he was one of three sons; the middle child. He told her his educational background, and how he had gone about getting a master's degree in forensic science and his job in a forensics lab. He even told her of his aspirations to work for the NYPD. They traded stories most of the evening; not thinking or even feeling the need for sustenance other than each other's company. When Chemah finally looked at his watch it was one-fifteen a.m. "I think it might be time for me to go," he said reluctantly.

"What time is it?"

"One-fifteen a.m."

"You could spend the night if you want. No strings attached."

"You know that's the same line I used on girls in college."

"It's not a line; you can sleep on the couch if you'd like. I just want to know that you're near me." The butterflies in his stomach were coming back; he was really feeling her now.

"Which way is the bedroom?" Chemah asked as he stood. Nairobi took his hand in hers and guided him down another hall to her bedroom. The bedroom was almost as big as her living room. Its space was not minimized by the few items she had in it: a king-sized bed with matching Ralph Lauren sheets and comforter (he had the same ones on his bed); a massage table next to the window facing the park; and a desk with a computer in the corner. The place was so immaculate it seemed she didn't use the room at all.

"We may have one problem," Chemah said. "I sleep in the nude."

"It's not a problem for me if it's not a problem for you. I sleep in the nude, too," she said.

"Are you trying to make me think that the two of us are going to be nude in this bed and nothing is going to happen?"

"I didn't say nothing was going to happen. No strings attached."

She shrugged her shoulders and pulled at his belt. Chemah took this as a cue that they would be undressing each other. He reached for the string on her sweatpants, but was intercepted by Nairobi's swift moving hands. She pushed his hands back to his sides, and as he was about to object, she put her index finger to his lips signaling for him to be quiet. Nairobi's eyes never lost contact with his as his pants fell to his ankles. Nairobi held his hips briefly and began lowering herself using first his hips, then his thighs to steady herself as she slowly descended to her knees. Chemah almost broke his silence to tell her that he didn't wear underwear but thought maybe she'd already figured it out. As she reached eye level with his penis, she broke eye contact with his eyes and stared admiringly at what he had to offer.

Chemah's excitement was becoming obvious; he started to thicken and lengthen right in front of her face, but all she did was stare. After a few moments of staring at his privates, her eyes and hands went to his feet. Undoing the bow in his laces she helped him take his shoes and socks off one after the other. She was then able to gently remove the remainder of his pants from around his ankles. Nairobi got off her knees with no help from him, and walked to the massage table neatly placing the pants on the table and the shoes and socks under it. Chemah felt silly standing there with nothing on but his Coogi sweater, so he pulled it off before she could turn back to him.

Nairobi turned toward him again and pouted as he extended his hand to her with the sweater in it. "I wanted to take that off you," she said. "I've been thinking about it since I first saw you this afternoon."

"So it's just been my body all along?"

"Noooo, it's just that you're so beautiful I wanted to unveil all of you myself," she replied.

"Well, when do I get to unveil you?"

"You don't," Nairobi said as she reached the wall and turned out the lights.

"I don't, huh," Chemah said, reaching for her in the dark, and missing. As his eyes adjusted to the darkness, he could make out Nairobi slipping into bed and out of his reach. Chemah carefully made his way to the bed and found his way under the sheets next to Nairobi. He felt for some part of Nairobi's body in the huge king-size bed, and found her hand. Chemah squeezed it gently and simultaneously pulled her to him as he pushed his body forward to meet hers. His eyes had fully adjusted to the darkness and he could see Nairobi's face by the moonlight coming through the window.

Chemah bent to kiss her and as their lips touched, her tongue entered his mouth searching for something soft and moist. Their tongues slipped in and out of each other's mouths as their kissing became more and more frantic. When he thought he couldn't take it anymore, he reached for the string on her sweat pants and pulled it. Her pants were immediately loose and he slipped his hand inside to touch her. Nairobi was very wet. Chemah easily entered her with a finger. Nairobi detached herself from his mouth and began kissing his neck as her breathing came harshly through clenched teeth. Chemah needed to gain more leverage to stimulate her with his hand, so he stopped touching her and used that same hand to tug her sweats off. As she felt him tugging, she lifted her hips off the mattress, and in one swift motion the pants were around her ankles. She kicked them off quickly; and he used that moment to tug her T-shirt over her head. Nairobi manipulated his penis in a jerky motion with her hand, as he kissed and licked her breast. Chemah slid his hand down her stomach to touch the moistness again. She caught his hand and guided it lower than he had intended to go.

"Get me ready, here," she said breathily, slipping his middle finger into her ass. Chemah had heard that some women preferred anal sex to vaginal sex, but he would have never guessed that Nairobi was one of those women. Either way as hard as she had gotten him, he wasn't going to argue. Chemah didn't know where she pulled it from, but he heard the tearing sound of a condom wrapper and the *thppt* sound you make spitting the remaining rapper from your mouth. Nairobi worked hard to put the condom over his penis as he continued to lave her breast and pump his finger into her ass using the vaginal juices that dripped out of her as a lubricant. Nairobi let him know she was ready to be entered by pulling him on top of her. Using his erection as a leash, she guided him to the space she wanted him to enter and pulled her legs far back so that her knees were against her shoulders.

Chemah had never had anal intercourse before, but like all men he fantasized about it many times. Initially, he was careful as he entered her, pulling back slowly, and entering her slowly again. Nairobi urged, "Do it harder, Chemah. Faster, faster. Oh God, make love to me." She grabbed a handful of his buttocks and pulled him into her. This kind of sex was everything he had imagined it to be. Raw and animalistic. Chemah came twice without ever getting soft or leaving her body. After the second time, he pulled out of her. Chemah was still rock hard. He knew it was the excitement of having fulfilled a fantasy and the newness of the relationship that was keeping him hard.

Chemah lay on his back trying to catch his breath. "Are you alright?" Nairobi asked, kissing his chest.

"Yeah, just give me a second to catch my breath, then you can show me to the shower."

"You're still hard," Nairobi noticed out loud.

"After I get out of the shower, we can make love again if you're not too tired."

"No, honey, I'm not tired; we can do it as many times as you like," Nairobi responded. She led him to the bathroom. He took a quick shower and came out ready to go again. This time he intended to make her come as fast as she had made him come. Chemah walked into the bedroom again and Nairobi was standing at the window staring out into the park. The room was still dark but he could see her silhouette against the light outside. She was still naked and looked beautiful. She had pulled her hair back so you could see her entire face.

Chemah came up behind her encircling her in his arms. "Hmmmm," she murmured, "that feels good," as he pressed his hardening penis against her backside. He turned her around to face him and saw tears forming in her eyes.

"What's wrong?" he asked. "Did I do something to hurt you?"

"No. You've been perfect from the moment I met you."

"Then why are you crying?" Chemah asked, not understanding her pain.

"Because I'm happy and I never want it to end."

"It doesn't have to end," Chemah said, lifting her into his arms and carrying her to the bed. This time he meant to make love to her slowly letting her know that his feelings for her were also very strong. They kissed each other ardently. Each touching and feeling the other with the intensity that is born with finding your soul mate.

"I'm a virgin," Nairobi said, unexpectedly breaking their kiss.

"Huh, what was that?" Chemah said stupidly.

"I AM A VIRGIN," Nairobi said, exaggerating each word.

Chemah stared at Nairobi through the darkness. "What are you talking about? We just got busy twenty minutes ago."

"We just had anal sex twenty minutes ago," she corrected him. "I've never been vaginally penetrated."

Chemah lay staring at her for a moment and then asked her the only question that came to his head. "Why?"

"Why am I a virgin or why do I have anal sex, or is your question why am I telling you now?" she said vehemently.

Chemah kept his composure. "Why don't you just tell me everything you want me to know on the subject of your virginity? If I have any questions when you finish I'll let you know."

"Well, it's very simple actually," Nairobi said. "My mother always told me that I should save my virginity for a special person. That person would be my husband. My mother's advice to me on my first date was that a boy would do anything he could to stick his penis into my vagina; so I should do everything that I could to not allow that to happen.

"My first date was John Delaney—blond hair, blue eyes, and a smile that broke through all my defenses," she continued. "I told John that I was saving my virginity for someone special, and John convinced me after a time that you didn't have to have vaginal sex to have fun. Sitting in my parents' living room watching TV after midnight on a Saturday, John and I started petting after my parents went to bed. John and my teenage insecurities convinced me that anal sex was okay. After all, Mom never said I shouldn't do it. Anyway he was the first, I enjoyed it, and all my other boyfriends since haven't complained when I offered them my buttocks in place of my vagina. I've since learned that almost all men fantasize about what I have always thought of as the natural thing to do. Including you," she said slyly.

"What do you mean, including me?" Chemah said, sitting up in her bed.

"Are you trying to say, you didn't enjoy the sex we just had?" Nairobi asked.

"I'm not saying I didn't enjoy it; I'm just saying that it's not my main concern when I'm having sex with a woman."

"And what is your main concern, Mr. Rivers?" Nairobi asked, reaching for his hand in the dark. Chemah was not ready to let Nairobi know all of his secrets yet. The white girl had him open, and she knew it. Chemah had to close the gap a little.

"I'm concerned about getting some sleep," he said, lying down and turning his back to her. Chemah could feel Nairobi smiling in the dark as she laid her arm over his body and ticked herself into the small of his back in spoon fashion. She softly kissed the back of his neck, and gave him one last squeeze before whispering a soft "good night" into his ear. He never fell asleep feeling that secure again.

Chemah awoke slowly feeling that he was still in the dream that he had just been disturbed from. He felt a soft moistness on his dick that was all too familiar. Raising himself onto his elbows he questioned the darkness. "What are you—" he started.

Nairobi continued to raise his nature with her mouth, but she gently urged him onto his back using her soft hands to put pressure on his chest. Her mouth never skipped a beat. Chemah could see through the window that the sun was starting to rise. The sky was a light purple, but it enabled him to see clearly in its glow. He looked down at Nairobi and saw that she was staring back at him. Her eyes dared him to try and hold back another orgasm. As his hips involuntarily began to jerk upward to meet Nairobi's mouth earnestly, she suddenly released him from her grip. The cool dawn air against his wet penis was uncomfortable enough to stop his orgasm. Chemah wasn't about to beg her to make him come, and he didn't have to. Nairobi kissed her way up his leg and on to his stomach, where she lingered to tongue his belly button. As she kissed her way up to his chest and then his neck, she simultaneously grabbed his dick. Chemah could feel the entrance to Nairobi's vagina dripping onto his hardness as she attempted to nestle the tip into her opening.

Chemah wanted to tell her she didn't have to do this. He wanted to tell her to save her virginity for someone who deserves her, but the only thing to come from his mouth was a breathless, "yessss." Chemah was in her raw dog (no condom, no contraceptives). It had been years since he made love to a woman without a condom, and the sensation that a woman's gripping vagina gives a man when it's skin to skin, almost made him weep.

He was concentrating on not cumming almost immediately after he was in her. She had already given him two orgasms and he didn't want to cum again until she got a few in herself. Whenever he felt himself about to blow, he would forcefully stop the thrust of her hips with his hands and go into a slower stroke that he could control. Chemah thought she had come as soon as she had impaled herself on him. She was shuddering and shaking as if she was having an epileptic attack, but he figured that was impossible. No woman comes that fast. They were both slippery with sweat and he couldn't hold it back any longer. Chemah felt his balls were about to crack open, they were so ready. "I can't hold it," he gasped.

"Give it to me, Chemah. Give me all of you. I'm cumming," Nairobi exalted. Chemah's cum blasted through him and into her when she made that announcement. They clung to one another, each riding out the other's orgasm. "Are you alright?" Nairobi asked as they lay holding each other.

"Shouldn't I be asking you that question?"

Nairobi smiled. "I'm happy."

"You're not in any pain, are you?"

"Shouldn't you have asked me that question two hours ago?" she said, raising her eyebrows.

"I'm sorry."

She one-upped him. "I love you." They both drifted to sleep lazily lying in each other's arms.